Lesley —

Love from all Th...

Alan Broad

Alan.

The

Paper Caper

Also by Tim Topps

The Bunny Run (Matador, 2014)
Too Long in the Business (Matador, 2014)

The
Paper Caper

TIM TOPPS

Matador
9 Priory Business Park,
Wistow Road, Kibworth Beauchamp,
Leicestershire. LE8 0RX
Tel: (+44) 116 279 2299
Fax: (+44) 116 279 2277
Email: books@troubador.co.uk
Web: www.troubador.co.uk/matador

ISBN 978 1784624 491

British Library Cataloguing in Publication Data.
A catalogue record for this book is available from the British Library.

Printed and bound in the UK by TJ International, Padstow, Cornwall
Typeset by Troubador Publishing Ltd, Leicester, UK

Matador is an imprint of Troubador Publishing Ltd

Remembering warmly the DC, Alan Fernyhough CBE MC; Staff Mac from Inverness, and my three consecutive Codonian warriors, all by now surely long retired from Fleet Street, like the Street itself. Also, of course, Simon and Mark, James and Ana, who've heard all this and still won't believe much of it – but then, nowadays, I'm not even sure I do...

TT

GLOSSARY

ATS Auxiliary Territorial Service – the women's army during the war, reformed in 1948 as the WRAC, to include regulars.

BBC British Broadcasting Corporation – my son Mark points out sensibly that in 30 more years, readers may need to be reminded!

BOD Base Ordnance Depot – like a smaller COD but designed to be immediately rushed overseas in an emergency. (This can't be 'restricted', it's so obvious!).

CIA Central Intelligence Agency of the USA – set up at the start of the Cold War, with orders to infiltrate everything, including UK military establishments (also students, as I describe elsewhere from personal experience. See "Too Long In The Business" by Tim Topps, 2014).

COD Central Ordnance Depots – two or three vast stores of military equipment in the UK, covering all sorts of stuff except the perishables like food, whose delivery was handled by the lorries of the RASC.

CRS Casualty Reception Station – first port-of-call if ill or injured. Males and Females had their own. Staffed by ATS nurses with visiting RAMC doctors.

CSM Company Sergeant Major – a very senior NCO.

CSO Chief Stores Officer – a senior civilian running a sector of the store-shed (and if you're not careful, a Union man).

DC Deputy Commandant – military Assistant to the Brigadier; a Colonel, usually doing most of the top work.

DUKW Amphibious troop-carrying vehicle, affectionately known as the 'Duck'. Pretty useless in peacetime (although a few have been restored for work as fishing vessels or pleasure craft) but awesomely remembered by some scarred veterans.

E&R Engineering and Radar Stores – in Building 5.

IPA India Pale Ale – a superior bottled light-ale associated with the Raj.

LRDG Long Range Desert Group – a daredevil unit swooping behind enemy lines during Monty's North Africa campaign.

LSGC Long Service and Good Conduct – a valued medal awarded after 20-25 years for just what it says.

MC Military Cross – a high award for bravery, given to (usually younger) officers only, until recently.

MI5 Military Intelligence, Section 5 – British secret intelligence service, countering those spying on us in the UK.

MI6 Military Intelligence, Section 6 – British secret intelligence service, promoting our own spying outside the UK.

NAAFI Navy, Army and Air Force Institute – network of canteens and restaurants at all military centres.

NCO Non-commissioned officer – promoted from the ranks to hold local authority as Corporal, Sergeant etc. Higher offices are CSM and RSM.

OCTU Officer Cadet Training Unit – the final six-week grilling that, all being well, ends up with you receiving the King's or Queen's Commission.

OS Ordnance Survey – splendid people who produce those detailed maps we all rely on (if we have any sense) to find our way around the UK, gleaning information as we go.

OTC Officer Training Corps – many schools had these before the war, which turned out in 1939-40 to have been very sensible; these days known as Cadet Force.

P&P Printing and Publications Dept., in Building 18, with the Codonian down the end.

PMC President of the Mess Committee – officer who runs the Mess (probably as I describe him).

RACC Army Catering Corps, then, but now Royal. Is the accolade because, for a year or two, their food didn't kill many people? To be fair, Kittie was pretty good, when sober.

RAMC Royal Army Medical Corps. Well-liked in general because they were chiefly laid-back and not too 'militant'.

RAOC Royal Army Ordnance Corps

RASC Royal Army Service Corps

RMP Royal Military Police – the Redcaps, to be avoided whenever possible.

RSM Regimental Sergeant Major – the very top of the NCOs, one big step up from the several CSMs in any regiment; greatly respected by any Officer with common-sense.

SIS Much too secret to tell you about.

SMO Senior Medical Officer – usually a Major or above.

TCV Troop-Carrying Vehicle – normally a wagon-like covered lorry with lots of benches.

WO Warrant Officer – the senior NCOs, like the Sergeant Majors. However in the RAOC (only) we had a terribly senior rank called a Conductor, but I never met one, he was probably too important.

WRAC Women's Royal Army Corps – new name for the good old ATS.

I t was going to be a strange new life, I told myself as, with the
shiny new pip on my shoulder, I changed trains at Stafford,
on to the wheezy Donnington branch line; and my first
contact with that new life was lovely Mac. The platform was
bleakly deserted, steam came up fitfully from the lone
obsolescent carriage which they were linking up to its tired
puffer-engine; it seemed to be empty, but halfway along I
caught her khaki-clad eye and she smiled.

As we were both in uniform and practically alone,
obviously headed for the same grim destination, I swung along
the corridor with my kit and suitcase, and made to sit down
opposite her. I would have been less chatty and relaxed if I'd
known that under her folded greatcoat she had a gun pointing
at me.

I suppose I'm safe, now, writing about it. When they made me
an officer back in late 1947 – I'd missed the war by a nailbiting
few months – I remember I signed some bits of paper, but
that's so long ago and they never gave me a copy... We were
all getting stuck into the Cold War, switching our hatreds and
suspicions almost overnight from the Nazis to the Commies
further North; and anyway, nearly everybody must be dead by
now. Even that tasty little blonde tilly-driver with the retroussé
nose (the 'tilly' was the neat utility-truck with quite comfy seats
in front, but a good six-foot space behind it) must be seventy
now... She used to drive me into Newport every Wednesday
afternoon with the copy for the Depot newspaper for setting-

up, and there was a lay-by on the way back and a mattress in that six-foot space… Naughty girl. But no! Dear God, she'll be in her eighties…

In fact, for anybody skimming these pages, you can assume either that I've had clearance from the War Office – or whatever soppy 'correct' title they give the building nowadays to avoid offending the sensitive – and I'm in the clear; or that I'll pretty soon be arrested and this book will then be a Collectors' Item. If you want it signed after that, it'll cost you.

She looked at my shiny new uniform, the peaked cap so obviously almost unworn, and the gleaming leather Sam Browne belt which was cutting into me horribly in any number of places after my long day of travel from Aldershot, that centre of officer-training universally hated at the time but now, briefly, seeming to have been a cosy nest for an embryonic Second-Lieutenant cruelly launched upon the military upper world.

"Officers," she said, "are supposed to travel First-Class." Perhaps coldly? No, there was another smile. She sounded softly Scottish, probably around Aberdeen where the purest English is claimed to be spoken. She was quite cute in a superior sort of way, but had a businesslike look to her. Then I noticed the stripes on her arm and on the coat on her lap. My word, she was a Staff Sergeant, no less.

"They must have forgotten to link on my special carriage," I said, as I stowed my case up on the rack.

"Your lot usually go down the other end, that's First, there where the steam's leaking out of the wee heater."

"I'm only a new boy," I told her, "you can tell that by looking at me. I'd be lonely down there, what I need is companionship. Not just that – I need advice about the Depot I've just been posted to. Let's call this a guidance interview, a teach-in on Donnington Depot; that ought to permit me to sit and talk to you. Who made these silly rules, anyway?"

Mac went along with that. We exchanged names and geography. She was from even further North: Inverness. I was from the Home Counties, but my brainwashed posting eliminated all memories of that, and so far as the Army's penpushers were concerned I had originated from their age-old hatchment at Aldershot; anything before, not just my civilian history but even my nine months of training prior to receiving my commission, was eliminated. They even gave me a new Serial Number (which I never learnt and never, ever, had to use; whereas to this day I can tell you that as a private soldier I was 19121302. Most of my contemporaries would tell you the same)…

We had been hatched at Mons Barracks in the heat generated by the terrible RSM Brittain, that almost literally monumental figure who had sat on us for the last six weeks, to bring us out as officers and maybe even, to an extent, gentlemen. (It was only years later, when he had retired and appeared in films as a caricature of himself, that I came to accept that in fact he was an actor and probably quite a nice chap under the uniform and the absurd bluster). But I can't be alone still twitching in bed when I dream of his volcanic yells across that parade-ground. "Mr Parnaby, that little round man, shall I slow the squad down for him or can he catch up, eh, Mr Parnaby?"

Parnaby, though equally decorated with braid and ribbons, was – I think – a CSM (Company Sergeant-Major) as against Brittain the Regimental ditto. But whatever, he seemed a far more approachable person: I am reminded of the difference whenever I watch 'Porridge' on TV and compare Mr Mackay with Mr Barraclough; I wonder whether the writers went through Mons?

★ ★ ★

3

"Oh my God," said Mac. "RSM Brittain. He came to our basic training once and we all wet ourselves". Trying very hard to shut the picture out of my mind, I attempted a bit of flattery. It was far-fetched but at least it was conversation.

Pointing to the insignia on her sleeve, I said: "Strictly speaking, from Staff to RSM you're only about four steps away from that eminence yourself, aren't you?"

"Eminence," she repeated. "Don't you mean Ben Nevis? No, to be honest I've no ambitions in the ATS. I came in as a volunteer because of the War, and I suppose it was the right time to go up in the ranks; but there's a limit and I'm not in the rat race."

"So you're not going to be as merciless to me as Brittain was?" It was quite obvious to us both that I was chatting her up, but we had to play it very cool; we talked about the Depot.

At that time, just after the War, Donnington was one of three Central Ordnance Depots. The others were both down in Oxfordshire, at Didcot and Bicester, and the latter had been cleverly equipped for quick transferral anywhere in the world, so that a complete Supply Depot could be on-site if required as immediate back-up to a sudden military operation... The Donnington Depot was mainly concerned with Engineering and Radar stores, where Mac was Assistant to a Colonel at the heart of an enormous building – a shed, really – holding all that equipment.

"Well, he's just a half-colonel you know, but he's a nice wee chap."

There was a lot more at Donnington: apart from acres of huge sheds, specialising in all sorts of stores, we apparently had our own printing works which churned out endless Government leaflets, guidelines, and a crummy weekly newssheet. Also, at the furthest end of the Depot, on "the lines" which were in reality a decaying series of overgrown and rusting railway sidings, we had a sad collection of tanks, armoured cars, staff cars and ambulances brought back from North Africa, still uselessly flaunting their desert camouflage as they ever-so-slowly crumbled away.

All this I was able to confirm later, when my two jobs led me to explore the Depot thoroughly. But for now I sat back and enjoyed the moment. She really was a very attractive girl: the dark hair neat under her cap, the tempting swell under the uniform, the fairly short Army-issue skirt... And those dreadful issue stockings didn't entirely destroy the charm of the legs. I know it was generally considered that the most enticing women's uniforms were for the Navy girls, the 'Wrens', but this wasn't bad; not bad at all.

Nevertheless, a hesitating railway journey through certain parts of Staffordshire in 1947 didn't exactly inspire brilliant conversation, and we sat in silence as the countryside began to lurch past apologetically. Not yet a great tourist area, although, as I ventured to tell Mac amid the gloom, almost anywhere can be interesting if you know how to look at it. She just nodded despondently. We chugged on.

After a steamy halt at a place called Haughton, our monocarriage train heaved into a station labelled Gnosall. "Great Scott," I said, "How the Hell do you pronounce that?"

"Ah," she said, and I've always treasured this as rather brilliant, "The 'g' is silent, as in blood sports." It was neat, and it took me a while to work it out. OK, send me a postcard.

★ ★ ★

"Have you always lived in the South?" she asked, out of the blue; I told her Yes, except three years overseas.

"In Europe?"

"No, East Africa. Why?"

"Oh, nothing, it's just interesting – other people, I mean."

I thought I'd try her with a joke. I was keen to know whether she had a good sense of the ridiculous, largely by which I have coasted through my entire life, and which was going to be pretty essential in those coming months stuck in a Depot twice the size of Epsom racecourse.

"I've travelled a lot in this country, though," I said innocently, "Did I see you in Pontypool last Tuesday?"

"No," she replied, bewildered, and then, as I hoped, she added: "I've never been to Pontypool."

"Neither have I," I said, "it must have been two other people."

Yes, I told myself, the sense of the ridiculous is fine. It is a great leap in the right direction. Though laughter at your jokes is always gratifying, the giggle of a lovely girl at something being shared just between the two of you will always instantly create a delicious sense of intimacy… So often, as they say, you can 'laugh her into bed', and this must have been the way so many ugly lotharios in the past got away with it – Casanova and that crowd – the recipe being wit plus wealth. In my case the wit was on its own. That joke must have had them rolling in the aisles at the Colosseum: "No, I've never been to Catanzaro" – "Boo! Throw him to the lions!" – "No, it wasn't too bad, throw him at the Christians."…

I wasn't sure I was making much progress with Mac, but at least we had found something in common which I could work on. Mind you, at Mons we had all been taught the dangers – indeed the official prohibition – of fraternisation between those of us anointed with the King's Commission, and the ORs (dismissed equally officially as being mere 'Other Ranks' and thus unworthy of our haughty attentions). It was a well-intentioned rule for obvious reasons, to avoid serious upheavals in the line of command; but, as I was now asking myself while we steamed past brickworks and pylons towards our destination, did that apply quite so much in the case of senior NCOs? Would I have been court-martialled if I had taken RSM Brittain to the pictures?

Perish the thought. But it brought me back to wondering about this strange new base Mons had sent me to: it would probably be my home for at least eighteen months unless they posted me abroad. I asked Mac about Donnington: was it a happy place?

"It's big. Two battalions, mainly storemen or engineers. A small number of radar specialists, boffins, who keep themselves apart." Then perhaps with a slight sniff: "And of course all the civilians."

"Civilians?"

"About five thousand of them, swarming... Didn't you know? They pretty much run the place, and did so especially through the War of course."

"What are the military here for, then?"

"Well," with a shrug, "so far as I can tell, the idea is to cover each of the big warehouses – and there are twentyfour Buildings numbered –"

"Good God, it must be enormous – "

"It is. Each one run basically by the senior civilians, with an officer attached, supposed to be his equal but really a sort of shadow. You see, if we get another war, the civilians will carry on, but the shadowing officer can go wherever the emergency Depot is moved to. Or," another shrug, "something like that."

I repeated my earlier question: "Is it a happy place?"

She thought for a minute. "The soldiers and the civilians tend to stay apart, they don't mix much off camp," and she trailed away.

7

"Yes, but is it –?"

"It's not very military, only drill parades and weapon training on a Saturday up at Humber Camp, that's a mile away up the hill."

I said: "You're not going to tell me, are you?"

She wriggled uncomfortably on the bench seat and adjusted the greatcoat which slid on her lap.

"Well," she said at last, "Security is tight just now. We're all a bit –" Then, brightening: "You'll be told. It's not up to me. I've been told too, because I'm at the HQ offices of Building Five. But you'll be seeing the DC tomorrow I expect–"

The DC was the Deputy Commandant, the Top Army Man apart from the Commandant himself whom nobody ever saw. What was he like, this DC?

"I think he's nice. I don't think he's married."

I told her that the man's marital status wasn't my main concern. But how like a woman to put that bit of the description first.

"He's not very military, I'm sure. Too friendly. Nice blue eyes. He looks a bit like Attlee but he smiles."

★ ★ ★

We were getting to our feet as the engine sighed along the platform. As she stood up, the pistol slipped from under the coat on to the seat. I stared at it, then at her.

"Christ!" I spluttered, "Do I *look* like a rapist? With all this stuff on, I'd ruin my new uniform..."

She put the gun away.

"You never can tell," she told me. But then she laughed and laid a hand on my arm. "It's nothing personal, but many of us are on special duties just now. I can't say any more but perhaps

8

the DC will fill you in if he takes a fancy to you." Walking along the carriage she turned: "Nothing personal, promise."

As we parted outside the shabby station, I looked across into the distance. To the West, the skyline was broken by an enormous solitary hill like a minor volcano. What the hell was it?

"That's The Wrekin," she said. "It's our local barometer. If you can see it, it's going to rain. If you can't, it's raining already."

"If ever the rain stops, can we climb it for a picnic one day? I'll bring the sandwiches and a bottle, you can bring your gun."

She nearly touched my arm again, then didn't.

"Too close to home," Mac said, gently, tapping the pip on my shoulder. And with a warm look she was away, the smart, crisp, lovely, gun-toting Staff Sergeant.

I watched her go. It was getting dark, but I think she looked back once.

||

lugged my cases half a mile to the Officers' Mess (registering
mentally where to put the apostrophe, although I soon saw
that one was free to omit it entirely). The mess was at the
very furthermost righthand end of the Depot – would be,
wouldn't it? – and outside the high solid fence. It was one of
those neo-Georgian brick-and-good-window buildings one
saw everywhere in mid-century, often the work of that
delightful Professor A.E. Richardson. I looked at it from the
front, as I rested my arms.

The central section was very good, textbook. But on to each
side, and coming forward to form an overall 'E-shape', were
two wings which had clearly been added in a hurry, trying to
look the same but obviously thrown up by a lesser architect,
even, maybe no architect at all but a local builder under
pressure in wartime, when a sudden rush of extra officers
would have been drafted in. Somebody must have been aware
of this discrepancy, because both wing extensions had been
tactfully smothered with Virginia creeper, and I had to admit
it looked very pleasing this Autumn. I was sure that the great
Professor would have given it good points for camouflage.

He himself had a genuine Georgian house in Ampthill. I
went there several times from school, and he rejoiced in telling
us his story. In the Army in the 14-18 War, he was marched
through that little town and spotted this lovely house. He
decided that when the fighting was over, he would come back,
somewhat more comfortably, and buy it. On his return, the
house was indeed for sale, but all the wonderful and original

Georgian furniture and fittings had gone to auction. He set about, as a lifetime challenge, buying everything back; and I believe he largely succeeded, because to walk through those rooms was a delight. So was Richardson himself: among the embellishments was a real original sedan-chair from the eighteenth century. At the end of World War Two, on VE Day, there were celebrations in Ampthill as everywhere else; he got friends to carry him in the sedan through the streets to join in the excitement of the crowd. But he came up against of the constabulary and, returning after dark, the local copper detained them for 'driving without lights'...

"No," Richardson argued, successfully, "I am not a vehicle. I am being carried. I am a parcel."

★ ★ ★

Protocol, I knew, required me as a new arrival to make myself known to the Station Adjutant, always accepted in the Army as being something of a caricature of himself: he would be a deeply-knotted militarian, full of long-past glories, rigid with discipline he had learned on countless courses, handy with the Bren and the Sten (to which he had lost half a finger, "in the face of the enemy" of course), and once able regularly to outrun all his boys on a three-mile assault attack, somewhere safe like Dartmoor or Catterick. But, one thought, he was still only a Captain. He would tell you all these things over a pint in the evening; but he was now condemned to sit at a depressing desk in a remote Nissen hut, loaded only with a heap of files that had no safety-catch and had to be discharged by Friday. He was surrounded by filing cabinets, and they in turn were surrounded by earnest young clerical soldiers aching to be demobbed so that they could go off to their drama colleges.

It came as a relief to realise that our meeting could be

deferred, too late to 'check-in' with that buttoned-up officer. So I asked for the PMC on entering the Mess. An orderly stowed away my cases and went to look for him: President of the Mess Committee, in charge of the smooth running of the place, and butt of all the complaints when the soup is too thin or the wine a bit too rough. He, too, is an officer and probably another sidelined Captain – a Lieutenant would be too young to be acceptable for welcoming 'visiting firemen' of which there would be many at a place like this, sometimes even Generals; while a Major would be seen as too much of a failure in life, achieving only this despite his twelve years in the rank. In short, the PMC was a minor hotel manager with a rifle.

To my surprise, he was nothing like I had been expecting. In fact, it was he who gave me my first encouraging glimpse of how astonishingly un-military Donnington was going to be. I warmed to him at once.

He sauntered in, tattered blue shirt and flannels that were losing their crease. Suede shoes, hair a bit too long, cigarette. He waved me into the long friendly Common Room and indicated a couple of comfortable armchairs over to the side. I noticed that he avoided the better ones in front of the fire.

Without asking what I wanted, he called for two large Scotches with ice and water. I took this as a compliment: I would only have done that with a stranger I had immediately sized up in a favourable light.

"Well," he raised his glass, "welcome to the Gloomy Depot."

I naturally took a deep draught, but felt I ought to pursue the line of thought. "I've only just got here," I said, "but you are already the second person to suggest that this place isn't entirely happy. It can't be just the shadow of The Wrekin?"

He settled back in his chair and I found myself looking for signs of a gun. This was ridiculous, we weren't at the OK Corral, but what was the bulge at his side?

"We do have a bit of a problem just now," he conceded, but wouldn't go any further. "You'll be seeing the DC tomorrow, I'm sure. Drink up."

I did. Tomorrow would be soon enough.

The PMC must have sensed that I was feeling a bit unsettled over my future year-and-a-half in this depressing place. He tried to break it to me gently.

"We're a long way from anywhere," he said sadly, "except Wellington and Newport and I suppose Stafford, but they don't count much really."

"Where does one go, then? I mean, you know –"

He waved his arms about; feebly, I was sad to see.

"This way, eventually, there's Shrewsbury, all very historic once you get there. That way, Wolver-bloody-hampton for Christ's sake. but there are some decent shops, maybe?"

He fiddled with his ice-cubes and we sat in silence for a minute. Then everyday business took over, just as I was going to ask about access to the Wrekin as a picnic place.

"By the way, Carter Paterson brought your stuff yesterday. A trunk, and would it be a typewriter?"

"Oh yes," I told him, "My only weapon – ", half-hoping that he would mention the evident need around Donnington for weapons rather more to the point; but he let it pass. We got back to the local geography.

"Will I be living here in the Mess?"

"Good God, no." I felt as if I had demanded a flat at Sandringham. "Up the road, off to the left as you came in, there's a long row of typical Army Officer houses. You've got a room in House Four; you share with three other subalterns, Topps, and you share a batman between you."

"When I came in, off to the right I saw another building, much like this one but smaller, across – what was it? – a small lake? And I thought I saw barbed-wire around it. Is that –?"

"A lake!" He was amused by this. "Great Scott, I think it's some sort of emergency reservoir left behind from the air-raids; but that building, nothing important, it's just the ATS CRS."

"CRS?" More bloody initials.

"The girls' own Casualty Reception Centre."

It took me a minute or so, it had been a long day. Then: "That's CRC."

"By George, so it is…"

Unasked, the orderly had brought us a refill, and so we worked away at this new problem for a while.

"Why is there barbed wire around it?" He looked astonished. Either he had never noticed this, or I was asking too many sinister questions – I began to wonder if he would pull his gun on me, like everybody seemed to.

"God knows, maybe left over from the War, to keep the Americans out, No, it's always just been their Reception place, but – " with a severe frown – "strictly out of bounds, of course."

"Of course. Might get measles."

"At least."

"Or chickenpox?"

"Certainly some sort of pox, har-har," as he finished his drink.

He walked me to the door, gave me the key to House Four and retrieved my bags.

As I set off, I had one of my few shafts of brilliance. I turned and called to him: "Station – "

"Eh? You're not running away already?"

"No. CRS – Station."

"It's still out of bounds," he called. "That crowd'll chuck you in the reservoir."

"Lake,"

"Claypit," he said and went back to his hotel managing.

I wandered along the avenue, or rather The Avenue since

14

it said just that on a signpost. It stretched away, curving to the right at what must have been something like House Thirty. Even more, I later discovered, because the numbers ran all up the lefthand side and the first house on the right, obviously a family home, was House Seventy-two.

I found my room in House Four. Room Three, upstairs. My nextdoor neighbour was Second Lieutenant Smith, he wasn't in but I could smell his socks. I started to unpack but was interrupted by a thin man in scruffy khaki, about thirty I'd guess, not much hair but a huge triangular smile which was repeated on his sleeve: this was our shared batman, Lance-Corporal Edwards. The PMC had told me very proudly that we actually had an NCO as our batman, and Edwards was indeed splendid. I often wonder what he did when he was demobbed: I would have taken him on as my butler if I had any money, but that hasn't happened yet. Maybe if you get your friends to buy this book instead of borrowing it?

He tidied up our rooms every day; he was excellent with our boots and equipment for the Saturday morning military stuff up at Humber Camp; he also worked away at my bloody Sam Browne for Wednesday Mess nights, and somehow made it look attractively old and battle-worn. This didn't fool anybody in Donnington of course, but it came in handy with the girls down south when I was away on leave…

Also, later on, Edwards would be an absolute master of deception when carrying messages from me across to the other side of the lake; and he kept his mouth shut. A good chap. For the moment, though, I thanked him but preferred to do my own unpacking, so I would know more or less where I'd put it all. (I still had to ask him sometimes, especially on Thursday mornings). I asked him what his name was.

"Just Edwards, sir." OK, I went along with that. What *did* he do later?

In the morning, happily reunited with my usual comfortable everyday battle-dress, though slightly embarrassed by the blatant newness of the single pip on each shoulder (must get Edwards to rub some dirt into them) I went through the guarded gates into the Depot in search of the Adjutant. I got no salutes from the guards, nor from the few hurrying soldiers I met on the way, but didn't expect any. We had learnt during our six-months of Corps Training, that all such bullshit was to be shelved in day-to-day operations, or it would become ludicrous.

Every so often a newcomer would take exception, pompously, to this; he would walk past the guards, hesitate, then call loudly for the Sergeant of the Guard and start to dress him down for insubordination, very loudly, hoping people were watching. The sergeant would have marched out stiffly and thrown an enormous salute at the start of all this, carrying in his hand the Brigadier's instruction, in short words "no saluting" but in very large print. He would then cry at the top of his voice: "And welcome to COD Donnington, Sah!!" and repeat the salute as if it was an Olympic event. All the people in the guardroom would by now have come out to watch the wretched officer slink away. Most of these self-important blusterers, it seemed, were superannuating Majors who had at last been commissioned from the ranks; sad, in a way; but the men joked about them endlessly, and through the drizzle the Wrekin quivered with mirth.

On the other hand, as officers, we all – even at a place so laid-back as Donnington – conformed scrupulously to the age-old tradition of politeness, which dictated that when you enter another officer's territory (whether his dusty desk in the far corner of a warehouse, or his tent on the battlefield) you salute. Even if you are the Colonel and he is just a Subaltern, you are the visitor and you salute first – albeit sometimes a touch sardonically. In return, of course, if in fact you are the junior, you rise to attention.

But oh! American film-makers, do please note, even if you get nothing else right about us: in the British forces we do not, ever, ever, salute if we are bareheaded. Even if we are reporting to Wellington on the field at Waterloo; even if we are required to hand something to the sovereign. No hat, no salute. Get it right, Hollywood, and stop spoiling my viewing.

I went in to the Adjutant, through a hive of outer offices, and at once I was disabused of all these traditions. I swung him a good salute at the door and he just said "Yes, Yes," and didn't even look up for a while.

I told him who I was, he searched and found me on a bit of paper; then he did glance at me and sort of twitched mournfully – one couldn't call it a smile. He was bald but he had a big untidy ginger moustache that was starting to go grey at the edges. I guessed that he couldn't afford to retire and they had allowed him to stay on, lingering in this backwater because perhaps he'd had a bad war: this happened in the late Forties. In the case of this chap, perhaps he was showing signs of slow disintegration?

To my disbelief, but as I soon learned, to general hilarity, his name was not just Captain Barton, but Dick Barton. That was too good to be true, but true it was. At that time, when the nation was restricted to a mere couple of radio stations, the airwaves were full of the incredible macho adventures of 'Dick Barton, Special Agent'. Even now, whenever I hear that galloping signature-tune: dum, diddle-um, diddle-um, diddle-um, diddle-umpty-umpty-umpty-umpty... I see the ginger moustache and bald pate.

The intrepid Captain filled in a form or two, having to buzz each time for a clerk to come in and fiddle with the papers; he managed to spoil one of them with wrong entries; then he heaved to his feet and showed me out. I was to see the DC at ten-thirty.

He sat down again heavily and I got the impression that he had now dealt with his workload for the day. There had been a bottle on his shelf, close to hand, as ginger as he was. He had glanced at it several times while filling in the forms. It was only nine-thirty.

I gave him the polite salute again at the door, but I don't think he noticed. Or he couldn't be bothered any more. Or he was simply a rather unpleasant man? Who could tell?

L ife, for me, really started with the DC. And, come to think of it, nearly ended there, too.

Mac's thumbnail sketch had been spot-on: the Deputy Commandant did look just like Clement Attlee though he smiled and his eyes had, at all times I can recall, a disarmingly humorous twinkle. As we talked I would always find myself wondering what he was doing in uniform? He ought to be at an Oxbridge High Table, or better, in a deep dusty armchair surrounded by old yellowing books with bindings that were curling away, greeting a sequence of tweedy bespectacled students through a haze of smoke...

Nevertheless he carried very well the relaxed open-necked battledress with its red tabs indicating a full Colonel, one who had evidently moved pretty swiftly through the levels of routine promotion, up to half-Colonel, then after a heavy session at Staff College, achieved the membership of the red-embroidered elite. It was quite new to me, this concept that the Army's Top People can be gentle aesthetes: in films, or in the Press, one always saw them as down-to-earth fire-and-brimstone battle-champions, as in your collections of cigarette cards or in the old photos of Haig, or Kitchener's wartime recruiting poster. Later that day, it occurred to me that many of those heroes must have been equally laid-back in their private moments. Clive, Wolfe, Kitchener himself? Roberts, and why not Rommel and Alexander for that matter – though probably not Montgomery – may well have written poetry in their secret hours. And I remember that Wavell had brought out a splendid anthology of verse 'Other Men's Flowers', a brilliant title harking back to Montaigne's 'garland'. And then, further back, how about Philip Sidney; or Raleigh's sad "Even such is time…", written in his Bible the night before they cut his head off.

The DC started with a few chatty questions about my background, since of course the Army files refused to believe that anyone had existed before call-up, so his briefing from Mons or Whitehall must have been short.

Then he said briskly: "I'm putting you in Building Five, that's our main Engineering and Radar stores, under Colonel Young." It is usual to abbreviate the title Lieutenant-Colonel in everyday conversation, it didn't mean promotion. Titles can become really topheavy, the higher up the ladder one goes, accumulating suffixes: our own Brigadier-General and Marshal of the Royal Air Force are bad enough but at least they spring lightly off one's tongue. The Germans must surely be the worst: how about the six syllables of Obersturmbannführer? If that doesn't actually get worse with each promotion, I'm sure Hollywood – more likely Ealing and Pinewood – will have played about with the idea sometime.

"I've alerted Colonel Young, so he'll be expecting you in a few minutes. But first," and he pushed a button, "I'm asking the ADC to join us." He explained that the initials stood not for an 'aide-de-camp', "I don't go in for those just yet," but simply Assistant DC. "There's something else I'd like to discuss."

A fat man with hair like a monk waddled in and looked at me curiously.

"This is Major Parrott. Sit down, Bill. Meet Mr Topps. I'm putting him in with Harry Young's lot. But there's this Codonian business, you know."

The fat man offered us his silver-plated cigarette-case, and a lighter which must have come from Egypt, I forget why I thought so. The DC very rarely smoked, as his assistant must have known; but I took one and lit it rather nervously. What was this 'something else; this 'business'?'...

"Topps," the DC picked up a page of close typing, "when you were at our training centre at Tidworth, you chatted to Captain Clements."

I remembered him well: six-foot-six, austere, a bit like De Gaulle without that sense of humour. But whatever could I have said which merited a whole page of comment?

"It says here," waving the paper at me, "that you're something of a literary bloke. Is that correct?"

In a flood of relief, I tried to look modest, but had to admit that I'd had some stuff published, from a six-part thriller in a Kenya Sunday paper at the age of ten, up to a short radio play on the BBC a few years ago – twice repeated, I meekly conceded. They looked at each other, then the DC went on.

"More to the point, didn't you edit your school magazine?"

At this, genuine modesty came to my rescue: "Well, sub-editor really; our headmaster always insisted that only he was the actual –"

"Yes," said the DC drily, "I've met the man."

The fat Major asked: "Have you seen The Codonian yet?" It meant nothing to me. "Our depot newspaper." He passed me the latest issue; it hung limply from my hand, eight pages only, so it was merely two pieces of double foolscap folded together; but well printed with plenty of photographs. It seemed to consist chiefly of hurried sports results surrounded by cinema adverts.

I looked at the DC in puzzlement. Were they really going to ask me to write for this awful thing, maybe report football matches between all our Companies?

It seemed to get worse. The Major asked: "Are you keen on sports?"

I wasn't, never had been, not in the least, a terrible waste of writing time. "Not really," I muttered.

"Well, thank God for that," and they both nodded happily. "Most of our young Subalterns get dragged into sports in the evenings, up at Battalion Camp by Major Thomas, whom you'll meet, eh Bill?" and they started nodding at each other again.

"But *you* won't, will you Topps? So you'll have plenty of time to work on The Codonian." I sank back into the chair and relaxed, a bit too soon.

"You're Editor," said the DC, and the blue eyes smiled.

Is there a word 'bemusement'? If so, that's what I was full of as I wound my way across the Depot, warehouse after warehouse, heading for Building Five. It took quite a while, but I had plenty to think about.

I had only been in the place sixteen hours and already I had two jobs, a quarter of a batman, and a possible girlfriend but only at long range and in violation of the rules. However, something told me that around these parts, the rules were likely to be fairly pliable. I looked across to The Wrekin. I couldn't see it.

The DC had sent me away to report to Col. Young and check-in to my day job. Later, that evening after dinner, I was to meet him again in the Mess to talk about my sudden elevation into the upper echelons of Fleet Street, or rather the supernumerary editorship of a weekly newsletter. It was typeset by people in Newport, but printed on site by the Printing and Publications Department, over in Building 18. I diverted to take a look from the road at the place where my editorial staff were based; far end of the Building, I'd been told. It looked quite impressive and I decided to call a meeting next morning, but not bother them meanwhile: the DC would be telling me how he wanted them organised.

As it became clear that P&P was diametrically opposite from E&R at Building Five, an incidental but valuable advantage occurred to me, something I had learnt as a private: as often as I wished, I would have the excellent excuse to be away from my offices, "on his way to the other". There was an important old rule, taught me by a Corporal at Tidworth: always carry a folder and a worried expression... This would not prove difficult, I would seldom have to fake it.

★ ★ ★

At E&R I found my tortuous way between skyscraping shelves and boxes of mystery, all scrupulously stencilled with descriptions of the contents in words that I could hardly pronounce, let alone understand. I had never in my life done a day of engineering, let alone radar, whatever that was: I thought it was something that ships beamed down to the bottom of the sea and measured the echo, or aircraft dropped like silver paper to confuse other aircraft. Maybe I would learn? (I never did).

Eventually, deep in the centre of the huge warehouse, was the HQ office, sort of prefabricated and stuck there with square panels and square windows and a handful of square people busy in their domain. I could see Col. Young at his desk, in his inner sanctum at the middle of it all. Suddenly I could also visualise him running a grocery store in Inverness and – yes, indeed – sure enough, in his outer office sat Mac. Things were getting better all the time.

I went in. As she looked up I raised both arms in surrender against her pistol. You don't salute NCOs, but I felt I ought to do something.

No smile.

"Good morning, Sir."

OK, if that's the way we must play it in working hours. She

gave a double push on a buzzer, the colonel looked up and beckoned me in. I saluted, he stood up and held out a hand welcomingly. Short neat hair, face still a bit tanned from overseas service, very clear eyes but hard to pinpoint their colour; he was a very small man, but probably, I sensed for no identifiable reason, a good cricketer – I still have no idea why I thought that, but do you know what I mean? As Mac had said on the train: "A nice wee chap."

If I say that my half-hour with him was interesting, I must at once qualify it. In my Corps Training prior to being commissioned I had learnt all there was to know about the handling of Army stores. My Corps was the RAOC – Royal Army Ordnance Corps – and had its origins in carting guns and ammunition from store to battlefield and, hopefully, back again... As the decades went by, we had become responsible for every sort of supply to worldwide Army units, except perishable stuff like food. When a Unit somewhere wanted something from us, a form would be filled in, in seven parts lying under each other so they only had to write the request once and carbon did the rest. It was, I believe, a system they had adapted from Marks and Spencer, and it was fascinating: the seven bits of paper, all different colours, went off in seven different directions to satisfy and record the order, the diispatch, delivery, stocktake, accounting and I forget what else; but eventually – from wherever in the world – they all came together again, and when we were taught all this, the denoument at the end was – it sounds utterly ridiculous – romantically exciting... How one can become brainwashed!

So all the Colonel had to do was explain how our Building Five, like others around us which dealt in different types of material, was in three sections: Receipts – Stock Maintenance – Issues. It was that easy.

I was to be 'in charge' of Receipts; fortunately, given my

ignorance, I would be sharing the office with a 'CSO', Chief Stores Officer, who was a fully knowledgable and long-serving civilian. In reality, as can well be appreciated, he – in my case the splendid Mr Stanworth – was the person in control, and I was to be his equal-status 'shadow' in case of alarms and excursion; also, if necessary, to make sure that our soldier storemen obeyed orders, as many of them didn't think much of the civilians. And anyway, covering the whole building was a very senior – almost over-aged – Warrant Officer known as a Conductor, much respected by the soldiery. It rapidly became clear to me that I would have plenty of time for my editorial chair…

★ ★ ★

… And I was going to need it, I would be telling myself by bedtime. After a very respectable dinner at the single long table, where about twenty of us met up, completely without ceremony, to enjoy a nicely-underdone steak which had been heralded in by an astonishing clear tomato soup (completely and utterly clear, you could see right through it like rose-tinted glass, with ribbons of the skin floating around); after all that I carried my coffee across the hall and took up a waiting position near the door, beside the big fireplace where a heap of logs was spitting at nobody. Several armchairs were ranged around the fire but none of us sat on them, and I remembered that even the PMC had kept to one side. From time I had spent in one or two other Officers Messes (see, no apostrophe – I was learning all the time) , I remembered that at most such places, despite the disengagement of protocol which specified complete equality in the Mess, all officers' ranks being politely ignored, nevertheless Orwell's Law still simmered below the surface and no less-equal junior officer would ever presume to sit in front of the fire unless specifically invited by one of the Top Brass.

The DC came limping in – I think he had taken a bit of shrapnel, low on the hip, at Benghazi or somewhere like that. He nodded and pointed down to the far end of the room; as I started to move there I noticed that he went over to the fireside armchairs and scooped up a highly-embroidered cushion and a matching antimacassar from the furthest one, placed by the Richardson window with its view of everyone coming or going.

Down the end, he swung left and we were in the wartime extension. From within it looked no different though possibly the windows let in a bit more draught. The chairs were the same; the carpet a bit worn, while those back in the main Common Room had recently been renewed. But there was another fire in a grate, and he waved me into one of the chairs, setting out his curiously-woven personal insignia on the other before sinking into it with an end-of-day sigh.

"I've ordered you a scotch, straight but with ice, on the recommendation of the PMC, is that all right, Topps?"

I thanked him, also the orderly who had followed us discreetly round the corner. I quietly noted the DC's meticulous choice of the right word: 'recommendation' was neat and just a touch sardonic; and anyway, 'advice' would have rhymed with 'ice' and sounded banal. If I was going to edit his crummy newspaper I'd have to keep my wits about me.

"Don't let anyone disturb us, Charles," he told the orderly. Then, to me over the top of his glass: "Settled in OK?"

I told him 'Yes', but it hadn't half been a busy twenty-four hours.

"You'll like Harry Young. Used to open for Worcestershire, but he was a hopeless fielder. Never caught anything, couldn't reach it."

"Yes sir, I like him already," I said, quietly preening myself on my brilliant ability to sum people up. "E & R will be interesting –"

"Bollocks." To my surprise.

"Sir?"

"Ninety per cent of the work we do here, certainly for the past couple of years, has been utterly boring, and will continue to be: there's absolutely no escape and I am sometimes amazed that we don't all shoot ourselves. I often wish we still had air-raids." At least he had the grace to look guilty on saying this.

"But then," with a long sip, "you can escape all that, Topps, lucky chap that you are. Through the Codonian, you see."

I began to sense that he was seeing the paper as his own sideline that might counteract the insidious Depot Boredom; I could go along with that, with this lively man.

"Let me tell you about The Codonian. It has been going for several years but really sort of dribbling along like something off a Company notice-board. The last editor Captain Tisdale has just been posted to Hong Kong but he was more of an HQ clerk really, heart wasn't in it, or if it was, he hadn't much heart. Weekly. Price, twopence. Circulation, around three thousand."

That was a hell of lot, I thought, for a weekly news-sheet; I told him so. "That is splendid, Sir. There must be a whole lot of really interesting news items, or articles? Or is it the sports pages?"

"Good God, no. But the civilians buy it all the time."

I must have looked perplexed. I'd never actually had to *sell* a paper, at school the mag. had a captive readership who got it free anyway.

"It's the cinema adverts." said the DC.

Some things in life are amazingly simple, when you think about it from a different angle. We were on to something here, odd though it was.

27

"It's much more expensive for the cinemas to advertise in the local Wellington or county papers, they charge the earth. And you must have seen, this area is lousy with picture-houses, mostly fleapits to be sure, but they're always full: nothing else to do except take girls up the slagheaps afterwards..." He seemed to go a bit dreamy at this point. I had already been told that these grassed-over acres were renowned locally as a courting-ground, so much space, room undisturbed for all, but if only they could have found a more romantic name for it... The DC came back to earth.

"So," he said, "you have a solid core of about three thousand civilians buying their movie dates and performance timetables from you for a weekly twopence. And now, you see," and he sat forward, "you must build on this."

"What about our soldiers," I asked. "Do they tend to buy the paper?"

Possibly, he told me drily, the few who can read. And he added: just for the cinema ads, you know, but they can see copies at the Company Office, anyway, for free."

I tried to pull myself together.

"Sir – if I'm going to edit it, how should I go about it? What do you want to do? I need to have your guidance."

He stared into the fire for a long while, then turned to me bodily, dislodging his antimacassar.

"The Codonian must be expanded, built up, so that everybody buys it, at least all the civilians. I'm not so bothered about the military because they come and go all the time." I couldn't see the logic of this at the time, but it soon became clear.

"I can expand on this and give you reasons soon," he went on, "But all that matters for you at the moment is – improve the appeal, bring in articles, correspondence columns, whatever you can come up with."

It was getting a bit late, and the DC was becoming mellow. He sipped further into his whisky.

After a while he told me thoughtfully: "This is quite good stuff, you know. The Catering Officer gets it from somebody up North he's got a hold on. Glen-something. You'll meet Kittie soon, he's brilliant but terribly out of shape. He keeps a barrel of it under his bed but he thinks nobody knows – ask Charles. Good chap though, Kittie. You'll recognise him, he looks like two poached eggs in a bucket of blood."

When Captain Kitson, ACC, came carefully into the Common Room a few days later, it's an awful thing to say but I recognised him instantly.

★ ★ ★

The DC wouldn't let me buy the next round, when I waved across to the orderly. "No, no, Topps, this is an official conference." (That was the same line I'd shot with Mac on the train, come to think of it). "You can treat me when your circulation reaches five thousand. But let me – Charles, as before please – let me answer your question in a bit more depth…"

I'd had the presence of mind to bring a notepad, and fished out a pen in readiness. But I put it away again, as his alarming answer sank in… Though I had to wait for it.

"What I want," he began, then went silent, either deep in profound thought or running out of ideas altogether. I felt I should try, drawing upon the enormous scope of my journalistic experience, to help him.

"Can you perhaps tell me, sir, whether your aim is – one, just to increase circulation; two, to boost our advertising income; three, to improve the news reporting; or four, to stimulate readers with provocative articles, get them to 'join in' with letters to the editor and so on?"

29

"Five," said the DC and drained his new glass completely. "To catch a spy."

★ ★ ★

Traditional journalism would say that at this point I took a deep breath and called for my sword and breastplate, sweeping back nonchalantly my tangled mass of flame-coloured hair; but we can't all match Chesterton. As I recall, I just couldn't properly breathe at all for a minute or so. Oh, and I spilt my drink, which I have regretted ever since, as it *was* a nice Glen-something and I miss it late at night when I have become pensive or whatever they call it. However, the fire crackled laughingly at me for those long seconds while the DC clearly enjoyed my reactions; and eventually I cleared my throat and air passages, and was bold enough to point to his battle-dress.

"Is this why," I croaked, "you are all carrying guns, forgive me for asking?" He ignored the question, for the moment.

"Tim," he said, and the unexpected use of my first name was clever and had the desired effect, "I think – and nobody else knows this except Major Parrott – we think The Codonian can have an important part to play, and for some time we've been looking for the right chap to run it covertly so that through its pages we can nail the bastard."

I opened my mouth but nothing much came out; he was standing up anyway.

"For now," he concluded our meeting, "just get to know the paper and feel your way. There's no hurry, no immediate secrets to defend; what we seem to have is called a 'sleeper', who has been planted here, presumably by Moscow, and might well be working here for years until one fine day they call upon him. So, build up the paper and make it an essential read for the Depot, whatever way you think best; but come and see me every week before you – what's the phrase? – before you put it to bed." He was very proud of that. "Goodnight." And as he turned the corner and reached the better carpet: "Oh, and write us a story or two."

That I will, I told myself as I walked home along The Avenue; and I'll go in the morning and give all the staff a pep-talk.

IV

I slept on the DC's alarming news, and as I walked to my Receipts Office next morning found myself looking furtively left and right, especially when passing civilians. Was that scruffy young messenger on his bike whistling the Volga Boatman? Did that little old lady behind the secret-laden desk have snow on her boots? How on earth was my flimsy news-sheet going to coax them all (for by now I imagined there was a whole sea of murderous Communists among us) out of their sneaky wormholes, and into the grim corridors of MI5, ultimately to the Old Bailey where the whole story would unfold in the National Press, and I would stay on in the Army as Editor of – perhaps? – the Royal Codonian Weekly, circulation huge all over Western Command?

In Building Five, sitting at his desk alongside my smaller wobbly table, was my CSO, Mr Stanworth. He was probably in his late fifties and had just had all his teeth out: perhaps senior Civil Servants had had no difficulty in getting extra wartime sugar. We smiled at each other, but painfully and with gaping embarrassment on both sides, only one of them figurative. We would get friendly in the months to come, no doubt, though I did look at his boots from time to time.

I then crossed the Depot to make my first and important entrance to the Codonian offices, in the remote Building Eighteen of P & P. (Before long it would be Building Five that I would regard as remote). The slender ATS clerk , sitting seductively but aloof and studiously disinterested in me at the reception desk, surely – and I was right – handpicked by her boss, buzzed me across to the building's HQ office where I was to meet the lady in charge of Printing & Publications: Junior Commander Chunk.

I approached her glassy office nervously; thinking perhaps she was part-Chinese, and I ought to look at her boots too. But never has a surname been more appropriate: Peggy Chunk was mountainous. I saluted of course, but it was ignored – I was a man.

She was sitting gigantically at her large but bare desk but, even like that, I'll swear she was taller than I was. What's more, her feet were buried under a large alsatian that immediately started sneering at me. I bet it was a bitch. This made any sort of fruitful social conversation almost impossible; and so it would continue for weeks, until we wore each other down.

When I told her I had been made Codonian editor and had come to meet my staff, she raised an eyebrow and pointed wordlessly to the distant corner of the building.

I sauntered over, between thunderous machines that were heaving out long streams of leaflets, instruction booklets, regulations, and forms, forms, forms… and came at last to a small heaped table which I took to be the paper's Reception Desk. It was covered with trays of cuttings and photographs and, mainly, cinema programmes. Behind it all sat a sensible-looking private. I spent a while looking at him and all the stuff around him. He didn't seem to mind. He didn't stand up and salute because the 'officer proprieties' didn't apply, and besides we weren't wearing caps.

I said: "Good morning. I've been appointed your Editor. I would like to talk to you all," and I looked around for the inner offices, and the hive of activity.

"All?" echoed Private Brown. "That's me, sir, pull up a chair."

* * *

David Brown was holding the fort, and had been doing so for nearly a year. My new colleague told me how he had gravitated during National Service from normal clerical duties into, first, writing an occasional sports report, then editing them all as other inarticulate sportsmen sent them in, being sure to obtain two reports for each match in order to balance the blatant lies; then ultimately somehow – he couldn't quite remember how – finding himself compiling the entire paper, writing the front page news story, collating everything else, and doing the layout then taking it by tilly to Newport to be set up. He got no recognition for this, but as he told me, it was better than working in a store and doing military exercises in the rain every Saturday. He had twice had a new arrival as an assistant, but each time they had been posted away to the Far East and he didn't want that to happen to him, so he decided to keep quiet about the workload and muddle on.

I told him I thought he was muddling pretty damn well. He then generously admitted his real reason, since I would henceforth be sharing it. The dozen or so local cinemas, thrilled with the inexpensiveness of their adverts with us, were sending him an inexhaustible flow of free passes. He confessed an insatiable love of the movies; and he was taking girls, every night of the week, apparently, to this picture house or that; and then, I silently supposed, up to the slagheaps.

This was clearly a positive thinker. We had to get together to build a powerful Codonian, to perform a real public service, to stimulate and inspire the readers around the Depot, and to get me a slice of the free passes. (Would Mac like to go to the pictures in, say, Shrewsbury?)

But of course, I couldn't tell Brown, or anybody, about the DC's secret plan, not least because I hadn't a clue yet, how I could begin to implement it. As he had told me last night, my first job – Stage One – was in every way possible to boost interest in the paper, especially among the civilian workforce. I would present this to Brown, quite acceptably, as my goal. It would be an enjoyable challenge in its own right, and I told him we must get together on it as soon as this week's issue had gone to bed. He had never heard the phrase.

On the way out I called back at the Chunkery, but the Junior Commander was out, at an important ways-and-means meeting. I left a thank-you-see-you-soon message with the slender ATS girl at the reception desk but she didn't smile back. I decided I wouldn't bother to offer her a night at the pictures, after all. Perhaps two tickets to Peggy now and then, or was she on to this little racket already?

★ ★ ★

When I got back to my Receipts office, Mr Stanworth had gone to an early Civil Service lunch, so I would be on my own for about three hours. I rang Mac on the intercom for the first time.

"This," I pronounced importantly, "is the Editor of the Codonian. Am I speaking to Staff Sergeant Mackinnon?" I could imagine her, not recognising my voice along the line, coming to attention as she sat.

"Yes, sir, that is I," she said in her best Inverness telephone voice.

"There is something we need to know, without delay, Staff."
"Sir?"

"We need to know," I said very slowly, and then speeded up as it became more ridiculous, "whether you have any knowledge about the man on the bus with four brown-paper bags full of fruit?"

Only a moment's silence, and then those lovely chuckles started.

"Tell me," she said eventually and with the utmost seriousness, "about the man on the bus with four bags –"

"Brown-paper bags."

"Sorry, sir."

"This man," I went on, "opened one bag, took out an apple, carefully peeled it, and threw the peel out of the window. He then sliced the apple – "

"Carefully, sir?"

"Indeed. Then he also threw all the slices out of the window. Next, he took a banana out of the second bag –"

"Did he peel it?" she asked, very concerned to get the facts right.

"He did. Then he cut the banana into thin slices –"

She interrupted me, how thin would those slices have been.

"Thin, very thin, Staff Sergeant. As thin as a Scottish shortbread. I hope you are taking notes?"

"Oh, I am, sir, believe me."

"Because then, and also with an orange and an apricot, he threw all the slices out of the window. After which," I concluded, "I really had to ask this man –"

"Why was he doing it?"

"Staff, you are so perceptive. Indeed, that is what I asked. I said to him: 'Why are you doing it?' And he told me he was making a fruit salad."

"That would have been a reasonable assumption. But why, then did he throw –?"

"He said he didn't like fruit salad."

As I've said, a shared giggle with an attractive girl is one of Life's blessings. Then still very serious, she added:

"You forgot to say what happened to the banana skin. You slipped up on that," and as she put the phone down, "Sir."

★ ★ ★

Looking back, it cannot have been pure altruism that led Brown and me to make our first improvement to the Codonian, an extension of the film adverts to the outer reaches of North Shropshire; but in those days many folk went to the pictures everywhere, incessantly; and we doubled the allotted column-inches. Then, one day as we worked our way smokily through our first large tin of powdered coffee, he said: "How about all the rest? People who aren't film-goers? We need an improvement that will make them buy."

"And keep buying," I added.

"So, an issue with a sensational scoop, advertised in every Building the day before we publish; and –"

"Yes! That issue containing a couple of series which they'll want to follow –"

"Like a competition with the prize –"

"Free film passes –"

"Announced next week…"

All this began to come together over the next few weeks. Our sensational story, if you could call it that, was a gift from the blue. Recently the famous personality Professor Joad had been arrested and fined for travelling on a train without a valid ticket, front page news nationwide; and very soon after, one of the Depot's CSOs was hauled up for the same offence. Naturally enough, the world's Press hardly thought this worthy of more than an inch or two, if that; but Brown and I sat and looked at each other. I went to see the DC.

"He got off," said the DC.

"The train?" I ventured.

"The charge, Topps, for God's sake." They found his real ticket in his other pocket. There's not much of a front page story in that."

I had to change direction quickly, and managed it.

"But Sir," I argued, quite adroitly I reckoned, "what if he

had been found guilty? Half the Depot are probably guilty from time to time of little slip-ups, minor, you know, misdemeanours, here and there. If one of our civilians does get into that sort of trouble, would they have to lose their jobs?"

"I see what you're getting at."

"They'll all be interested to know how far the matter could go, where would the line be drawn, between staying in work or being booted out."

"Yes, Topps, they'd buy that issue for twopenn'orth of legal advice, wouldn't they? Well done, I'll get Cripps to write you an article."

With him looking like Attlee, I was disconcerted for a moment at the thought of the stygian Sir Stafford homing in on us; but he must have spotted this because he explained that his Cripps was not only unrelated but an earnest young lawyer at our Tidworth HQ. (And the article came, just a week later, aimed directly at the Depot civilians, and headed: "What If Joad Did It? Legally, How Far Can You Go?" Sub-title "Keep This, In Case".)

"Hold it back for a couple of weeks," the DC went on, "and hint at the story in advance, to get them buying when the time comes. And do keep me in the picture, Topps; I'm on your side, and you and I know what we're doing, but I've got one or two crusty colleagues around the place, senior people in fact, who aren't keen on your changes to the paper, and they'll be watching."

After a pause: "You've noticed, I suppose, that some of us are armed?"

Earlier than you think, I said to myself, remembering my train journey.

He scribbled on a piece of official paper and handed it to me. "It won't do any harm, now you're in the thick of things." Thanks a lot, I thought. "Take that to the Adjutant, if you can find him, best to go in the morning."

Yes, that figured.

"Oh," as I headed for the door, "and don't shoot yourself in the foot." Then that twinkle: "I'm speaking journalistically."

★ ★ ★

As I may have already indicated, Captain (Ginger) Barton was difficult to take to one's bosom at the best of times – which had to be chosen carefully. He had managed to construct around himself a maze of clerks and assistants to cover most eventualities; and when you had negotiated all these, carrying your thread with you if you were wise, you found at the centre of the maze, an idiot. He evidently thought that in requesting a pistol, 'just a small one, please', I was being unforgivably both presumptuous and precious. I felt it, too: I'd never asked anybody for a portable death-weapon before.

"What! You?" he puffed. "You haven't been here five minutes, you're the least important person in the whole bloody Depot. Sodding upstarts – just because you went to a public bloody –"

I handed him the DC's note and walked out. Oh yes – I saluted.

A nice little automatic was delivered to me, with thirty rounds, early next day, at the Codonian office, and Private Brown was watching as I signed for it. I could feel him thinking...

"I know we're planning to run some series on people and places, and things to make the readers come back for more," he pondered, and we had certainly been brooding over this at the odd moment. "But what if – How about a serial? An adventure story –?"

We went once more into our double-act. It kept things alive.

"Yes, set in the Depot –"

"Naming the actual buildings, real locations –"

"Blood and thunder, but jokey?"

"Real people, real names, maybe not –" Whichever one of us said that, withdrew it. But then:

"A sort of skit on 'Dick Barton, Special Agent'?"

"My God!" I cried; with a single bound I was back at the centre of that maze of officialdom. "Our Adjutant!"

This just couldn't wait. That very evening we both scribbled on in glee, until past midnight; and the next week began a regular half-page of excitement, the thrilling exploits all over the Depot of our starring hero "Bart Dixon, Special Detergent (A Soap)".

We wrote it in turns, mischievously ending each episode with a cliff-hanger that presented next week's writer with a tricky problem. It ran for weeks as the valiant Captain fought his and the world's deadliest foes in the most unlikely local venues. There were bombs with smoking fuses in the NAAFI, we blew up a couple of latrines, store-rooms soaked in deadly fumes, but our gallant hero sailed through, although in one early instalment all his hair was blown off by a Red rocket missile. In the end the DC put a smiling stop to it.

But I did manage, in our final episode, to have Bart miraculously survive his closest shave: "The bullets went right through the middle of his head, missing the brain by just a few inches." I was bought several drinks in the Mess that week, for some reason.

★ ★ ★

"Have you heard about Mrs. Lambert?" I asked Mac over the intercom next day. She hadn't but as the Colonel was out, she'd like to. This was a silly story I'd been told years before, about the man who knew everything about women and had all the information filed away in his office, "in section and part-

40

number order," I added, to give it local colour. It is best told standing up, with mimes of opening cabinets or unlocking drawers and so on, and over the phone it was going to be a challenge.

A visitor came to his office one day and asked: "Do you know Mrs Lambert?"

"Just a moment. (Sound of filing cabinet, paper rustles) Yes, yes, I know Mrs Lambert."

Visitor bristles. "Did you go out with Mrs Lambert?"

"Dear me." (Pages being turned) "Yes, I went out with Mrs Lambert."

Visitor agitated. "Did you – kiss – Mrs Lambert?"

(heavy ledger noises, many pages). "Yes, I kissed Mrs Lambert."

Visitor, (heavy breathing, low growl) "Did you –sleep with Mrs Lambert?"

"Ah, let me see." (keys jangle; door creaks; huge ledger; pages turn) "Yes, I slept with Mrs Lambert."

Visitor shouts: "Well, I'm Mr Lambert and I don't like it!"

"Just a moment." (pages turn) "No, neither did I."

That must have been the only time all the filing cabinets in Receipts had been opened and slammed shut on the same day, and then only for sound effects; but it worked and I noted a high mark on the gigglemeter.

It had been told to me originally as 'The Mrs Lambert Story'; I never knew why, and surely that is most unfair, not to say dangerous. If your name happens to be Lambert, please put down the phone: it wasn't you, it must have been two other people, as I've said before.

(However: long ago now, we moved into a house in Cambridge, and that evening at our house-warming in the garden, over my third glass, I asked in a loud voice if they'd heard the great joke about Mrs Lambert. You won't need telling

41

the name, we later discovered, of our new neighbours on the other side of the fence).

★ ★ ★

It was nearly Christmas, and I volunteered to stay on duty at the Depot, and take my leave over the New Year. As I had no near family immediately at hand, this made good sense: life around the Buildings would be very easygoing, also up at Battalion Camp with a skeleton staff and lots of turkey. I looked forward to the Christmas Day tradition which dictates that the officers serve the men (in my grandfather's cavalry days they fed the horses first), before adjourning to our own hedonism at the Mess. That thought about the horses gave me the idea for the first Editorial of the coming year: care of the horses had given way to care of the tanks and all those other vehicles we had littering the perimeter: should they be oiled and groomed on Christmas morning, just to preserve the old Army traditions?

I thought I might have a chat to the officers, involved with Vehicle Maintenance, who had their own Mess (called Armaments Mess) right up at the far end of The Avenue; so I trudged up there three days before Christmas. There could perhaps even be a series in this: the 'lines' were cluttered with every sort of horseless carriage, as I had seen on occasions when seeking new ways to traverse the Depot between my two offices. Certainly there were tanks and armoured cars, still in their desert camouflage, but also motorbikes and sidecars with or without machine-guns; lorries and PCVs of all dimensions – What? Oh, Personnel Carrying Vehicles – and tillies, those nice little Utility Trucks, usually driven by nice little ATS girls hand-picked from the Driving Pool and firmly believed, at least by us subalterns, to be 'Subalterns, for the use of', and I'm not sure that just meant the van. Then there were the rows of old beaten-up khaki-and-sand ambulances, lines and lines of them, and so full of forgotten stories and agonies; not least those in which some of those nice little ATS girls would have ended up, far from the battlefields, the vehicle known to all, including black-jokily the ATS themselves, as the 'Blunder-bus'. "Har-har", as the PMC would say.

I had never been to Armaments Mess before, but I had been warned that it was full of Irishmen, known for their chaos and their dangerous hospitality. Also, it seemed, for their democratic lack of pretension.

As I approached, past a fierce-looking DUKW landing-craft from D-Day proud of its bulletholes, a tall thin man in his shirtsleeves was mopping the front steps.

"Where can I find your PMC?" I asked.

"Sure," he said, "I'll be wid yez in a minute."

He was a colonel. Inside, he introduced me to several other officers and I got my story. But wait: Once you have accepted an Irish Coffee there is no easy escape. It slides down you un-noticed, and before you know it, so does the third. Some years later, I have to tell you this, in my business life I found myself lunching with an Irish politician at Jury's in Dublin, and over the pudding he began to sing, to himself, loudly. The restaurant was full, but nobody cared… However, the Maitre d' eventually came steaming across, and I feared the worst. He stood for a while beside us magisterially. He fixed my carolling friend with his eye. Then:

He joined in.

This disarming effect of Gaelic Coffee was also at work that evening at Armaments. Christmas being only a few hours away, as they put it, what better than to spread the goodwill around the houses? Carol singing must surely be the answer? So about ten of us set off, well muffled against the snow, led by that elderly but youthful Gaelic half-colonel and a young medic whose name might have been O'Hara. We worked our melodious way along The Avenue, greeted by officers, wives and offspring all the time, though we found that more than once we had to retire to the Mess to warm up: translated as 'refuel'.

At last, and it must have been past ten, we ended at my own HQ Mess, but nobody was in except Kittie who was asleep by the fire and the PMC who was hiding from carol singers. We hovered outside, reluctant to call it a day, when young Doctor O'Hara remembered that he had arranged for hot drinks over at the ATS CRS.

We managed to circumnavigate the pond or whatever it was, and also the barbed wire – it couldn't have deterred many resourceful Americans in the War if they had been sober – and we were welcomed in.

In the friendly entrance hall of the little hospital, all trimmed femininely with a tree that glistened and had, on top, at a precarious angle, a fairy with battledress and three pips that looked very much like O'Hara, we were greeted with warm mince-pies and steaming coffee; and by four charming ATS nurses.

We all sang, ostensibly for the handful of patients who listened through an open door, but mainly for ourselves. I shared a songsheet with a very, very likeable and attractive girl about my own age who had also been a trained dancer, she certainly had the figure for it; and she went, just a touch irreligiously, through a tap routine to some of the less lively carols.

Then we all kissed them Goodnight and Merry Christmas and dispersed. I don't know about all those Officers Houses, but we ourselves weren't short of the seasonal Goodwill. At the steps of the Mess, I stopped short, as soon as none of the party were looking. I had left my gloves on a chair, how silly of me.

I went back, around the lake as it now seemed certain to be. The moon was shining on it, as I remember.

My tap dancer answered the door, as I had hoped she would. My gloves were in her hand. Her name, she said, was Bobbie Roberts, and we both felt we ought to repeat that wish of a Merry Christmas. I noticed that over the last few minutes she had put some mistletoe in her hair.

V

You don't need to be told that after Bobbie had gone for Christmas and I, then, for the New Year – we hadn't met again after the carol night – I wasted little time in phoning the CRS. A crisp gruff voice which I assumed must be female told me that Private Roberts had gone: posted away to the Military Hospital in Chester. So that was that, snuffed out even before it had started. A great pity: I have always believed that two people can often correctly get the feeling straight away that they would be good for one another. Ah well, I thought. You lose some…

On the other hand, my flirtation with Mac, went from strength to strength along the wires: I rang her every day, launching straight into a joke without any preamble, though strictly only once a day. At that time I still had a long list of punchlines, dating back to long hilarious sessions at school with my father whenever he was home on leave from the Empire; he was a born raconteur much in demand as an after-dinner speaker at the British Council or the Overseas League meetings – even, I suspected, the Masons – wherever around the world he was stationed. Always brilliant, but perhaps always the same speech, a sort of Diplomatic Musichall act? One never knew, and certainly I never asked; anyway, why not, if it worked and showed the witty side of The Flag?

Nevertheless I stole all his best jokes, and the punchlines filled a page. I've lost it long ago, but by then my inside jacket pocket had rubbed out most of it. There's nothing worse than an endless list of disconnected punchlines.

Mac and I never made much progress in any intimate physical way. I took her to the cinema a few times, as you can imagine, given free seats, free icecream, handshakes from the management – but at least I had the decency to take her to a pub on the way home. It never got beyond an almost brother-and-sister relationship... Well, hang on, not quite. There would be a goodnight kiss, which was the way things began in those days; a lingering one, in a swirl of feminine scents and perfume, but was there any hint of promise? Those kisses, as a rule at the start of a potential relationship, would have two-dimensional proportions: medium length but little depth, if you know what I mean.

The joke-phoning was stopped in the end by Col. Young bowling me out. He could hardly help seeing Mac through his window, creasing up with the giggles every morning, and I now reckon he was envious: after all, she was terrifically attractive and so witty – and I saw his wife once.

But I did manage one closing success. The colonel was telling me, in front of Mac and with others around, that these long calls had to cease. He claimed that the engaged line had twice interfered with important calls from the Brigadier, that remote entity one heard of... (It's only now that I have seen the fault in his argument: the Brigadier would surely have phoned the colonel's direct line, not via Mac? Unless... Oh, no, not the Brig? But then, read on).

I said sadly: "May I just end, Sir, with one last joke – the shortest in the world?" Everybody in the office stopped what they were doing and looked at him. He found that he couldn't deny me. I said, with the last syllable in a high falsetto: "Mind that Boathook!" (the falsetto is absolutely essential).

Wherever you are, Bill Carrington old pal, thanks for that one. The whole office, the Colonel, his number two the pleasant Captain Critchell, Mac herself, and a couple of privates setting mousetraps all collapsed, and I marched proudly back to Receipts and told Mr Stanworth. Much of his sense of humour had been crushed under a lifetime's strata of red tape and Union memoranda, but an outcrop still remained and he nodded a lot and bared all his new teeth at me.

Next day "through the usual channels" a small package was delivered to Receipts. It had been fully documented via Issues Section at the far end of the building, and addressed to me marked "Re-taken-in, to be signed for." It was about the size of a packet of Players. Inside, with a bow of blue ribbon around it, was a dead mouse; and a message in nice feminine handwriting: "A dear wee mouse for a dear wee boy."

I sent one of my storemen to Mac with a saucer of milk.

★ ★ ★

It so happened that the end of my Mac involvement came, alas, only a few nights later. I was sitting quietly in the Mess, toying with the Telegraph crossword I expect, with a subalternine gin-and-orange at my elbow, when the fat Major Parrott lurched in with some of his cronies and settled in high spirits at a table nearby. After a while I heard him say: "Hey, have you heard the story about Mrs. Lambert?"

So that was that. Mac was evidently on her way to higher things, however grotesque they might be. Well, good luck to her, I decided. I didn't blame her in the least, and I suppose the Major wasn't all that fat really: it just pleases me, even now, to think so.

★ ★ ★

Over at the Fleet Street sector of my duties, we had quickly decided, with the approval of the DC and the disbelief of

Gefangenlagerkommandantsmitarbeiter Chunk – or Tschunk as I had started to spell it, confusing my Fascism with my newly-feared Communism – to go up from eight pages to twelve. This still only meant three sheets of doubled foolscap, the extra cost was more than covered by the increased cinema ads, and anyway – I told her with a big smile as she was printing it – there were three double-fools working on it, weren't there?

Brown no doubt noticed that I was talking about 'ads' now, having shaken off the prissy amateur 'adverts' which dated back to my immaturity of editing the school magazine. (I always wanted to ask Brown whether he had edited his school magazine, if there had been one, but was afraid to in case he upstaged me). The extra pages allowed us to develop many of the 'expansion' ideas I had been discussing with the DC. I couldn't tell Brown any of that, just that the powers-that-be had decided the Codonian should be built up as a "Mouthpiece of the Depot". In fact, he thought up that caption and we ran it as a banner thereafter.

Our Personal Column now took up a full page. Then I think we launched the rather lame series on Depot Personalities. The DC has wanted us to omit the military, at least for a start, and this left me with a problem which I should have foreseen if I'd been around the place longer: none of the leading civilians had any personality whatever. Nevertheless it did sell some papers, chiefly, I suspected, because every such leading civilian we featured would buy a stack of Codonians that week to distribute around his office and often the entire building. And the DC conspired with me at one point: he wanted me to include in the series a profile of one of the CSOs who was known to be a complete pain-in-the-arse: Fred McMurdo, self-proclaimed to be the most incendiary loudmouth of the Trade Union to which they nearly all belonged, or in many cases were unwillingly chained. I had this done by Brown, who gritted his teeth and came up with a good article of apparent praise of the man, though one or two bits of irony could be detected between the Codonian's prim lines, if you knew where to look. McMurdo saw it as a terrific win for the Reds, of course.

"Don't print it yet," said the DC. "Now he's read it, put it on hold."

"We need to ask him for a photo."

"Yes, take one but throw it away. When the time is ripe, we'll print a cartoon, don't you think?" There were many times that I felt he ought to have been on Fleet Street, more than any of us.

★ ★ ★

Crazy as it sounds but typical of Donnington, I did in fact once take the DC to the pictures. I've said how the Depot was unworldly, topsy-turvy at all times; but this was bizarre. He, and the almost-slim Major, and little Padre Jones were all sitting listlessly in the Mess one evening, and over in a corner was me, probably working on my next editorial or fiddling with the crossword. It was February, getting dark, and nothing whatever was happening, nor would it. We might have been lying in wait for Kittie because the meal hadn't been much good, but I expect he knew this and had slunk upstairs to his barrel...

Suddenly the Padre, scanning his Codonian I was pleased to see, said to nobody in particular: "Carnival is on at Oakengates."

It was a very well-reviewed film, just released, and it had a good cast but, never mind all that, it also had Sally Gray whom everybody fancied, like anything. (Indeed she later married into the Peerage).

There was a momentary pause, then they all looked at me. I put down the crossword, or whatever it was.

The DC said to the Major: "Call the car."

So the big Humber staff-car, the Supersnipe still with its North African sandy camouflage and the red tab insignia, transported the four of us to Oakengates; and the DC said our driver must come in, too. I had to lead the way, and wave my credentials at the box office; we all followed the overwhelmed Manager who ushered us into the back row with free ice-creams., a full Colonel, a warworn Major, a Senior Padre with his instructions straight from God, and Second Lieutenant Me who was only temporary and mainly engaged in chatting-up other-rank ATS girls. Oh, and the driver, who enjoyed the show, I hope, but must have been even more bemused than I was. I wonder what happened to him – he's probably still talking about it as much as I am.

★ ★ ★

When the Supersnipe dropped us back at HQ Mess, it was past eleven; but I knew the DC was a late-night person, and this was my best chance to get him on his own, and find out more about his plans for The Codonian, once I had managed to notch up the readership and their loyalty. I asked for a few private words.

He took his illuminated comforts off the big corner chair, purely from force of habit, as there was nobody around except Charles the perpetual orderly who was really part of the furniture and seemed never to sleep; and we went round the corner at the far end again with our pistols in our pockets. Well, you never know, do you?

Midnight, in front of a good log fire, in a comfy armchair after a good film with a good female lead, in good though unlikely company, isn't a bad time for a decent drink. I was getting a bit fed up with Kittie's Glen-Whatever, it was good but I needed something different and I was trying to wean myself off that elementary G&O; I had been doing some homework. Besides, I seem to remember that Kittie had polished off most of his Glen-stock over New Year with some thirsty visitors from the Black Watch, after being on strenuous duty all over Christmas. Somebody told me he had lain down for fortyeight hours, and then emerged, alarmingly palefaced. Palefaced? Surely not Kittie? My informant couldn't believe it, nor did I, but it was a very powerful warning against drinking with Scotsmen when they are on detachment in a foreign land – those Irish up at Armaments Mess were bad enough.

Before I could attend to my latest need the DC started talking business, worrying the logs with a bent brass poker.

"I reckon your Codonian's coming along OK," he coughed amid the wood-smoke. "Since New Year I've enjoyed your innovations: the local history's been quite interesting, and I suppose those bits about our self-important civilians are thrilling to the general mob, even when they see their hideous portraits. Then there was your assassination of my Depot Adjutant –"

"He did survive that shooting, Sir."

"Only in fiction, Topps. Not in the opinion of most of us." There was that glint in the old eyes. "But be that as it may, I think we may be close to moving on to Stage Two."

"I'm ready, Sir, when you are." But he waved me down as if he was slowing the Humber. "Softly... We must always bear in mind, and Whitehall drummed this in to me only this week, that behind our 'sleeper' there will be, somewhere not too far away, a controller; and if we get the controller in the middle of his web, that will lead us out to his other sleepers. It's, a bit like playing chess with ice-cubes: we mustn't heat it up until we get close to checkmate."

That was a good metaphor which jerked me back to attention: it was a bit late and my mind had begun to centre upon another problem. I had been looking at that poker... I knew many iron pokers that had become bent, only natural, but how easy was it to bend brass? The question was fast becoming incredibly important and I hadn't even had a drink yet...

"Topps!" said the DC. "It was you who asked me to spare you a few minutes."

"I'm ready, Sir, when you are."

"I'm told," he went on rather slowly and precisely, "by Junior Commander Chunk whose name you cannot spell, and who sits on all statistics as few can, that your circulation has been edging up steadily and is now a smidgeon above the 5,000 of our target –"

"Which means," I began feigning enthusiasm, "we can start our plan right away, to flush out –"

"To flush out," said the DC, "the drink you owe me. Five thousand sales, eh? One thing at a time."

"Does a Laphroaig appeal to you, Sir?" I had been doing some research. I buzzed and an annoyingly bright-eyed Charles loomed around the corner.

"You do good homework, Topps my boy, so already you know it is my favourite whenever Kittie isn't looking."

"It's like licking the back of a fireplace." I told him.

"Better," he agreed. "Hotter, and the sparks are inside you."

We sat quietly for a short while. The DC, I'm sure, was luxuriating in his new and off-camp role in the management of a newspaper. I was back to the poker: had Kittie been trying to lever his barrel up to his room, or had a disgruntled diner wrapped it around... I tried to re-focus.

"We need a code-word." This was the DC suddenly.

The drinks had come, and we chinked glasses.

"Charles," said the DC, " service round here is terrible. Where have you been?" Charles knew this was a joke, because he had delivered our drinks within thirty seconds, and I guessed he had presciently parked the bottle just around the corner. (A few days earlier, he had raised a fatherly eyebrow at me and said "Tsk Tsk" when I switched from the G&O.)

I enjoyed astonishing Charles further when I reached out for the chit which he was about to hand to the DC. I signed it with a flourish, and passed it back to him; his mouth was open and I said "Tsk Tsk." as he walked away.

I put a splash of water in mine but the DC took it neat, and knocked back half of it right away. "Yes," said crisply, "A codeword."

I looked at him and my expression was asking: "Why?"

"All the great military or intelligence operations have to have a codeword," he explained.

I was half flattered and half overcome by the absurdity of this.

"The Brigadier insists, Topps. He has to sell our Codonian spy honey-trap to the War Office, and they can't do anything unless it's filed under a codeword. Don't look at me like that."

"If we give them a code-word, will they cough up some money?"

"Good God!" he cried and I feared the worst from my presumption. "Of course they will. Sky's the limit," draining his glass.

"In the desert," he went on reminiscently, "we had lots of them. Codewords. All that to-ing and fro-ing; Even the Long Range Desert Group used to label all its excursions – I'll have to ask Major Parrott, he'll remember, he was out there for years–"

"What?" I was incredulous – you could never believe the facts about an old soldier's submerged past. "Are you saying Major Parrott was in the LRDG? I would never –"

"Good Lord, no." The DC was tickled to death. "He was much more likely in," and he looked at me wickedly over his glasses, "the Short Range Gezira Group". (That was the luxurious club in Cairo frequented by those officers who were having a 'good war' well behind any frontline danger area).

"So," he continued, "we have to give the War House a name to file us under. Obviously we can't employ the word Codonian… I've been chatting to the Brigadier about this, but he didn't help much. He's an addict of the Telegraph crossword–"

"Me too," I interrupted proudly – warming to the Brig despite myself.

" – And all he could suggest was something that escaped me entirely: something about a fish and a Scotsman… Escaped me…"

I decided, in about two seconds, not to pursue this.

"Something catchy, we need, Topps. When you write about this one day, and I'm sure you will, it's got to be catchy even then, let alone now."

"You could write it yourself, sir." Oily, a bit, perhaps; but I'd heard rumours; and anyway he was enjoying his Codonian connection.

"No, more boring – I'll be working on some military history, the story of the Corps, one of these days perhaps… When they let me out of this place."

"You used the word 'catchy', sir. Can we bring that into it? After all, we want to catch our sleeper?" This was beginning rather quickly to get silly. "How about 'catchword'?" I went on.

"Too obvious," and I knew he was right. Stupid suggestion. But then the DC waved across the room to the eternal Charles, who at once did the decent thing, and – as Wodehouse would have said, I think – shimmered towards us… The fumes from the whisky must have aroused my sleeping Muse because almost at once I was inspired.

"The latest American thrillers are describing their characters' schemes as 'capers'," I told the DC. I waited but he didn't say anything, he wanted me to go on.

"Would 'The Sleeper Caper' be any good?"

"It ought to be one word, to suit the filing clerks in Whitehall."

I didn't think one word 'sleepercaper' would seem very memorable; and in any case we ought not to use 'sleeper' because it gave away to some shrewd intruder what we were up to. But we were going to use a newspaper to trap our sleeper, so how about bringing that in? I told the DC I would work something out that was apparently quite innocuous…

"By the way," said the DC as he got up and stretched his good leg. "The Brigadier wants to take a look at you, and he'd like to be there when I give you our final instructions on setting the trap." We walked back to the main part of the common-room, nodding to Charles who – I saw as I looked back – thankfully picked up the bottle and headed to the cupboard with it; "I'll set up the meeting in a couple of weeks, once he's cleared everything with the War House and they've opened their file on –"

It came to me, while he was replacing all the regalia on his Number One chair.

"On the Paper Caper, Sir?"

Yes, he liked it. Two words, but the civil servants could run them together if they wished.

"That's it, Topps. Well, goodnight all in one word, and thanks for the cinema."

He limped off. I sleepily watched him go and wished he was my uncle.

VI

I forget whether I've mentioned my Local History series. The romance of old ruins has always called to me, and while still at school, as Spitfires and Messerschmitts wove their deadly patterns overhead, I had spent a glorious ten days – unashamedly self-centred as I now realise, looking back – on a cycle tour to the Welsh border, my route based entirely upon the red dots on the Ordnance Survey maps which indicated antiquities, all with collapsed towers and crumbling walls covered in ivy; and not a tourist in sight.

It wasn't therefore difficult for me to start a single-column series on such places within easy reach of the Depot: and as you surely know, looking West (if I could see round The Wrekin) I was spoilt for choice. But I felt I should begin with the simple better-known stuff. I wrote one week about the Battle of Shrewsbury and recommended a visit to the church on the site; I also featured the Roman City of Uriconium, then still being excavated by the tall gaunt man whose name I forget but who had shown me around on my bike-trip; and of course the everlasting highway Watling Street which swept up to the Severn ('Sabrina' to the Romans) passing so close to Wellington that, as I told my civilian readers, they might well have Roman blood in their Salopian veins. That brought in a few letters.

I found that this Local History research was becoming astonishingly interesting; and when I was uncontactable at either of my offices ("He's on his way, Sir"), in truth I was probably sitting immersed in the Public Library at Wellington, with my tilly patiently waiting outside and its driver either told to come back in an hour, or invited in to help, more likely. Mostly, I was wading through the incredible Victoria County Histories; which had been born, as indicated, at the end of the 19th Century and churned out by a committee ever since: further volumes were still crawling from the press. Shropshire had fared quite well, it seemed; but its poor relation Herefordshire was less fortunate (I can't think why, it's a wonderful county). Volume One sat lonely on its shelf, dated 1906[1].

★ ★ ★

In civilian life you would take a member of your staff across to the pub or a local greasy-spoon for a drink and chat. In the Army there was no easy way to achieve that corporate togetherness: I couldn't take Brown to the Mess any more than he could take me to the NAAFI. The Sally Army canteen tried to strike a balance and open its suffering-children arms to all comers, but one would sit there in embarrassment rather than the intended relaxation. Apart from the hovering padres, any officer seemed entirely out of place and suspected of acting patronisingly, and this would be death to his or her perceived status up at the Company HQ.

So I rang for a 'tilly' and said I had to go to the County newspaper works in Shrewsbury to discuss getting our printing done by them instead of Newport, and I had to take Private Brown with me for obvious reasons. I contrived to get my favourite tilly-girl from the motor-pool; and a few miles short of the town we stopped at that delightful hostelry The Mytton and Mermaid. "This will take an hour or two," I told them, "Then we'll drive back. Let's say Shrewsbury was closed."

"They'll check my petrol," said Helen.

---

[1] Volume Two appeared in 2009!

"OK, so leave the engine running," we suggested. She told us how stupid we were, whatever our rank; and it ended in me promising to get a chit from my friend the Brigadier when I saw him next week. That had the useful effect of subduing both of them and stunning them into the realisation that this meeting, however unorthodox, was going to be serious.

I bought the drinks of course, I forget what they were except that I had a pint of bitter in my down-to-earth plebian way.

Helen, more businesslike than either of us journalists, asked: "What's all this about?" And Brown nodded at me equally questioningly.

Having stung them both into semi-paralysis by name-dropping the near-mythical Brigadier, I went straight into overdrive.

"We have to find ways to rescue The Codonian," I told them, "and I need to know something about the woman-appeal." I turned to Helen. "Give me your own personal views. When you are back at your barrack-room after a long day driving people, what do you find yourself thinking about? What sort of thing are you most interested in, apart from listening to the radio and going to the pictures? If you're sitting in the tilly waiting for someone, where do your thoughts mostly lead you? What do you girls talk about – "

Helen picked up her drink and headed for the door. She turned to us, bewildered.

"Who is this Caledonian?" she asked.

"God," said Brown, "she's never heard of it."

We sent her back to her tilly, and took her a top-up from time to time. As for ourselves, we went into conference or whatever you call several pints around a log fire, with another big round slice of tree trunk serving as a table.

I had to keep remembering that Brown mustn't know

anything about the DC's ulterior motive and our 'paper-caper' plotting which hovered in the background and trailed away into the mists of Whitehall. Forget the suspected 'sleeper' – this meeting was simply about further ways to boost our circulation, although presumably I was permitted to say we were getting financial support from the War Office. That should be enough to satisfy the elementary enquiries of a Private.

"I think we'll have to skip the military," said Brown, "don't you, Sir? After all, we deliver a small bundle of Codonians to each Company Office every week, so there's no incentive for any of them to buy it. I know – I've seen them of course – they come into the Office and rummage around, just to read some match results but mainly to check what's on at the Garrison Theatre and the Brownhills Electric or whatever…" A pause while we thought.

"But suppose…" This was still Brown. My mouth was full. "Suppose we print some vouchers for them to collect, each week, dated, and when they've got, say, six with all-different dates we give them a prize –"

"A prize?" That was me.

"Well Sir, it's got to be free cinema seats, hasn't it?"

It had; and it was, it worked instantly. I believe our – OK, Brown's – voucher scheme alone must have boosted our circulation by a couple of hundred at once, and the same again as the news got around. We still sent the same bundles to each Company Office, but now the CSM's clerk would be ringing us for more, before the weekend. Our only problem was with the layout: our tame printers in Newport (who just set up the type, they didn't do the actual printing, Tschunk's people did that) had to be sure that the vouchers backed against something ephemeral like a football match report, not upon – just for instance – anything memorable and worth preserving like – just for example – my Editorials. Brown was annoyingly clever at coming up with captions for those, by the way. I initially headed them myself, but after enduring his suggested alternatives for a few issues, I asked him to do it in future as I was so busy. Well, I was, wasn't I? The DC would understand.

"Your series on our backwaters, those remote parts of the Depot," said Brown, draining his glass in the Mytton and examining his trousers for a spark that had shot him from the fireplace, much pleasing me. "These railway sidings, little sheds, outbuildings…I know you've only just started it, Sir, but do you think we could happy it up a bit?"

"Happy?"

"Perhaps, every week print alongside your article a full sketch-map of the Depot, and invite the reader –"

"Are you suggesting, Brown, that I will have only one –?"

" – All our readers to send it in with the position marked, of the place you're talking about and showing in your photo. With a reward for the first one –"

"But somebody working there themselves will obviously win it?"

Brown shook his head more vigorously than necessary.

"The first one we *open*, will be at the end of the week, so that makes it fair for everybody, all those thousands who have been wrestling with it."

I ignored that, and went to order some sandwiches: cucumber out of their kitchen garden, with salmon apparently hauled that very morning out of the Severn just across the fields. I still don't quite believe that; but it was a good sandwich. What? Yes, yes, of course we took one out to Helen, stop being so 'correct', what are you, a Communist sleeper or something? I also did the decent thing and took her some reading-matter: a Codonian.

"So," Brown started again after half his sandwich, "The 'Remote Award' will be more cinema tickets?"

I didn't see why not. They were our very own limitless currency.

Full of ideas, he went on. I began to wish I had bought him something non-alcoholic, or at least dropped something lethargic into his beer to slow him down while I had a chance to think of helpful suggestions.

"And," he said unstoppably, waving his quarter-sandwich at me, "in your weekly article about local history, why not include a deliberate mistake, with a prize for the first person to spot it?"

I had to tell him this was brilliant. I also knew damned well that he was hinting there were already some un-deliberate mistakes in my articles, and offering me an escape.

"A substantial prize," I agreed, "But rarely awarded."

On the way back in Helen's tilly, as full of beer and sandwiches as a Trade Union Conference at Downing Street, Brown seemed to have gone rather quiet and philosophical, gazing out at the countryside and puffing on a rather aggressive cigarette.

"Pity we didn't get into Shrewsbury."

"Why?" I asked. "Aren't you familiar with our lovely old historic towns?"

"I was at school there," he said.

That shut me up.

★ ★ ★

Next evening was one of the Wednesday Mess Nights, which meant unusually good behaviour, no talk of religion or women or politics, full Service Dress with a polished Sam Browne, to wear along the road but to be taken off when you got there; and deep boredom, almost always.

My quarter-batman Edwards was on leave (instead of the usual request for 'compassionate leave' which we used to listen to at Company Office, the joke at the barracks was to ask for "passionate leave, please, Sir"; when is the baby due, Private, we would ask. "In nine months, Sir")

Anyway, I had to shine up the damn belt myself. As I worked away at it, I wondered why on Earth the Army imposed this unnecessary 'bullshit' on its officers. After all, we had polished, and blancoed, and dubbined our kit month upon month in our early days up to OCTU and then continued all the way to getting a pip on our shoulders. Couldn't it stop now, so we might be released from the idiocy, to get on with things more realistic?

There was usually some boring guest of honour: a 'visiting fireman' who would turn out to be perhaps a cobwebby old General, long-retired and awash with reminiscences of young colonial days in Potschefstroom or Upper Topa; or a stiff-necked Civil Servant from the Ministry on his Tour Of Inspection, secretly terrified by the regimental traditions lest he commit a social faux-pas, using the wrong spoon, and nervously on his guard against the corruption by unfamiliar alcohol of the purity of his Report, due for filing next day.

But this time, happily, it was different. A much more welcome celebrity, the singer Anne Shelton was appearing down the road at the Garrison Theatre on one of her incessant tours of the troops, no matter how boring they must have been for her after the wartime excitements of singing through monsoons under gunfire. Brown had found a respectable-looking photographer from somewhere (who went on later to be a star of magazines like Vogue and never really came down to earth again); and with the drink-purchased aid of the PMC we smuggled him and his camera through the door to the dining-room when everyone was on the cheese and coffee. And port.

The photo looked good on next week's front page, I thought. But as I might have guessed, we received a load of caustic letters from our underprivileged left-wing civilian readers, about how the upper classes in the Army spent their time and all the ground-down taxpayers' money...

Stung by this, Brown had gone a bit quiet again. For several days he left his desk earlier than usual, but I noticed he took the Codonian camera with him. I waited.

By the end of the week he came round to see me at E & R Receipts, where I was holding the fort for Mr Stanworth, whose jaw had gone a bit peculiar. Triumphantly, Brown showed me a set of snapshots of our top Trade Unionist, Fred McMurdo, dining very well indeed at Wolverhampton's finest restaurant and looking a bit bleary on it, with somebody's little hand on his thigh.

I posted one copy to Fred "for information", and filed the rest, just for now.

★ ★ ★

I suggested to Private Brown that he might like me to have him made up to Lance Corporal but he declined. It would inevitably get him involved in further duties and military obligations and he preferred to stay put and concentrate on The Codonian with all its concealed advantages. I can't say I disagreed with that. In truth, I suspect I secretly rather envied him. While he did all the hard work planning the competitions with their 'vouchers' and cinema-seat prizes, I was listing my 'backwaters'. The first was among the broken-down vehicles beyond the far-flung railway sidings. Brown's tame photographer snapped a huge gun seen against a wrecked khaki ambulance. My next was just a chaotic jumble of cardboard boxes and dustbins and general detritus at the back of the

NAAFI; nobody won that prize, so we invented a fictional winner, a civilian delivery man, and put the £5 into our Petty Cash reserve. But the third one changed my life.

★ ★ ★

I asked Brown what he thought about featuring, among the 'remote places', the ATS CRS. With its anti-GI barbed wire, and access across the lake or claypit or whatever, it was surely remote enough? It would be well-known only to those few ATS girls who had been trundled there with some dubious disorder or other, as the PMC – har-har – and I had envisaged that day back last Autumn; but it was a pleasant-looking building which could easily be confused with others around the Depot (usually pseudo-Richardson as I told Brown, and to my great pleasure he didn't know what I was talking about). So the ATS CRS was chosen as our next 'remote place'. It would either set a difficult problem for all our readers, or give an easy fiver to some ATS reader, thus boosting readership among all those girls.

So I rang the ATS CRS again, in fear of that Teutonic voice I had experienced last time. But now it was different: a gentler sound I seemed to connect to mistletoe with just a hint of the Lake District.

"This is The Codonian, the Depot newspaper. Who's speaking?" "Corporal Roberts, sir."

"Bobbie, you're back!" Pure joy – my little mistletoe tapdancer! I was over there on my army-issue bicycle in five minutes.

Yes, I got my story about the CRS, to feature a few weeks later; and Yes, I got some useful stuff about some of the Depot Medical Officers, including that largely unprintable Irishman at Armaments Mess, but also the recently departed and much-loved SMO Major Hallam, who would soon therefore feature as one of our 'Depot Personalities'. But all this official journalism seemed, as we talked, to be some sort of unimportant shadow projected on to the brilliant background of a vivid and overwhelming personal attraction. She was delightful – and she liked me, too.

You won't need to be told that we went to the pictures that night. In mufti of course, because we both knew the rules. And from then on, we would meet up whenever possible, usually just for the cinemas in outlying towns, with a meal or a drink before or after – or both; or for a walk along the lanes behind the Mess and CRS, but of course, never at or near either of those places. At the weekends, whenever we were both off-duty at the same time, we would travel further afield. And we talked, endlessly, about so much that we had in common: we were the same age to within a week, and we loved the same things. To my surprise Bobbie had read my local history pieces, liked them and from now on she would collaborate with me on them. We also colluded in planting errors in them, to see if we had any readers sufficiently keen to write and correct us.

I asked what had happened to the fierce woman on the phone, who had disenchanted me for several weeks. Oh, she had gone back to Chester and Bobbie was now back to replace her, made up to Corporal "but only acting, until they bring in a Regular, I'm being demobbed later this year." That was brilliant news, it meant we could eventually act as open human beings instead of skulking in the military Army Regulation shadows.

She later confessed that after that first evening, she had caught the bus into Wolverhampton to buy some civvies for our dates; and then I, too, admitted to a new Harris tweed jacket and a pair of slacks. They all had plenty of good use.

★ ★ ★

The DC's office was somewhat over-heated for late March, and I supposed that our delitescent Brigadier was unhappy in cold weather.

"Topps, Sir."

The DC introduced me, at five past ten a week or two later, to a tall, gaunt man with a long grey face and sad eyes. He was heavy with medal ribbons and bristling with red tabs – for a moment I was reminded of an American NCO but that was ridiculous: our Brigadier for all his forty years' displayed too few medals, not enough insignia on the arms… However, this was our very own local Supremo, the ultimate Master, Under God, of the good ship Donnington. One never saw him, normally, except passing through distantly in his staff car.

But – you know? – curiously at that moment I found that I wasn't all that much impressed. I recalled that I had, myself, only a couple of weeks ago been to the pictures in a big Humber staff car with a mixed group of high-ranking potential renegades with so much more life in them, even that less-than-obese Major for whom I had to admit I now had astonishing new respect. Looking back, I seem to remember regarding our Commandant much like those superannuated and decaying schoolmasters who had to be kept on during the war long after normal retirement age until such time as the younger teachers could come limping home. (But we suspected some of those suede-shoed limps, didn't we just?)

In particular, the Brig. reminded me vividly of old Mr Henderson, our Vice-Master, who in 1945, in the absence at Speech Day of the Head Man away at a conference, said: "And now we will sing 'God Save The Queen". Yes, in 1945. OK, then, look it up: forty-four years behind the times – no wonder he taught the Classics.

"How do you do, Sir." What else does one say to a phantom? I had already saluted to the DC because it was his office. He had once saluted on entering mine… It crossed my mind to invite the Brig. round to E & R Receipts one morning for coffee, just to get him to salute me.

"Sit down, Topps," said the Brig. "I'm going to leave it to the Colonel here to brief you, now that we've had the go-ahead from the War Office. He will work with you closely. I will just be reporting back to the War House and MI5."

He was still standing, and evidently wouldn't be staying long – the DC's words a fortnight ago had been precise: the Brig. just wanted to look at me. What was he checking for the benefit of Whitehall – my dress-sense, my haircut? my accent? Ought I to spoon up some soup for him? Whatever it could have been, I seemed to have passed muster, because he came over and patted me on my one-pip shoulder.

"First of all," pat-pat, "I need to tell you I've been watching all the improvements in The Codonian. This was the essential first step, they said in London: widen the interest, boost the circulation, get it out to everybody; then we can use it."

"We reckon now," the DC put in, "with your circulation, Topps, almost every civilian in the Depot will either be buying the paper, or at the very least sharing it with another reader."

"So we have an innocuous channel of entry now, to the entire workforce," said the Brig. "We can feed them anything."

"With respect, Sir," I risked saying, "D'you think Codonian should get political – "

"Topps, this doesn't concern politics," said the DC, looking even more like Attlee. "This is about nailing a sleeping spy."

I wasn't in the business of trying to separate non-Politics from anti-Communism, so – very sensibly in view of later developments – I shut up. The Brig. saw a gap in the conversation and moved into the empty space.

"Feed them anything," he echoed, "but innocently, too,

because the way your paper is run, with a young National Service short-term newcomer in charge of it, as editor, and with a range of unimportant and localised chatter, I don't think anybody, even our sleeper, is going to suspect the Codonian of being dangerous. It is so amateur."

I had shrivelled word by word. The DC could see at once that I was having difficulty in swallowing my pride, and he put in: "And, Topps, you've achieved that effect quite brilliantly, has he not, Sir?"

"Oh, yes, yes." said the red-tabbed old man as he moved to leave us. But then, out of the blue, came the moment I will always treasure as being – what's the word? – the zenith – the acme – of my Army career. He paused at the door.

"Oh, Topps," he said, "Not for me, you understand, but I wonder whether you – er – my wife and our daughter are very keen on – er – do you sometimes have free tickets or passes for any of the local –?"

"Absolutely, sir," I said. "I'll send some to your office regularly."

Without looking, I could describe the DC's face as the Brig left.

"Nevertheless," said the DC drily, "and if I may bring you back to solid earth, Topps my boy, we have a campaign to plan: a 'caper' did you say?"

He was clearly enjoying this departure from the everyday boredom shunting stores around the planet. He settled deeply into his upholstered office chair and for the first time I noticed on the back of it a brightly embroidered antimacassar which was the twin of that one on his dominant fireside chair at the Mess. Somebody, at some past time, must have given them to this bachelor, and I thought: is there a story in this? If so, it wasn't for The Codonian, was it?

The DC lit a cigarette and offered one to me. I took it with a strange feeling of mystic occasion, which I only identified later: I had never seen him smoke before. Perhaps he only lit up on special occasions, and he saw this as one? I had a passing vision of him covered in sand, sheltered behind a tank as the barrage began at Alamein, surreptitiously flicking his lighter...

"First," he began after a couple of deep drags, "as I'm sure you've read, the Americans are completely paranoid about Communism, and this is now beginning to infect us in Whitehall. Ever since Winston's speech over there a year or so ago – that "Iron Curtain" speech you know – we've been getting dragged in. The current official view is that there are Reds under the beds, all over the place."

"Do you believe that, Sir?" He spread his hands.

"Our own secret services seem to be going along with it. Call them SIS if you like, but now we've got MI6 looking after secret stuff overseas, and MI5 who take care of anything nefarious here at home; and they're the boys we are dealing with."

"And the Americans have told us –?"

He pulled on the cigarette again, almost viciously.

"The bloody Yanks have told MI5 that this country is riddled with spies, but they would, wouldn't they? Over there, they're even starting to weed out Hollywood actors. Any minute now, they'll put Snow White in jail for –"

Like a fool, I interrupted him, so I'll never know what was coming next.

"But we have to remember," I suggested, "they have dug out some pretty dangerous people." They had recently sent a couple to the electric chair. "And I suppose those spies in Canada do reflect back on us in the UK?"

"Well..." Dragging again on the long-suffering Capstan. "We've got to go through the motions anyway. As you know, we're on Red Alert here in the Depot and carrying weapons purely because of this warning. They think we have a – a mole, is that the expression? Or, as we've been calling him, a 'sleeper'. Maybe yes, maybe no…" He sighed. "But I've been given three months to root him out, Topps."

"Through the Codonian?" (incredibly, I thought – and still do).

"Because, you see, behind this man there will be a controller."

He had said this before, and I could see my job was going to get more tricky, but I kept quiet and let him go on. The Codonian was sailing into deeper water, stormier, and I had a nasty vision of rats leaving the good ship, let alone moles.

"And that hidden controller, they tell me, may be in charge of a dozen or more other sleepers, a sort of ring of them, radiating out from him and hanging on his words and ready to strike when he says – could be years that they lie low." He waited my reaction. "No, not all here in Donnington but, don't you see, a network covering all our central depots, Bicester, Didcot, Long Marston, Preston, Watford –" He was putting on a distraught tone, but I noticed he had the places all neatly in alphabetical order. "Everywhere, infiltrators…"

"And," he ended, sitting back as if to convince me, "The CIA have told MI5 that we here seem to be the hub."

"CIA?" I queried.

"Oh, just a new little outfit they've come up with in the States, to cover these Communist scares. But only over here, not in the US. It won't get them far, they are too trigger-happy these Americans." He shook his head sadly. "And so unsubtle. They can't understand non-democracy. One day they might learn how to handle other people, races, creeds, like we did so brilliantly for two hundred years. I mean, look at Tunisia…"

It would have been good to look at Tunisia and know what on earth he was talking about, but he went on.

"I met one of them once, in Harrogate –"

I sat up. "A Tunisian, in Harro –?"

"No, no, Topps, one of these CIA chaps. They've opened an office in the West End – trust them, no expense spared – to be an HQ for their undercover work in Europe – oh, and I'm told they're in Holland too – and this chap was up there for a conference. Weirdo; must say: looked like an undertaker…" He chewed that over. "Well, cadaverous, you know? More like the undertaker's client really, come to think of it, but ladies' man though. Amazed me: he's been at an English Public School too… Midlands somewhere… Radley was it? Rugby? Malvern? One for the girls, very American… Cheltenham? No, not Cheltenham… Very odd, though."

I had to get the DC back on track before he drifted off to Henley and Twickenham and Lords. Or Shrewsbury.

"Sir – the paper-caper. How do you want me to play it?"

He got up and went across to a cabinet in the corner of the office, where I caught a glimpse of glasses and bottles.

"It's still Laphroaig, I hope?" as he started pouring.

I looked at my watch and he caught me doing it.

"I still work on Central European time," he told me defensively, "which means it's well past midday. And anyway, it helps me to think, and I'm bloody sure it does you, too."

It crossed my mind fleetingly that somewhere in the DC's past there must have been somebody who used to nag him. But he was right: it did help. It always does.

The alert from the Americans had come after they, with our people, had sifted through a heap of documents and back-of-envelope stuff following one of their midnight swoops. All they could suggest to us was that (i) our local sleeper was probably early middle-aged, and had entered the depot just after the end of the war, on his own and apparently unmarried; and (ii) that his controller had been based in the UK right back in the Thirties, joined the forces but soon came back, and now seemed to have set up a network of sleepers around the Midlands. There were no further clues, except a code-name that might or might not be significant: 'Wilhelm Krein', our snake-in-the-grass.

"So we're looking for a German?" I asked naively.

"It's not very serpentine really," said the DC. "You're always doing crosswords. W Krein is an anagram."

"That's pathetic."

"Yes, but possibly tells us something. About the controller, I mean. If he is making up names, perhaps he's actually inventing people. Like that brilliant spy we read about recently, named after a film-star; he created a huge network of agents and sleepers, got funds to maintain them all, and none of them existed, not one. Disappeared with a colossal fortune. Splendid!"

We sat and enjoyed for a minute or two the memory of that great caper. Then I felt we ought to get more businesslike.

"If our sleeper is real –" I began.

"We have to proceed on the assumption that he is."

"Then don't we have security checks on all new civilians coming here?"

"Well," the DC shifted uncomfortably. "Until the war ended, of course, we were very careful, or so I'm told. But what with the relief and no more bombs and all the chaps coming home –"

"We dropped our guard?"

"It appears so. It was just before my time," he added rather quickly, picking up his cigarette packet and putting it down again.

I rather enjoyed sitting pensively for a minute, sucking through my teeth.

"I think, Sir, I ought to have from Admin a full list of all males who have joined us since the end of the war –"

"That'll be a couple of hundred."

" – So I can delete from it all those who have, or have had, relatives already working here. I reckon that's reasonable for a start."

"How about age?"

"Yes, that must be the next step. If the CIA say our man is middle aged, given they're Americans and therefore probably wrong, we ought to bring that down to the thirties to be safe; so we can eliminate any really young newcomers, like most men returning from the forces? Could you set that up for me with HQ without them knowing what we're up to?" He could, and our short list would be very short indeed. This wasn't in the least foolproof but it was promising – the best place to start.

"Next, Sir –"

"There's more?"

"I'll need lists of all new members since the war joining all the civilians' clubs and societies that people like to join: Music Club? Jazz Club perhaps? Keep Fit? Chess? Bridge? Drama Group? Darts?"

The DC had opened his mouth, then shut it again.

"Oh," I added, "I'll keep off all the Sports Clubs. If our sleeper's described as middle-aged he won't want to attract attention by being hopeless on the pitch."

"Bowls," said the DC and for a moment I misheard him.

"I play bowls," he explained; and I agreed we needed a list of that club membership. Always an intelligent crowd, we told each other.

The DC had been doing some thinking quietly while I was steaming on; and now it was his turn to take the stage, on a subject that, from my half-page articles, he knew fascinated me.

"Our spy will have been ordered to put roots down, to merge into our traditional English ways of life. Given that code-name, we can assume that he is well dug-in in Shropshire or hereabouts. I think, if he's thinking like me, you should look at Local History societies."

"Absolutely, Sir, it would give him the ideal excuse for prowling about the countryside –"

"Looking at all our sub-depots. But I don't believe we have a society here that covers it."

"I've already started one, through the paper: we're featuring local sites every week, and from next week I'll be including one deliberate mistake each time, with a prize –"

"Oh, I say, that's a great idea, Topps."

"Thank you Sir." One day, I tell myself, I'll apologise to Private Brown, but I'm sure I'll never get round to it. Anyway, he'd declined promotion when I offered it, hadn't he? And I'd bought all the drinks. As you can see, I'm still embarrassed by stealing his thunder, so let's move on, as the politicians say... The DC's journalistic urges were coming to the surface alarmingly.

"I'd like to join in," he said. "I've been to Ludlow."

Everybody's been to Ludlow, I nearly said; but stifled it. Financially, we did really need his enthusiasm.

"And I know the excavations at Uriconium," he added, to my surprise. "You know, those Roman remains hard by the river and that great pub where the Roman road crosses –"

I said Yes, I knew the place. I didn't tell him we had featured the site already, let alone that I'd been drinking there with two Other Ranks that very week. What I did say, by way of diversion, was that all these elaborations to The Codonian would require an immediate and permanent expansion to sixteen pages. But we daren't put the price up, or our main core readership would at once abandon us and get its cinema programmes elsewhere. We were twopence and the cheapest local rag was threepence and upon this ridiculously simple fact my whole Codonian experience depended.

"Twelve pages?" the DC echoed, bewildered by the arithmetic.

"No, Sir. We have that already. I need sixteen."

He looked puzzled. "How can you fill sixteen pages?"

I explained that our Personal Column was attracting many replies and I intended to build on it. The ads could easily be doctored in whatever way he, the DC, may want in future weeks; and to make that more believable, we needed to build it up in anticipation.

Also, we were getting letters from readers, criticising this or that article we had run provocatively; and to establish the paper as a reader-friendly medium, we must encourage this. I knew he could hardly argue against that, and he didn't.

"Thank you, Sir," when he agreed the sixteen pages; but then, "One more thing though. If you are planning to set some sort of trap through our pages," and that little pomposity delighted me, "ought we have the whole paper typeset in-house, just for security?"

The DC agreed at once, which indicated to me that something serious was afoot. I asked him whether I should notify my friend Tschunky, even though I had a worrying glimpse of snarling females.

"No, no," emphatically. "I'll tell her myself, right away. You can't even spell her name – or won't." A glare, but there was a smile beneath it.

"So," he said, relaxing back into his antimacassar and summing things up, "We should be able to pinpoint our sleeper by all this narrowing down, and then by finding activists in our Depot clubs or societies, eh?"

"No,"

"No?"

"I think the opposite, sir. We are most likely to find him among people who have made a point of joining as many societies as possible, to establish themselves, but who have no real interest and therefore no record of attendance at most of them. Like at College," I explained, "where you join all the clubs in your first week, mainly to meet girls, then whittle it down to the one or two that truly interest you."

"Or whose girls seem more promising?"

"Absolutely."

"Well," the DC said thoughtfully, "you may well be right, Topps. Anyway, we're right into our paper-caper now and they've opened a file with that name in Whitehall. It'll be a classic military two-pronged manoeuvre: we build up the Codonian readership, and we trim down the suspects. It's neat."

He waved me to the door.

"Then, Topps," he said, "I'll tell you about my trap." He looked at my side pocket. "Don't lose your pistol."

As I left the room, he was lighting another cigarette; that was the most worrying thing of all.

VII

Whatever the DC's trap was going to be – and apparently I would be told in a couple of weeks – I was now administrator of his two 'prongs'. My nights were spent in cross-checking the Depot's lists (which had come to me very quickly) of new male entrants aged over 30, plus membership "required by Security" of all the civilians' Clubs and Societies. I smuggled Bobbie into House Four to help with this, sandwiches or fish-and-chips on the table alongside the bottle and glasses, one of us reading out names and the other crossing them off.

It was tiring. Easter was near, and we planned to take a few days off on leave, to explore the Welsh Border and – how did we primly word it? – to get to know each other…

But my days were equally busy: the second DC prong remained, to establish the Codonian as an unmissable weekly publication, now that its actual setting-up had been handed over to Printing and Pubs. at Building Eighteen, even The Tschunk was sometimes smiling – though stiffly – as I walked past; and her dog just quietly slobbered at me over her shoes, though that svelte receptionist was still hard as nails and jealous of every kind word I exchanged with her boss.

Brown had pretty well perfected our Personal Column which now took up an entire page; all because of his outrageous lies. I would hear every day his side of phone-calls to our office Reply-Line: "The £5 portable radio? Oh, I'm so sorry, it's just gone, but there will be more." – "The cottage in The Lakes, £12 off-season? Ah, what a pity, madam; but if I can drop you a hint, try next week's Column."

With a view to whatever the DC held for us in the future, I started to invent one or two coded messages from the forsaken or lovelorn. One of them read: "Came from South-West (Devon); lonely up here, attractive, friendly, thirties, seek partnership for meals, outings, etc…" and a box number. I must confess I rather liked that row of dots, and in madder late-night moments I almost wanted to answer the ad myself. But it turned a bit sour, I remember, because I had omitted the gender of the advertiser, and we got a few curious responders, all heavily underlined on the envelope 'Private and Personal'. He never told me, but I suspect Brown sent a few mischievous replies: I happened one day to see on his desk a box of scented notepaper, and I found in his bin a sheet on which he had been practising different handwritings. I didn't say anything, but filed away in my mind the possibility that this gift of his might come in useful sometime. You had to seize on to everything.

My Local History series seemed to have started well. My first deliberate mistake was an easy one, to test my readership: I called the great Roman road Ermine Street instead of Watling Street, and we were delighted to be told off by dozens of phone calls and a pile of helpful or outraged letters. That was my cue for telling readers the following week that we would be making this sort of error regularly, and the first person to (how did I put it?) "correctly correct" us would get free cinema seats for two.

But when you are lifting chatty tourist information at the library, and inserting an obvious error into it, it is easy to get complacent. And I did. I was being too incautious in checking my facts, so we suddenly had an alarming crisis and a blank front page, entirely my silly fault.

Browsing through some recent newspaper articles about the war days, not long past, I discovered that in 1940, when evacuation plans were being drawn up for the Government and

Top People, should we have been invaded – which seemed very likely, as all our readers would vividly remember – the Royal Family would be re-housed at "Donnington, Shropshire", with Churchill and the Cabinet nearby. This snippet of information meant nothing to anybody I spoke to: the DC hadn't heard about it, and he asked the Brig., who didn't know either (or else he was at the cinema, I forget which). But then, this was secret stuff, only now being released.

So I planned a colossal scoop. I hinted on page one that the full story would appear next week: "Royals At Donnington War Retreat? Truth Now Told!".

It was an HQ clerk who rang me, kindly I have to admit. There are two Donningtons in Shropshire, and the prepared hideaway was the other one. Not too far away, though, I comforted myself: just a mile south of Uriconium the Roman town, and very handy for the Mytton and Mermaid in case of the royal gin-and-Dubonnet running out. I wriggled out of the faux-pas the next week by making a page two joke about it as part of my Leader; but for a while it scarily left me with a blank front page. I forget how I filled it – perhaps an old CSO had died, or some unimportant visiting Major-General was astonished to find himself so well-known and is still telling his grandchildren.

I have just mentioned my Leaders on page two. As Editor, I wrote one every issue, sometimes bland, sometimes a bit contentious, and I enjoyed both. Brown and I used to compete to find *mot juste* for its headline. On one occasion around this time I had gone to the local Garrison Theatre on my own because I planned to write a feature about the rundown place; it was not a live show that week but a rather seedy film full of long legs and pert breasts, and I could hardly follow the plot, let alone hear any dialogue, for all the raucous howling and whistling. I wrote a good editorial, condemning the antisocial behaviour, and Brown came up with a splendid headline: "The Call of the Wild."

Also, remembering the DC's encouraging suggestion, I took the opportunity to print my own short story, and invite readers to submit some of their own in the form of a Competition, closing date six months ahead, three prizes.

To my delight, it was Bobbie who supplied the copy for my piece on the dear old departed SMO Major Hallam, with whom she had often chatted in the CRS kitchen over a mug of coffee, when he had finished his Army Medical Corps duties for the day, and was wearily about to start his local hospital visits. He would reminisce about wartime and once showed her his DSO about which he was otherwise very reticent. It gave me an idea for an extended article, on all those Army medics who were still returning from their ghastly nightmares in the jungles and the deserts, to resume their traditional and more gentle duties healing the slightly indisposed with codeines-and-Dovers until their time came for retirement.

And believe me, they worked, those pills. If you had a 'feverish cold' (nobody seems to get that nowadays, I wonder what flashy new name they've found for it?), you took two massive codeines and two brown Dovers pills, had a hot drink and went off to bed with a hot-water-bottle under a big heap of blankets. And you would sweat. You would sweat until you could wring out your pyjamas into the washbasin; then sleep deeply. In the morning you would be perfectly well. What went wrong with that rough-and-ready sort of treatment? You can't find Doctor Dover's powder any more and most GPs have never heard of it. Or of him, whoever he was. Perhaps his invention was bought out by some huge drug company, suppressed in favour of something more expensive, and the old Doctor left to end his days as an ignored Victorian charlatan? I must do an editorial about it...

★ ★ ★

The Spring that year was particularly glorious, as I remember it. Well, anyway, mine was. Bobbie and I were heading for the Marches – but the Southern end, as up beyond Shrewsbury the maps seemed to be less inviting: yes, there was the top end of Offa's Dyke but so what? And we'd already had a day at Old Oswestry. We agreed that we were far more interested in the Norman castles, whether standing or flattened, and the little black-and-white villages that still huddled around them. We arranged to travel separately from Donnington for the usual evasive reason, and meet up at the railway station in Shrewsbury.

I got there early, as I had business in the town with the printers that morning. The platforms were crowded as this was Easter and people were heading off on leave, mostly in uniform. Waiting in the buffet, I saw a train arriving from Wellington and things suddenly got interesting. Dressed pleasingly in the latest fashion, an attractive girl I knew to be a Sergeant descended, to be greeted enthusiastically by Major Parrott in his carefully-ironed civvie suit. I kept my head down.

The next train brought Bobbie, dressed and equipped for our hiking-plus-local-train holiday; and we pulled out our OS map and caught the slow stopping train to Ludlow, picking out things of interest and spotting the passing hills and villages as we crouched side by side at the steamy window. It was a warm day but – who remembers this now? – if you put your head out of the window, you'd get a speck of soot in your eye as likely as not.

It is difficult to convince today's young people, how comprehensive the railway network used to be: those branch lines went everywhere, linking the villages, stopping at 'halts' to pick up the farmer's churns, and weaving a long white canopy of smoke that would hang like a shroud in a windless sky as dawn came up. That was the daily milk train. The locals would set their watches by it during the war when the churches were silent.

Those little trains were friendly, too, before the aggressive harshness of the diesels. At one point on that Easter holiday, we were sitting on our own in the closed-door compartment, as one now sees only in old films; the conductor came along, slid the door open and passed the time of day before punching our tickets. We had another half-hour before reaching our destination; summing us up very quickly, he said: "I'll call you," winked at me, pulled down the blinds by the corridor and stuck a 'Reserved' notice on the door. You don't get that often these days, do you, on the milk-train from Paddington?

★ ★ ★

Anybody with a drop of romance in their veins would have loved Ludlow as it was in those unspoilt days. Well, look what A.E. Housman had to say: amazingly, he even managed to make an execution there sound romantic ("Eight O'clock") in his own morbid way; and the last time I went there I found myself thinking, as I'm sure Housman did, that – like so many of our historic places – it would be a wonderful town if only it wasn't full of people. I think AEH was willing them all to go away and get shot before they reached their thirties.

We soaked it all in, from the castle itself in the magnificence of its ruins, up to the small miracle a few miles North, of the castellated family home of Stokesay; from the timbered importance of The Feathers, down to that delicious private house just across the bridge… We had decent rooms at a small hotel on a side-street, and a huge country breakfast, doubtless an inherited supply-chain from the local farmers, dating back through the years of food rationing…

The best things in life need to be kept secret. We headed

West, on foot through the trees along the South bank of the Teme, and excitingly away from the world. We had a solid bag of sandwiches with us and a bottle of Tizer, and for the whole of that day we walked amid woodland and clearings, mossy twigs and spring flowers, cutting through The Chase until we caught up with the riverbank again and followed it. We never saw a soul; deer and rabbits, yes. The silence of every step grew more wonderful: a sort of hushed awesomeness. And at every step we found a more sensuous knowledge of this secretly-shared discovery; at every step we were falling more in love.

So often, an experience like that can cut abruptly short into disastrous anticlimax. Some little thing, unimportant and extraneous, can go wrong and the vision is shattered. But that day, the dream went on growing silently more and more magic and came to a climax as we came down a slope and through a spinney alongside the rushing Teme, hissing over the shallows. We stopped with a gasp.

Right in front of us, crumbled white walls leaning into the river, its huge wheel broken and covered in moss and the long sloping roof sliding down into nettles, was a deserted old watermill. A large yellow butterfly was hopping among the Spring weeds. A wide planked door hung sideways off its hinges but it smiled at us, and inside was a heap of hay...

We didn't look at each other but I felt for her hand. We knew we would be staying there. Our first night. The river chattered on.

★ ★ ★

"Topps, I'm talking to you, Topps!"

It was the DC, at his office in the HQ building. I pulled myself into the present, first day back at work.

"Yes, sir, yes indeed, our likely suspects." I fumbled for the notes I'd just picked up from Private Brown and tried to focus on them. But I kept seeing worn flagstones supporting grey-ridged oak timbers and, on them, a deep scatter of warm hay...

"You will remember, sir," I began with a mild threat, "I'm sure, that you thought we might have had about a hundred male newcomers to the civilian staff since the end of the war and the start of this 'Cold War'?" He nodded, in that textbook way of somebody who doesn't remember. "Well the precise figure, after eliminating –"

"Oh, do get on with it, Topps." I think the DC had also been on leave.

" – is just twelve. Those are the complete newcomers, without any prior link with the Depot or with any family connection with us."

"These twelve – are you opening a file on each one?"

"Not all, sir, because five of them have come out of the Forces to be near a newly-found wife or sweetheart; and another three have moved up here to be close to aged parents who have no Depot connection."

"And all this has been verified?"

Far away, a pile of logs was flickering and crackling through the small hours, in the steam of a damp old inglenook: an owl had hooted...

"All verified," I echoed. Brown and the Tschunk had liaised in getting confirmation from the Personnel people in Building Ten; I had maintained security by telling them both we were going to print an article about where people came from. They had both pulled a face at the utter boredom of any such subject. "So we must now conduct an in-depth –"

"On the remaining five," said the DC whose maths at school may have been interrupted in 1914.

"What I propose to do, sir, is carry out some covert checks on our final four."

"Ah, four, yes. But surreptitious, very surreptitious. Remember we're ultimately after his Controller. So – softly, you know, till I spring my –"

I knew. I told him I planned to have them and their movement patterns watched and noted; and I was recruiting, very surreptitiously, the patriotic services of certain local dignitaries.

"The Chief County Librarian is giving me a full list of all books taken out by male readers who have joined since 1945 and have addresses within ten miles.

I think the DC said: "Not bad" at some point; but my head was full of an old re-discovered blue tin washing-up bowl, swirling away into the distance when I'd tried to fill it from the river. We had stood and watched it all the way: somehow it had seemed so sad, that morning.

"And," I went on, "the local Postmaster has been told we want to know about all letters coming or going between here and Eastern Europe, and his discretion will be rewarded." The DC raised an eyebrow.

"Desperate times – " I quoted to him, but I was recalling a time so peaceful, unencumbered and un-desperate that it could hardly be reconciled with reality… I saw in my head a young couple deeply, deeply in love, actually going through the ridiculous routine in the morning of tidying up that derelict room, empty for decades, before reluctantly walking on. All swept clean with bracken, but a final log on the fire as we left.

"All right then," said the DC. "If any of these four people are – is – the sleeper, stuff like that may help. But we need to check them out more thoroughly, don't we?"

I had an answer to that.

"Through the Codonian, sir, I think we can arrange some sort of search."

He was intrigued.

"Suppose," I went on, "I can contact each of them – er, surreptitiously and say the paper is interested in our hand-picked civilian workers. It must be kept confidential, for some reason we can think up; and then I can send someone along to their house, to interview but also to take a good look round and report back?"

"They're going to be very suspicious, especially if one of them is, in fact, our sleeper."

"The Brigadier said, didn't he sir, how amateur and lightweight the Codonian is? How remote from the important things that matter?"

"Well," said the DC apologetically, "I don't know he meant –"

But I was far away, walking hand-in-hand and watching the swooping glint of a kingfisher, and looking back, when we came to the Rainbow Bridge, to a dreamlike spiral of blue-grey smoke from the old Hay Mill.

"I think you ought to go to bed," said the DC, "and sleep off whatever it is you've got."

"Yes, sir, codeines and Dovers," I muttered. But they couldn't help, this time. What could?

It was then that, finally dragging my mind back to the subject in hand, I had one of my sparingly-planted bright ideas; and it blossomed even as I spoke: I was making it up as I went along.

"Just before I go, sir," I turned at the door, "I think we can make the approach to our suspects a bit more subtle."

He beckoned me back to the chair, and as I settled down he went across to the cabinet.

"Laphroaig, isn't it?" He knew perfectly well. Unfortunately, as he was pouring them I looked at my watch and for the second time he caught me doing it. "Not a word to the troops," he cautioned. "It's Central European Time, for so many of us round the Depot, you may have noticed? It dates right back," he concluded.

"The wartime stress, coming up through Italy?" I had often taken a peek at his various campaign medals, as one does. I knew Italy had been difficult.

He nodded, but added lugubriously: "You've got that as a sort of hangover even before you've opened the bottle. And then, boredom can itself be stressful, you know. If there is another war, I'll go at once. If they've retired me, I'll re-enlist as a private, or go as a mercenary, or –" He brightened, "I'll go as a journalist, eh? Foreign correspondent for The Codonian."

He cooled down and asked me what my more subtle idea was: I had spent the last few minutes working on it.

"Suppose in our Personal Column I advertise for local civilians to make a spare room available, at a decent rent, for visiting staff coming in on a short detachment? Or make a special box ad. Since it's official?"

"Yes, but –"

"I know, sir, our suspects won't have replied to it but we can call on them by mistake? Then spend a few minutes chatting as though we're talking them into it."

"H'm. Won't they be suspicious –"

I took one of my deep breaths. They had served me well on many occasions.

"Not," I said, "if it's an attractive young woman pretending to be an Accommodation Agent."

★ ★ ★

It would take several intensive days and nights for me to convince Bobbie that I was doing all this for our own mutual long-term benefit: I uselessly mentioned promotion; I waved a figurative Union Jack, even the Royal Standard with medals hanging from it; but most of all I pointed out that as she had been to Drama School and done well, here was a fine career opportunity.

"I'm not going to tapdance into all their bloody houses," she told me quite reasonably, when I put my brilliant idea to her. But you just have to act, the same scene to all of them. Put that wig on, to get in the mood. She had a long blonde wig and we had fooled around, with her pretending to be some sort of vamp – she did it well.

Meanwhile, over the drinks, the DC was intrigued; and I knew I would have to make some admissions. Then it got trickier.

"This young lady," I began confidentially, but then hesitantly because the slim Major Parrott had been buzzed in to listen. As well as being the Assistant Deputy Commandant he was the Senior Depot Security Officer and as such he understandably liked to be told most of what was going on.

"This young lady has been trained as an actress, and will visit our suspects –"

"Suspects?" the Major queried. "Suspects of what?" It was only now, I believe, that the DC realised he had kept his assistant completely in the dark. He waved him across to the drinks cabinet, where the thin Major busied himself awhile.

"Tell you later," said the DC. "Go on, Topps."

"She'll call on them, a few days after our ad. asking for accommodation for our visiting radar experts on special duties. She will assume they've seen and replied; while she chats to them and flutters her eyelashes, she'll observe all she can about their home – what pictures on the wall, what sort of books and newspapers they read, envelopes with foreign stamps, all that sort of thing; and ask a few questions, which we can brief her on –"

"Who is this woman?" asked the Major over his glass.

"Just someone I know."

"How well do you know her?" He was pulling out that lighter from the back-streets of Cairo.

"Pretty well," I smiled at him. The DC was watching this with interest.

The Major didn't smile back. Never did: he was the Security Officer.

"Where does she work?" This was the one I had been waiting for, and I now knew how to deal with it, thank goodness.

One of my deep breaths. The Major's tobacco reminded me of woodsmoke in an old damp inglenook and it gave me strength.

"She is an NCO," I didn't say 'temporary acting unpaid', "at the ATS CRS."

Major Parrott bristled, and I got ready.

"What's her name, this ATS girl?"

"Let me see," I pondered. "Would it be Mrs Lambert?"

He went a delightful shade of pink and said nothing. The DC was understandably bewildered.

"No," I ended, "she is Corporal Roberts, and in fact she's due for demob in a month or two. I think she will handle this role perfectly, if I work on it with her."

"Very well," the DC stood up and stretched his leg as usual. "I'd like to meet this girl, she sounds nice." Pause. "Off the premises, of course, and in mufti. Perhaps," he looked at me sideways, "we can go to the pictures?"

★ ★ ★

Suffice it to say, Bobbie and the DC got on splendidly on our visit to the Newport Olympic. I rang in advance to make sure we got the best seats and the coldest icecream. The driver had seen the film before so he went to the Greyhound; he must have been an unromantic fellow because, had it been me driving, I would have come back in, any number of times: it was Hitchcock's 'Notorious' with that splendid plot and wonderful cast. And above all, that delicious kiss scene between Bergman and Cary Grant, which goes on for ever (and they only stop for breath, every now and then, which apparently met the censor's requirements – very crafty!). It put Bobbie and me into an agony of self-control while the DC sat stoically next to us. I found myself wondering, in the calmer bits of the film, what must have been going through that ageing mind, and remembering those hand-embroidered mementos on his chairs. There has to be a story there, I thought as the baddies drove off with Claude Rains. Must be. But I never found out.

I ran the ad. in a box on the back page. Nearly as good as the front, of course, when the paper lies unopened. It asked anyone with a spare room to contact us at the Codonian, "Box: Radar 21", since we would be getting a flow of specialist visitors for a few weeks' stay. We had seventeen replies but of course we didn't want them, and wrote back to say we would doubtless be in touch when the occasion arose. Brown knew something funny was going on, and had done ever since he'd seen me signing for my gun, but knew better than to ask questions. All in good time; and for the moment I told him I was somewhat involved at present and had to leave the everyday newspaper stuff to him: which pleased him.

Given the DC's blessing and Major Parrott having been circumnavigated, Bobbie and I together planned the entire covert operation, to accumulate whatever information we could about our four suspects. We made our base, in civvies, at The White House, a small pubby hotel well away from the Depot, where we kept our files in a locked upstairs bedroom and – tell it not in the Mess – very often stayed the night…

So where other naughty couples might have pillow-talk, ours was more caper-talk. First, we listed the essential details we needed, on each of our four. Where did they come from? How do we check that? Who did they give as references when joining, or when first applying for work? If any qualifications, where acquired? Check that, too. Test, somehow, for any knowledge of foreign languages. Check them against the DC's lists of Depot club or society memberships. Whereabouts in the Depot were they now working, or had done in the past? Was their house/flat owned or rented? If rented, whose name did they give as reference? What about their social life? Were they married, engaged; any children? Where did they go for holidays (must ask the Travel Agents in Wellington, now that overseas travel was beginning to become possible)… What newspapers did they read (make a joke about "all you need is the Codonian")? Finally: what is their reaction, and their body-language, when we let slip the fact that their short-term visitor will be "a radar specialist on special duties")?

I showed all this preparatory stuff to the DC and told him that Roberts was ready whenever he was.

"I like this 'special radar' bait," he said. "It's going to fit perfectly with mine. Start her visits right away, because I want to spring my trap in a couple of weeks."

"Is it possible, yet," I asked for the umpteenth time, "for you to let me in on the trap secret?" I knew the answer anyway.

He smiled but shook his head.

"The War Office won't let me. But keep one column clear on your front page, the week after next. I'll tell you, the day the paper goes to bed."

"Oh," he added as I was going, "You'll be getting a lot of phone calls from Fleet Street. Better get a bottle in."

He was chuckling as I shut his door, but no cigarette this time.

VIII

"How about this?" I wrote across the top.

Name:	*Origin:*	*Arrival:*
Address :	*House/Flat*	*Own/Rent:*
Depot Dept:	*Head of Dept:*	
Marital status:	*Family:*	*Where:*

War Service:

Pre-War History:

Personal Description:

Reaction to approach:

Reaction to Radar mention:

Rooms contents: (eg – newspapers/magazines; books; pictures; letters)

Club & Society Membership:

Bank:	*Library:*

Telephone:

Drink:

Women: (Men?):

Travel:	*Past:*	*Present:*

Next Step for us:

★ ★ ★

It was eight a.m. and I'd been messing about with the report-form most of the night, up in my House Four room, after waking up full of bright ideas at about two. My neighbour Lieutenant Smith had come in the worse for wear and chucked off his boots, releasing as ever the pungency of those awful socks. Hard work and strong coffee were my only antidote; and as the sun came up I finally felt fairly happy with the end product which would be an aide-memoire for Bobbie's visits and then our record of information gained. I had typed two fair copies, each with a carbon, so she was now equipped for all four visits.

I folded everything into an envelope and sealed it; wrote on it: "Going back to bed, see you at six, our 'office'. XXX.", and took it downstairs, where I could hear Edwards my quarter-batman crashing about with crockery. I directed him across to the CRS to hand it to Corporal Roberts with my compliments, looking him straight in the eye. He saw the 'XXX' and although I was closely watching his eyebrows, he had them under control. A very good chap, Edwards...

Our four suspects were a mixed bunch:
1. *Robert Blackmore*: Age about 40. Single. Driver. Flat in Newport, comes in by train. Joined depot early 1946. Gave a London charity as reference. Always dresses well.
2. *Henry Colman*: Age mid-30s. Accts Bldg 12. Clerk. Modest house in Wellington; believed married, wife works in shop. Joined late 1945. References from school in Kent, Polytechnic in South London, and Army (Pay Corps).
3. *Paul Klenov*: Age 40-50. Single. Small flatlet/bedsitter in Donnington close to depot. Typist and filing clerk, HQ Building. Foreign accent. Only reference the Red Cross dated 1941, and covering letter from American Hospital 1945. Joined Depot 1946.
4. *Ian Ap-Something (unreadable, unspellable, unpronounceable)*: Age maybe 40, but unhealthy and overweight. Storeman/supervisor, Union official. Welsh-Londoner. Believed divorced. References from previous Union. Flat in Oakengates. No record of war service. Joined 1945.

I am going to give Bobbie's own wording of her visits to these four, mainly because she completely ignored my painstaking report-forms.

1) *Robert Blackmore.*

He is a very attractive man and knows it. When I rang the bell of the flat, in a classy block on the outskirts of Newport, he answered after a couple of minutes (what was he doing?) with a big smile; he very obviously looked me up and down. I told him I had come from The Codonian, and he invited me in at once, without asking why I'd called on him. (Perhaps he has a big ego and assumed he was to be interviewed?). Or was it just personal (I was wearing my blonde wig!). I told him we were following up his reply to our advert, seeking digs for visiting Radar experts. He said he didn't remember replying to us, but laughed that he may well have done, he tends to forget everything after a good night out, "Don't you, love?". He offered me a drink. It was only ten-thirty. I accepted, in the interests of research.

It was a dry sherry, not the best but acceptable.

He said he had a spare room but didn't want any long lettings: in an emergency he could put somebody up. He showed no great interest in who they were: when I mentioned Top Secret Radar specialists he didn't react at all.

I tried to swing the conversation on to his background but when I asked about his war service he said it was secret – and he went over to a desk and got out an MC, you know, with that lovely ribbon. He said it had been given him "after Burma" but he couldn't talk about it. I asked him which regiment he had been with, and I noticed a hesitation, but then "General Staff" – but he didn't look at me when he said it, and re-crossed his legs a couple of times. A bit nervous? Suggest we check the MC records. There were several magazines on the table: Country Life, Field, and one on motor sport. They didn't seem to have been opened or read very much.

On his mantelpiece were a few old Christmas cards signed by well-known people in the Sports world, but I didn't have a chance to check them. But why leave them on show, months later?

Robert asked to see me again, and – all in the cause of the Empire as you've told me – I didn't say no. Further instructions awaited…

2) *Henry Colman.*
He was out (gone fishing in the canal) but his wife let me in. They have a small rented house on a modest side-street. Dustbins. Kids playing in the road everywhere – it was Sunday – but they have none, yet. Wife is Italian, they met when he was with the S. France invasion forces: she was in Nice on forced labour. Pleasant young woman Marina, dark, good English; works in a Wellington shop. Forgot to ask where. He was a Pay Corps sergeant.

Pre-war: at College in SE England, accountancy and economics she thinks. I saw a Sunday Graphic, well-read, and a Sunday Times not opened yet: hers or his? On the wall, pictures of Italy cut from magazines I expect: I recognised the Milan Duomo and something that might have been Florence. No sign of Catholicism anywhere. One of the Nice promenade on mantelpiece, a postcard; I took a quick look while she was making tea, humming happily in the kitchen, but it just said "Ciao again, H." and a row of kisses like one sometimes gets from a sardonic batman NCO at 8.30 a.m..

Books about boring financial and economic stuff, and

some back numbers of The Economist gathering dust, on the shelf along with a couple of the one-inch OS maps. But spread on the table was another OS map, our local one, with some little blue ink circles on it. I was looking at this when she came back. She said she was getting Harry interested in old ruins after your articles in the rag. They were going to cycle to see some of them. She said she had been on a tour, as a girl before the war, of hilltop Norman castles down the spine (I think she called it) in the south of Italy. Is that the Appenines?

They have a spare room ("At present," she added coyly) and would be happy to oblige if necessary, she was sure, but would have to ask Harry. No glimmer of interest when I mentioned Radar Experts. She did shyly ask what sort of rent they ought to charge, what about laundry, any meals to be provided, things like that. I said I'd be in touch again, to get the OK from the Fisherman. Oh, there were two books about fishing, much used and with margin scribbles.

3) *Paul Klenov.*

This one treated me with enormous suspicion. No, of course he hadn't replied to The Codonian: accommodate strangers, how could he, look at the size of the flat. I did, he was right. Most of the room, which smelt of beetroot, was taken up by a cello and (curiously) a violin-case – no, no tommy-gun inside it, I looked. Anyway, I'd "better come in for a minute" (the wig always works; and it was raining). First things first: how did we get his address? At the depot, nobody has it except the pay office.

I dithered a bit, but then said some joker must have done it, knowing how he likes to keep himself to himself. Perhaps a friend? It hurt me a bit when he sadly shrugged and spread his hands: "I have no friends". He is widowed, looks older than the reported 40s, no family so far as he knows. When he said that last bit, it dawned on me that he is Jewish, and lost his people under the Nazis. The smell of beetroot from his kitchen was terrible. I coaxed some more detail out of him by admiring his cello and talking music. At once, he lit up, and we spent over an hour on the 19th century concertos. I remembered that you'd once told me (was it that night in the ruins of Lilleshall Abbey when you told me certain other things too?) that you had been at a BBC Orchestra Adrian Boult broadcast at your school, as the only audience, and sat between Max Rostal and Stuart Hibberd during the first number – L'Arlésienne, with the saxophone, right? – and then listened to Rostal playing Max Bruch. So I told him all that, he made me some sort of Polish coffee that tasted of even more beetroot, and we chatted one-sidedly for another half-hour. Music is clearly his life, and he is great to listen to: his accent is a bit of a trial, his English is rather like Sam Goldwyn's but it's worth the effort: you must meet him. About one music critic he said "He can't tell his Gluck from his Glinka," which I really must remember. (PS – I can't tell, either).

Nothing much in the room apart from music stuff. Daily Mail, local paper, Tit-Bits. A book about electronics… I asked about this. He said that he had an occasional "shaft of light", sometimes when sleeping, that seemed to suggest that in his pre-war life he had a connection or interest with that sort of thing; and had bought the book in case it sparked anything in his muddled memory. It hadn't.

But he works in HQ building on communications. Should I go back and dance his secrets out of him?

4) *Ivor Ap-Something (can't read, let alone pronounce it).*

I want double pay for this one. Objectionable, is hardly

a strong enough word. I rang the bell, early evening, just as a rather cheap-looking girl was leaving. He came down, in a vest and scruffy trousers, scratching himself. No, he didn't read The Codonian, let alone reply to it; but come in and have a beer. Was I a member of the Union? I said I was saving up the subscription, my pay as an Accommodation Clerk was so disgustingly low, and what was he going to do about it?

I was pretty sure he'd be making a pass at me, so while he was cracking the bottles I took a quick look around me. Reveille, Mirror. No books worth noting, just a pile of paperback novels with lurid covers and usually a well-thumbed chapter somewhere in the middle. On the table, though, several letters from Germany: one postmark was Berlin, the rest I couldn't read, one started with K-something, a long word but all smudged. On the walls, nothing much, but a framed photo of a town almost flattened by bombs. We drank the beer, he told me he was a Londoner from Ancient Britain then Ilford, called-up halfway through the war, Royal Engineers, worked on building Bailey Bridges.

I'd never heard of them, at first I was going to ask: "Who is Bailey Bridges" but luckily didn't. Married 1940, came home to find another man in the house. Hit him hard: two years inside… Divorce.

Has a spare room "But nobody's going to like it much." A flicker, when I told him about the secret Radar connection; but only a flicker.

On his second beer he began to leer at me and heave himself closer across the tatty settee. What is it they say in the News of the World? I made my excuses and left.

★ ★ ★

I took all Bobbie's reports to the DC, and sat there while he read through, passing them page by page to Major Parrott alongside. At the end they both looked up and nodded.

"Your friend has done well," said the Major. "But we'll have to watch all four of these people for a while –"

"But not for too long," the DC interrupted, "because of my trap." He handed me a sheet of paper. "This is a news item for next week, a column on the front page, please, and I want the headline big and bold."

I began to look at it, but he waved it away.

"And then, the very next day, all the nationals will be sent a denial."

I then really did look at it.

"HUSH HUSH : Coming Soon" it said, in a typeface alien to us; the copy told of a top secret Radar device that would outdate all existing equipment; it had been developed with maximum security between us and the Americans and the finishing touches were now to be added at COD Donnington, Shropshire. The article had been written (presumably by boffins in Whitehall) so that it would just fit one of my front-page columns. But we would have to re-set it in our normal font, or it would look like an advertisement, I told them.

"But we mustn't give away, to anybody at all, that this whole story is a concoction."

"In that case," I said, "we'll have to set it ourselves"; and for quite a while I sat, again looking at them meaningfully.

The Major, as Security Supremo, spoke first. He asked where, at present, the Codonian was typeset. I told him it had recently been transferred to in-house at Building 18.

The DC asked whether that ATS Officer, Chang, Chung, Cheng, could do it. I said that J.C. Chunk was a very forceful personality but I wasn't too sure about her background –

At which point the Major squashed the whole idea: "No,

she's a problem for us, there's a possible security weakness in her personal life…" He trailed off. I found myself wondering whether his Sergeant had tipped him off about the nubile receptionist in Building 18, or whether the Major himself had at some time explored those possibilities and been rebuffed. A good story I'd never be able to publish. One for Private Brown perhaps, when he went on to Fleet Street?

It was left to me to come up with the only sensible solution. "Suppose I write an editorial about the mysteries and tricks of type-setting, and expound on the professionalism required, and invite Top People in the depot to try their luck, under the guidance of the Tschunk? We can turn it into an interesting article later, but it would at once enable us, ourselves, to set the Radar piece."

I looked around at them.

"Just the three of us, on a short-course? Two or three hours, maybe twice in a week? Then one evening in the Building when nobody's around?"

It was so absurd that they both agreed at once.

★ ★ ★

So it was, that we sat through a session of manual typesetting instruction, to which I brought along Private Brown to add authenticity, and Corporal Roberts to relieve the boredom; and the paper would go to bed that Wednesday with the sensational news-item complete, its bold headline designed to catch the eye of all those gutteral foreigners now, in my imagination, infesting the depot.

"Friday," said the DC, "we tell Reuters, and all the main newspapers individually, that your front-page column was entirely wrong – misguided – more than that, utterly misinformed and you have been suspended."

"Surely," I asked, "none of them will even have heard of The Codonian?"

"Of course," he smiled, "That's the point. Our official denial will bring your paper to everybody's attention. As I warned you, you'll get a host of media enquiries. Just bat them away, play dumb, so that they'll be quite sure you've made a bad mistake and have something to hide. Just keep using the words Radar and Donnington, otherwise concede nothing at all."

And that is how it evolved. I told The Tschunk we were going to run a feature on typesetting, and she confirmed there was still a variety of fonts available in the good old mono-process 'pie'. (Building 18 was currently and somewhat agonisingly going over to the smug superiority of lino., where a whole line would be cast in a single slug of molten lead; I knew that she considered it to be "quicker, but less fun" than picking individual letters out of the 'pie'; I remembered pondering on her idea of 'fun', but what did I know?).

EDITORIAL page 2.

FINGERS IN THE PIE

Your Codonian is, every week, literally "put together". For five hundred years, ever since Gutenberg and then Caxton began to fiddle with little lead slugs of individual letters, compositors have slaved away with trays of what they call "pie" – selecting every letter and blank space between, to build up the message in every book or newspaper you read – even the Codonian. This function is now performed for you by our own in-house printing staff in Building 18.

To demonstrate the skill and dexterity required (and that perhaps cuts out the left-handed if you know your Latin?), we recruited a team of high-class amateurs to attempt the task of setting up at random a news item, just in from the War Office. To confuse the issue, we raided the Printing & Publication stores to mix a variety of typefaces (as we call them) or 'fonts' (as the aesthetes prefer); and here on our front page is the result. Its confusion must serve as a tribute to our regular compositors who do, in contrast, know what they're doing!

COLUMN FOUR page one.

HUSH HUSH : COMING SOON

Donnington has been chosen by the War Office to be the base for development of a Top Sercet Radar Device. This will outdate all existing sytsems and render them obsotele. Maximum security will apply to the chosen section of the Depot, which we cannot yet divugle.

★ ★ ★

It was Private Brown's idea to exaggerate the typesetting errors, as we worked away at our compositing that evening. "Catch their eye with a couple of misprints," he pointed out, "and everybody will read the whole thing closely, looking for more." This was especially true when viewed along with our Editorial, and we sent the paper to bed very happily. The Tschunk deplored all those errors but knew we were up to something that she wasn't yet going to be part of; I saw her distressed look, and with a melting heart I told her she would know all about it later. But at the same time I suggested – probably unnecessarily – to Major Parrott that she ought perhaps to be watched.

He was also a bit worried by my inclusion of Brown in

our caper. I had anticipated this by suggesting to the DC that my Private, being a highly-educated young man about to head off to either Oxford or Fleet Street or both, might in either case be of future use to the country, and therefore should be invited to sign the Official Secrets Act despite his self-inflicted lowly rank. The point was taken – it would also tremendously flatter him, and score him any number of bonus-points when he was demobbed into national journalism. It also, quite incidentally, helped my and Bobbie's covert researches…

I said to Brown, once he had signed and been briefed on everything that was going on ("Do I get a gun like yours?" had been his only reaction), that we had four prime suspects, they being the only men who had joined the Depot recently with no prior connection.

"We will be looking out for any response from one of them –"

"Or more, or all of them?"

"Unlikely," I told him. "Major Parrott's men are keeping an eye on them all, and they never meet – in fact they're all in quite different parts of the Depot".

Private Brown weighed up this information; he turned to me with a glint in his eye which should have warned me.

"Suppose," he said, eyeing the gun-bulge in my side pocket, "Suppose they have dug a tunnel that links all their flatlets and bed-sitters, so they can come and go without –"

"Shut up," I said, "for God's sake."

Brown shut up, after a final helpful suggestion: "Why not, Sir, shoot all four of them?"

"Here," as I handed him a piece of scribbled paper, "is the list of them. If any of them rings the Codonian, make full notes of the conversation and tell me at once. You are also going to get enquiries from all the papers, nationals, sundays, BBC, Reuters, everybody, about our revelation. We'll be denying it in a couple of days, so they will all smell a rat – which is what we want. Do you understand now?"

But Brown was looking at the piece of paper with the four suspects' names. Blackmore, Colman, Klenov, Ivor-Thing. He looked up at me, mouth open.

"Paul Klenov." he said. "That's your man."

IX

It was early on the Thursday morning and Junior Commander Chunk's presses were churning out the six thousand copies of tomorrow's Codonian, throbbing with its implanted message… And here was my Private telling me that he already knew who our 'sleeper' was…

"Klenov," he went on, looking at me as if I ought to know. I shook my head.

"Music," he uselessly prompted me. "I bet he's a musician."

I looked at Bobbie's notes: cello, violin case, an hour talking about concertos. I nodded feebly.

"Paul Klenov," Brown told me ever so patiently, "was the pseudonym used by Sir Henry Wood when he wanted to hide his identity as the composer, or rather the arranger, of a piece by Bach, just before the war."

"So – " I began.

"So," said Private Brown, "this suspect is hiding behind an alias which he has chosen because not many people," he looked at me, "are sufficiently knowledgeable –"…

As I stalked out of Building 18 he was still telling me about it, and the machines were still pumping out Codonians ready for our cunning spy-trap tomorrow.

★ ★ ★

"We have to go back into the dreaded beetroot belt," I told Bobbie, and explained. "It looks as though your Sam Goldwyn soundalike is our man."

"It's unlikely," she said. "To me, he seemed too" – she searched for the word – "world-weary to get involved in our politics at all, let alone into active spying."

"Ah – the worst possible kind," put in Major Parrott who was sitting-in on the conversation. "I've seen all this before. He's our man all right. Sticks out a mile. In HQ building, too!"

We agreed that I should cycle over with Bobbie and call on this pseudo-Klenov at once, visiting his flat because we mustn't arouse any suspicion by tackling the dangerous character anywhere within the Depot, especially not in the HQ Building where he sat at a desk filing all our documents and answering the telephone, doubtless listening-in to endless Top Secret conversations: keep it quiet, said the Major, "mustn't frighten the horses", he added in the confident tone of someone in Supply who had never in his life been within twenty miles of the Cavalry.

We knocked on Klenov's street door, which opened on to a dingy flight of uncarpeted stairs, at about six that evening; across the road, down his side-street and in the road behind, the Major had stationed twelve of his best security men: God knows what they were armed with, I only hoped they could shoot straight if the time came…

We could hear him coming down to answer our knock. I listened to the slow, heavy and erratic footsteps on the bare wood and I remember thinking that if this was a dangerous sprightly Communist spy planted in our midst by the KGB, he was a pretty good actor, not even knowing who had been knocking…

"Hello Paul," Bobbie said with a bright smile as the door edged open. "I've brought my friend to see you, like I promised; this is Tim, he knew all those BBC Orchestra people." The door opened wider, but I noticed that Klenov glanced up and down the street while letting us in. Why would he need to do that? I hoped the Major's men were well hidden, as we went upstairs creakingly.

My first impression was that Bobbie's report had been too kind: the smell of beetroot was everywhere, oppressive like an invisible maroon blanket which draped the room and everything and everyone within it. I knew we had to conclude our business quickly, so I didn't hang about.

"Paul Klenov," I began, "I must tell you that this house is surrounded."

"Forgive," he said. "Not understand. They will pull it down?"

I began to get a bad feeling.

Luckily, Bobbie stepped in.

"Paul," she said gently, and so he listened as carefully as he could, "We want to know why you are using the name 'Paul Klenov' because it is a name invented, isn't it? Please, can you tell us?"

He looked at her with relief. "I have to have a name," he said with a helpless spread of his hands. "I have done wrong?"

We declined the offer of coffee, but sat while he told us all he could remember about his background – and it wasn't much. The terrible events in the Warsaw ghetto, from 1939 onwards, had cut him off from everyone he knew. Whatever horrors he had seen, had so mentally paralysed him that when the Red Cross found him two years later, huddled in a blanket amidst mountains of brown coal, in the hold of a rusty ship docking at Malmo, neither he, nor the crew, nor yet the Swedish authorities, could tell them anything useful. They found no papers on him; his memory had almost completely gone, but he lit up on hearing classical music – "significantly," the Report said, "Chopin" – and extraordinarily, anything by Vera Lynn.

He knew that this was funny and we all laughed, while

picturing to ourselves privately the image of a terrified young man in hiding, tuning in to his secret radio to pick up BBC broadcasts to Occupied Europe.

The Red Cross had dusted him down, fed him up, and asked him where he wanted to go. He didn't know who he was, so he had no homing instincts whatever; and with enormous understanding they had seized upon the Vera Lynn clue and arranged for him to come to England. I found this sensitivity immensely touching, and made a note to praise Red Cross in a future editorial and indeed whenever I got the chance.

Once in this country, evidently nobody quite knew what to do with him. He was put in a remote hospital somewhere in Staffordshire, to recuperate in the forlorn hope that his memory would come back, by well-intentioned medics who obviously had more urgent things to worry about as bombs dropped on Birmingham, Coventry and Stoke. A Polish fighter-pilot was brought in from an airfield in Lincolnshire to chat to him, and he found that Paul's fluency in his native language was unimpaired; they discussed music; the airman also reported to the doctors that, once prompted subtly, Paul seemed to be fairly articulate in speaking English – he must have studied it in school as well as listening to the BBC – so it was agreed that he should be given access to the local library's music department... But there seemed to be no apparent memory.

So it was, that when the question arose of his name: "We've got to call you something other than Mr. X Polish, don't you know?", he dipped into the book he had been painfully reading, and said: "Henry Wood."

The young nurse had a bit of basic musical knowledge, and also read the papers.

"You can't do that, he's a real important person and anyway, he's just died."

So, this likeable beetrooty little man told us, he had read Wood's obituary, and found the Paul Klenov connection, and with his Slavic sound it seemed ideal.

"Hence the pyramids," I said to Bobbie, hoping that Paul wouldn't hear the expression and ask me to explain, because I couldn't.

We smiled our way out and down the stairs. I only hoped that Major Parrott's twelve marksmen would recognize us and hold their fire.

★ ★ ★

Friday morning, the Codonian with the DC's page-one, mono-set, sensational column, leaking the secret news of our Radar involvement, was released upon an apathetic world.

On my desk when I got in later that day was the DC's apologetic Press release to all the national papers, marked with an important-looking War Office handstamp "Most Urgent: Immediate", which I thought was pretty good – completely phoney, Fleet Street will seize upon it. And they did.

"NEW RADAR DEVELOPMENT: MISINFORMATION or LEAK? A local Army Depot newsletter has mistakenly published erroneous details purporting to reveal astonishing advances in Radar defence systems, and claiming that research within the UK is putting Britain well ahead of all other nations in this vital area. Whitehall has dismissed the item as 'fictitious' and the editor, a junior National Service officer, has been reprimanded."

Fame at last, I thought; but one evening in the Mess I had been browsing through an article about the pre-Raphaelites and came across Holman Hunt's sad 'Scapegoat'... I sensed that I was about to join that poor animal in the desert.

Attached to my copy of this Press release, "for information

only', was a handwritten scrawl. "Topps," it said, "you'd better run a small paragraph next week. Don't make it too contrite, just say you got the location wrong. In fact, our radar boffins are at Hut Seven in Wem, but that's not for general information: just say it's all happening somewhere away from us, at one of our sub-depots: should satisfy the nosey". This all seemed somewhat superfluous but I supposed the DC had to keep all his loose ends tied up, even if they were imaginary – I gave the stuff to Brown to put in the files, and he did it with one hand while juggling the phone with the other: reporters had been phoning ever since he got in, and he was enjoying this greatly. I counted three half-empty mugs of cold coffee; both ashtrays were loaded, one holding a half-smoked Players while he was already lighting the next… He grinned at me happily.

"What are you telling them?"

"Chiefly," he said with his hand over the mouthpiece, "I'm explaining how I've been put in charge of cleaning up my Editor's terrible *faux-pas*."

I took away his new cigarette and dragged on it, pointing him towards the still-smouldering old one. I noticed that he had a large sheet of paper in front of him, full of names and London telephone numbers. Whatever was that?

"Contacts."

He was going to go far, this opportunist. It struck me that in a year or two, if I got kicked out of Oxford I could probably ask him for a job .

Meanwhile, we had to await developments. I wondered how likely it was that the DC's bait would be taken; and if not, what would his next trick be? After all, you can't keep spinning obvious lies in a paper week after week, especially when you've already had to make yourself look a fool. Oh, I don't know though.

When I feel deflated or a bit depressed, I react by withdrawing, going into my shell some people call it, though in fact I am merely using my brain, such as it is, to re-charge my batteries; and with me, this always means reaching for the typewriter and starting on a short story. Bobbie quickly came to understand this, and as soon as I called her to say I'd be back at House Four for the day, she just suggested a quick drink after my Mess supper, down at the nearest pub, "if I was feeling ready for it by eight"…

The junior officers' houses were pretty empty during the day, unless they were pristinely changing for sports at about two o'clock, or sweatily washing off the mud around five. The Admirable Edwards usually finished his services by lunchtime unless one of us had bribed him into extra duties. So I had the place to myself. I was very glad for this: I needed thinking and typing time. I had landed myself with a minor but embarrassing Codonian problem far removed from the Depot's seething pit of spies: nobody had won my short story competition…

It was worse than that. In my early editorial enthusiasm I had over-estimated my readership's levels of – how can I put this? – no, there's no easy way – let's just say that if Thomas Gray had visited Donnington instead of Stoke Poges, he would have been in the wrong churchyard. If there were any mute Miltons hereabouts, they must be more inglorious than the average. To be sure, we received a handful of entries; but after eliminating first the illegible then the unintelligible, we were left with two finalists, one of them too rude to print even in Shropshire, and the other (as Brown fortunately pointed out) had been copied word for word from O. Henry…

But The Chunk had told me we had a surplus in the Codonian account, and I had offered prize money…

So I wrote three short stories, or rather, I rehashed some I

113

already had; using three aliases, I ran them as the three winners. And yes, I did, here I confess: I paid those three winners – £10, £5 and £2. And I spent the final £3 on a jolly good lunch for Peggy P&P, her lissome friend, and Brown, an excellent way to inveigle them into keeping quiet about it. I still tell myself it was all for the good reputation of the Codonian, and though I say it myself, the stories weren't bad (one of them, under my own name, was later broadcast by the BBC's Home Service – twice, actually. You have to say 'actually' after an announcement like that, don't you?)

The DC never commented at all on those stories, and that itself makes me suspect he knew what I had been up to. Probably he was uncomfortable about the scapegoat thing, just a few weeks earlier, and felt that I deserved some sort of compensation. I did.

I skipped supper in the Mess, and met Bobbie for a sandwich in the pub down by Donnington station. We weighed up the situation about our four suspects.

"Why just these four?" she pondered. "We're sitting here amid several thousand Depot workers, aren't we?"

I began to spell out again our thorough processes that had eliminated all the less likely: only new entrants, males without any local connections prior to entry… I had to concede that any number of existing staff may well have come over all communistic during the war, enthused by what the public had been fed about Our Glorious Allies – anyway, until the Russians raped Berlin and everyone in it – but she and I had been charged with concentrating on The Four, hadn't we?

"And yet," I added, "it wouldn't do any harm to spread our net a little bit wider. Tomorrow's Saturday, you're off-duty. Why not nip into Wellington and ask the Bank managers about any noticeable or repeated exchanges of foreign currency, say from Eastern Europe? And the Travel Agents, too?"

"They won't talk to me about things like that."

"You're a reporter, you're an Accommodation Agent, you're a Corporal and don't forget, you can get a Letter of Authority from the DC, too. Not only that, you're a vamp. Get out there. I'll talk to the DC first thing."

We finished our pub sandwiches at about ten, and I was back in House Four by – that's got nothing to do with you.

★ ★ ★

Quite early the following morning things had begun to develop. Nothing started too soon on Saturdays, indeed some sections were closed down for the weekend: the civilians to go to the shops and the football, God help us, and the military to do their military once-a-week stuff on the barrack square. I often had to play a minor part in this, up at the camp, where all our clumsy soldier-storemen were trained to kill. As a subaltern, I was in charge of a platoon, that is a group of about forty men: in battle, which the Good Lord forbid, they would divide into four 'sections' – three of ten men under a corporal, armed with rifles plus a machine-gun operator, and the fourth being the HQ section where I would lurk with my sergeant, mortar-man, radio operator, RAMC man and runners – those under-rated bravados who had to carry urgent messages to and fro under the hail of enemy fire, so that each operational section's corporal could, with a bit of luck, know what was going on... I would absorb all this in a state of quiet desperation as I looked around at my dishevelled Saturday charges, and force myself to remember their earlier colleagues who had stumbled out of their depot store-rooms to defend Hong Kong and Singapore, not so long ago.

I am the first to admit that, as a soldier, I was – er – unorthodox. A certain stuffy Colonel, not mentioned hitherto, nor hereafter, and no friend of mine, would have said – did say – "unacceptably unmilitary"; but come to think of it, he was only a half-Colonel who had reached his ceiling, he had come up through the ranks and taken twenty years about it, and exchanged feelings of hatred with almost everybody, so far as I could see. His one self-proclaimed fame was rooted in his single good non-military idea: to set up local Depot newspapers. He had done this, I think, at all our main Ordnance Depots: Bicester and Didcot, as well as our Codonian, but his intention had been merely to spread propaganda to the civilian workers, linking football reports with banal round-the-depot chat, in four limp pages. Given his background, one can perhaps understand him despising National Servicemen, especially those of us who, because of our intense OTC training at public school, came into the Forces already halfway qualified to hold a commission. We could shoot; we could map-read; we knew everything about parade-ground drill, indeed many of us had taught it for six terms! More to the point, we had learnt, over sometimes anguished years, how to handle and cope with – live with! – the vagaries of our peers and contemporaries. (After all, sharing a house with forty other people for up to nine years, you simply cannot avoid gaining a good insight into various human prototypes and realising, perhaps painfully, that "It takes all sorts"). It is not difficult to empathise (as we were also taught!) with the likes of that Lt. Col. But such feelings were not reciprocated – are they ever?

★ ★ ★

I was saying: quite early that Saturday morning, having side-stepped the military parade with some excuse I now forget, probably an urgent indent from somewhere like Malaya for engineering equipment, I put in my routine visit to E & R, which would keep Mr Stanway happy. After reporting to HQ office and grinning at Mac through her window where my Lt.Col. glowered at me, I got an agitated phone-call from my new and unlikely colleague at Building 18, the Tschunk. She, I had to admit, was now "one of the team" involved in our Paper Caper, after our rather ridiculous typesetting feature and its spycatching ulterior motive.

"We've had a break-in," said Peggy Chunk.

"What sort of break-in?" I asked, though I realised at once that this could well be somebody taking the DC's bait. I didn't wait for an answer and a few minutes later, thanks to my decrepit Army-issue pushbike, I was at her desk and Private Brown was beside me. Both of them now had the basic story of our suspects, the DC's trap, and the Codonian's part in all this.

"Overnight," said the enormous Peggy. "Broken window, forced cabinets –"

"Was anything actually taken?" I wanted to establish if this had been a search for information rather than just for goods.

"I don't think so." Peggy, predictably, looked across to her receptionist, as did we all. This delicious woman slowly unfurled herself and went through the erotic motions of checking a handful of foolscap sheets in her 'Pending' tray – I noticed that the other two, In and Out, were both empty. A good day's work done, already at twenty past nine? The under-employed receptionist at least had the awareness to feel a bit embarrassed, and swayed across the room to make us coffee.

Once she was out of hearing, Brown said: "My filing cabinets have been forced."

"But has anything gone?"

"I don't think so, but I must re-check." He went over to his nest in the corner of the building, where the same small desk was nowadays framed by not one but three large cabinets. I knew his meticulous methods and we waited quite a time, halfway through our coffees, until he came back thoughtfully and said to me: "Could we have a word, sir?"

You don't want to insult a woman as big as Peggy Chunk, especially not in front of her girlfriend, but he glanced at her and explained: "Codonian editorial business, Ma'am, can't really wait." And we walked back to the nest.

"It's the caper file."

"Caper file? You mean you've opened a special file –"

He looked at me with that look he had.

"Sir, everything has to be filed, I can't just leave it all lying –"

I had to stop him shaking his head like that.

"Yes, yes, Brown, of course. But what about it?"

"It's gone."

"Are you sure?" But of course he was, I suppose I was playing for time, before asking the obvious. "What was in it?"

"Oh, all the copy for yesterday's issue and your notes from the Deputy Commandant. But nothing that's important now, I suppose. After all, he's shown hand, hasn't he. I mean, breaking in–"

"How did you name the file?"

"Well," said Brown, regaining his confidence as usual at my expense, "I thought it would be quite a good idea to give it the title we all know it by, 'Paper Caper', rather than something like 'Secret Radar Sensation All Revealed Within', you see. Sir," he added acidly.

"We're not writing funny editorials just now," I reminded him. "Is anything else missing?"

There didn't seem to be, although all three cabinets had been forced; but admittedly that hadn't been difficult: throughout Building 18 they were old prewar wooden things which we had recalled from around the country after issuing the modern metal ones.

"Oh, and he helped himself to our petty cash float – two pounds four and tuppence. And probably theirs, too," he nodded across, "when Gloria Goodbody gets round to buying the milk." He looked at his abandoned coffee mugs, and right on cue there came a screech from the far end of the building.

"Well, of course," I reasoned, "that's a typical cover-up to hide the real reason for a burglary: it's in every Hollywood movie –"

"You should know," we both said to each other pointedly. We sat and thought for a minute; then: "Good God, have the free tickets gone?"

★ ★ ★

I had to report to the DC and presumably Major Parrott, but on the way I stopped at Peggy's desk and asked her to leave the matter to me; but I guessed correctly that she had kept quiet and instructed all her Printing & Publications staff to do the same "for reasons we can't explain at the moment, but only the Petty Cash has been stolen".

Peggy didn't know of any stranger who might have come into her Building after the Codonian was issued yesterday, Friday, looking for us and presumably 'casing the joint'; so I asked Gloria Goodbody, who automatically moved a few paces closer to her boss before venturing any reply.

"Well," she said, "Well, yes, there was a funny little man came in teatime –"

"What did he –" But Peggy muscled in at once; this was her PA (or whatever) and she would do the interrogating.

"What did he want?"

"He wanted to know where the Codonian 'offices' were," and with that sarcastic plural I decided I didn't much like our Gloria, or whatever her real name was. "So I showed him over to the corner. But Private Brown wasn't there, so the man went away."

"Can you describe him?" This was Peggy again, getting in a split second before me. "Sit down, dear, and think carefully."

Dear sat down, crossing her legs voluptuously but pointing them away from me.

"Well," she began, preening at all this attention, " quite short, a bit scruffy –"

"Age?" I said it first.

"Ooh…" A thoughtful pause with various facial expressions as though she was in an audition for Hitchcock or one of that crowd. "Forties? But getting fat, under his overalls his shirt was hanging out…"

"Hair?" Peggy prompted, but Gloria shook her head.

"It was only hanging out a bit, I couldn't see his stomach."

I glanced across but Peggy wouldn't look at me.

"What colour would you describe the hair on his head?" she asked in a voice that was just ever so slightly strangled.

"Sort of dark, gone back a bit at the sides. I can't tell you any more about him."

"Try." That was me.

"What was his voice like, dear?" That wasn't.

"Well… A bit – sort of – rough, really." She was embarrassed by this class thing but had to deal with it. "A bit – sort of – common. Oh, and he called me 'Brother'."

I ran out of the Building: a short, scruffy man in overalls, a shop steward… He had 'flickered' when Bobbie told him about the Radar stuff. I went directly to the DC and found Major Parrott there as well, waiting for my report since I'd phoned him early on.

120

They sat and listened to the whole story, ending up with this evident exposure of the distasteful Ivan Thingski.

★ ★ ★

"You must call on him at once," said the Major, gathering some papers together and getting up. "Make it midday when he gets home, I'll have my chaps standing by. A Communist – he's our man all right – worst possible kind. Seen it all before," as he went out.

The DC gave me one of his smiles and waved me into a chair.

"Well, we're making some progress," he said, "and the national papers fell for it – they're all making comments about your stupidity in giving away secrets." At this point, at least he went over to the corner cupboard. I didn't look at my watch, I knew what time it was in Cairo.

"Tell me, Topps," as he took a sip, "what do you reckon to this Thingy fellow? Is he the guilty one?"

"From what everyone says, he's not the sort of person I'd take to –"

"The Cafe Royal, no, or even the Royal in Oakengates. But apparently he's a leading Trade Unionist now, came up very quickly, I hardly know him, though of course I have dealings all the time. But these people all get elected, perfectly respectably... If he was going to look at your files, surely he could do it surreptitiously from the inside – nobody would ever need to know. Why draw attention to himself by walking in on the Friday and smashing a window at the weekend?"

"Create a diversion?"

He shook his head, picked up the phone as it rang, then passed it to me across the desk.

"It's your Private Brown, says it's urgent."

"Yes, Brown?"

"Sorry to interrupt you sir, but I've been scouting around. The break-in was last night after eleven. There's fresh mud by some of the cabinets and on the windowsill by the broken pane, and footprints just outside. Good ones. It's been dry and didn't rain until about eleven p.m. but then there was a downpour, if you remember."

"Good man, take some photos of the footprints, I'll be over soon."

"One more thing. There are two sets of them."

"Two!" The DC leaned forward.

"A very large man, and then a smaller one, lighter in weight, didn't sink in so deep. I'll do my best to take a decent snap, but the glass may cause some reflection."

"Glass? On the *out*side? On *top* of the prints?"

"No doubt about it, sir."

"OK, Sherlock. Thanks."

I passed the phone back to the DC who hung up without looking what he was doing. Staring at me and deep in thought, he almost knocked his drink over. I simply stared back. It didn't seem to get us anywhere, until he had a new idea.

"The guardroom," he said. "A lot of vehicles come and go during the week but after closedown on Fridays the place is pretty much deserted these days except when we get alarms and excursions from the Far East or somewhere in the Empire." He picked up the phone again and asked for the guardroom at the main gate: "The only one open at night," he said to me with his hand over the mouthpiece. Then:

"Sergeant? This is the Deputy Commandant. I'm sending Lieutenant Topps over –"

I sensed the "Who?" coming from the other end.

"Topps. He's – er – at E&R Receipts, but – you know – he's also editor of the Codonian and I want him to check one or two things from your records of last night." A slight splutter over the wire. "Yes, Sergeant. Who was on duty last night, after dark? Thank you, he'll be with you shortly."

"Well," said the DC happily, "now we're getting somewhere. But let's not forget," wagging a finger, "it's all got to be hush-hush. Our bait has been taken, but all the time we are after Mr Big in the background. These little men around the depot – even if there are two of them or more – they aren't much more than chickenfeed. So, absolute secrecy…"

The DC, during all this, had not been idle with his bottle, and for the first-ever time I sensed he might be succumbing, ever so slightly, to its soothing but dangerously-relaxing effects. I felt like telling him that it was closing-time at the Gezira Club, but instead I got up. He waved a hand to stop me leaving just yet: there was some philosophy coming.

"Mr Big," he started. "Good name… The big men hide well. When I was at school," he went on, "Our old housemaster used to tell us rude stories… But a lot of sense behind them." He looked at his empty glass, then at the bottle, then shrugged. "He used to warn us, and it's true, Trupps, it's true. He said: Every time you sit on the lavatory, remember the Biggy Paradox – 'The bigger the shit, the smaller the splash'. Isn't that just true?"

I told him Yes, and went gently out.

X

I hurried over to the guardroom, trying to weigh up the few facts we had. Paul Klenov was probably in the clear: not many Jewish people, surely, would want to work for the Russians, certainly not Poles. Yet, if he really had lost his memory and all his family, he might be vulnerable and coaxed or threatened into pro-Communist work by somebody subtly gaining his confidence. How about the Polish airman he had been introduced to? How about somebody Left-wing in the music world? Why was there a nice cello but the case for a violin? Why did he look furtive when he opened the street door?

And now: how about this nasty little Thingyman? If he was Welsh perhaps he could sing his name to us? Him, I had to see at once. Bobbie had noted in her report, the connections in his room with "East Germany", that new hotbed of Soviet-dominated Communists, still in post-war turmoil with the ruins of Berlin sunk like a modern Atlantis in the middle of it, under multiple control and quartered against itself. Was Ilford Ivan in touch with top people in the Russian Sector? And would I spot our missing file if I sprang my visit upon him?

Once Bobbie had come back from her Wellington calls, we might have a bit more information about the Singing Storeman's movements and perhaps an inflow of Deutschmarks or whatever lightweight little plastic tokens they used for money over there... Then I remembered I was going to ask the DC to give her a Letter of Authority, and ought to get it done, as we were already well into the morning.

I did this as soon as I got to the guardroom, using their phone to call the DC direct, which greatly impressed the Sergeant of the Guard, (so much so that when I left later on, I received a powerful salute!). I called Bobbie at the CRS to pick up the Letter from HQ Building, and while she was there, to take a look at Ivor's desk by the telephone switchboard, just in case... She had been awaiting my call, and drumming her fingers as she was keen to visit both the Bank Managers before one o'clock when, of course, it being Saturday, they would close...

The grey-haired old Regular who was the Sergeant of the Guard that day, had been waiting patiently during it all, and allowed himself a twitch of a smile as he heard this ATS corporal berating me. He had appeared bored when I first arrived in his domain, because that was expected of him, his job definition perhaps after more than twenty years as a Military Policeman (I noted the Long Service & Good Conduct ribbon on his uniform at the tail end of peacetime Palestine and the usual WW2 ones covering North Africa and the Home Front: why not Europe? Perhaps wounded and blightied amid the desert sands? My mind wandered: desert sands... Would a scapegoat get a medal?)

But the Sergeant's grizzled interest had been aroused by the snatches he had heard: an ATS girl going in to HQ to see the Colonel, this young whippersnapper on personal terms with both the high and the low? His instinct to serve was stimulated. Was this the glory moment he'd been waiting for, ever since he joined the RMP straight from Colchester in 1930?

No.

Nevertheless he did all he could. Last night, sir? After eleven? Depot pretty much closed, only one gate open, this one, sir. A few folk come and go on special duties. All entered in the book, by the overnight Sergeant, I'm sure sir. No, sir, I go off at eight. Night crew then: keep their own records, for security you see. You'll have to come back after eight this evening. Night Sergeant: Corporal Campbell, sir.

"The sergeant is a corporal?"

"Sir?"

It was all too difficult for this whippersnapper, so I thanked him warmly and went off on my bike to catch out the nasty Dagenham Celt, as he sat in his murky soviet hovel, humming the Red Flag while he ate his stewed cabbage and hit the vodka…

★ ★ ★

I called on our in-house Communist at his expectedly grim little flat, just as he got back from weekend shopping. The Major had stationed his men at various 'strategic points' as he would have called them, which meant that two rather solid-looking men in dirty civvies were leaning against convenient lampposts and four more in a tired Hillman Minx down the road. Only six this time, I thought to myself.

Of course, I hadn't met The Appy Singer before, but Bobbie's earlier description of him was spot-on. So, I had to admit, was Gloria Goodbody's – his shirt *was* hanging out when he came downstairs to answer my ring. And I made a mental note to tell her, some time when the occasion presented itself, that he did have hair on his stomach, quite a lot of it.

"I'm from the Codonian," I began. "You've met my assistant –"

"Yeah, nice little thing. Come on up."

He heaved up the stairs ahead of me, and I was subjected to a fat rear-end exposed above the dirty trouser-top, bulging left and right at each step. Even before we reached the landing,

I was becoming convinced that this could hardly be an enemy spy. No controller in his right mind would run the risk of being in charge of such a lump. This was just an old-fashioned lazy-minded pre Anglo-Saxon brand of self-delusional idealist: the ones who used to swallow Russian workers' wild boasts in pre-war newspapers, and thumb avidly through all those grey-paper magazines full of hydro-electric dams and muscular concrete statues...

We sat down and I accepted his offer of an IPA. It came along with a grey-streaked tankard, but I drank it straight from the bottle: not only was that much more hygienic, but I felt it would identify me as one of the people. That seemed to work.

I'd been looking round the room. Bobbie's description couldn't be faulted. Today's Daily Mirror was open on the floor. A paperback featuring a semi-nude blonde holding a pistol by its barrel and writhing orgasmically was on the table; the book, too, was open, and I could guess what sort of chapter it was open at... The framed photo of the bombed town was Dresden, unsurprisingly; but would anything else be proved if it had been Stalingrad or Coventry? You can't leap to two-minute conclusions, but I sensed that our Ap-Singer was a man of no great commitments, happy to drift along with fashionable left-wing opinions. Given that, and given his physical condition, I was sure he was an organiser rather than an activist. I decided it was sensible to get straight to the point. Anyway, there was no sign of our missing file...

"What's all this about?" Ivor The Terrible asked after knocking back most of his pint. He was perfectly relaxed, and after all, he only knew that he had been approached by us after his (faked by us and non-existent) response to an advertisement for in-coming Radar experts, this having been in the Codonian which he said he never read. He started scratching himself, and I didn't blame him.

To my alarm, I found that I was itching, too. All over. Nerves…

"You work as a storeman? Building Five, Engineering and Radar?"

"You know I do, in Issues," he said, bewildered. "You're there too, up in Receipts. Is something wrong, has one of my members –"

"No, no. Nothing like that. But I'm also running the Codonian, you see."

"I don't read it. Well, not usually –"

"Yes, I know." This wasn't getting me anywhere, I'd have to come clean. "You told my assistant that."

"Nice little girl. Are you and she –"

"That's entirely beside… Well, yes, actually…"

"Yeah," the Contaminated Celt said. "After she came and asked me about putting-up some new arrivals, I didn't think much about it at first…" He shrugged, and pulled out a half-empty pack of cigarettes. I'd like to say they were Woodbines but this is supposed to stick to the truth so in fact they were Embassy cork-tipped; the pack was, however, crumpled, as all good fiction readers will expect it to have been. I took one, then another as the first had cracked across the tip. We lit up. Then he asked again: "So, what's it all about, really?"

"You said just now, that 'at first' you didn't –"

"Yeah, well," he said, "after she'd gone, I realised –"

"When you'd thought about them being Radar experts, and with you working in Building Five – " I stupidly prompted him.

"Nah. Nah. Whatever… What building doesn't matter, the Union doesn't care a fig about that. But she said they'd be coming into the Depot, so then I reckoned I needed to get in touch because they'll need to join the Union, you see, Mr Topps."

"But then you called in at Building 18, Printing and Pubs?"

"Course I did – I'd bought your rag, for the first time ever, just because your little girl worked on it and I thought I'd sort of follow it up, with all due respect of course now that we've met, Mr Topps; then I read about the Radar intake and thought you people at the paper would know how I could get the Union membership man in touch as soon as they arrived. They *have* to join the Union, it's their democratic right."

"Of course it is, of course it is," I found myself saying.

"But the tart at the desk told me nobody was there from your paper, so I went off, I'll be calling back later. What's all this about?"

I decided to exercise my democratic right to get the hell out of there. I just said we like to follow up every visitor as part of our service to our readers. As I got up to go, he asked me to remind my 'nice little thing' to join his Brothers as soon as she could; but at least I could knock that one on the head.

"She's not a civilian worker," I told him, "she's in the Army, special duties." Then, as I reached the bottom of the stairs, I called: "And she'll very soon be an officer's wife."

Something upstairs fell to the floor as I went out to the busy street. I don't know whether it was the dirty tankard or the dirty book.

★ ★ ★

It was five thirty and I had a couple of hours before calling at the guardroom, while Bobbie would be 'on call' overnight at the CRS. I went to the Mess and sat skimming some of the magazines that were scattered about. Browsing, through 'Country Life', I was astonished to see a reproduction of an oil painting of our treasured Hay Mill, on the Teme west of Ludlow and close to Leintwardine, where Bobbie and I had spent our memorable first night... (I wrote to the magazine, they passed it on to the owners of the picture, who kindly sent me very soon a reproduction).

I sat and thoughtfully watched some of my – hardly the word surely? – mess-mates… Of course, I and quite a handful of others were not really fully-signed-up members of this exclusive Club: we had been clawed into the Army by Government decree, we were just "National Service", and officers only because there happened at our school to be a Cadet Force well-run: in my own case by an ex-1914 veteran Major whom I also went to once a week for 'English Essay' and whose sardonic comments in our end-of-term reports were worthy of Wilde, but he was also, to a great age, our top rugby coach: "I'm sure he has great ideas but they tend to emerge in the scrum rather than on paper." I met him again on a visit to the school fifty years on. "Good God sir," I said, "how do you manage to keep going?"… "Drugs, dear boy," said Beve.

Over there sat our Catering Corps supremo, Captain Kittie. The DC's thumbnail sketch had been cruelly accurate; but I looked at him and found myself pondering the facts behind that figure. What experiences had led to his awful red-faced goggle-eyed persona? He must be in his fifties; how was he at twenty? OK, let's assume he was driven to hit the bottle early on, but even then, how was he before, and what caused it? I was beginning to assess people according to their experiences. It was a good lesson to learn.

The PMC was fussing around, too. There, I contemplated, was another story that wouldn't ever be told. He must have come into the Army full of youthful ambition; he was ending up in this backwater job in a backwater establishment far from any action or excitement. Had there been, in fact, any excitement for him at all? You always hear about the heroes, the gung-ho soldiery who find themselves in peril and blaze their way out of it and win all the medals… But the vast majority of servicemen fall into two different categories: those who never see any meaningful action, and those who do meet the peril, but don't heroically survive it (one way or the other).

It then occurred to me that one of those majority was the Sergeant of the Guard whom I'd met earlier. Long Service, Good Conduct, nothing to report, sir. The Army used to have a way of commiserating with such old-timers: if they were still around, ten or twenty years after the LSGC medal, they got another one, for Meritorious Service. And it worked: I remember my grandfather being mightily proud of his, arriving in the post one day when he was on his deathbed.

And it would soon be time to walk across to that gate.

★ ★ ★

But meanwhile, Bobbie reported back. She had gone into both the Banks in Wellington, and by waving the DC's letter, managed to get close-and-personal with their Managers, and thus their Foreign Exchange clerks. Of our four suspects, only Heavy Ivan had applied for currency: a mixture of dollars and deutschmarks last year to cover a fortnight based in Bonn. As regards holidays or visits abroad over the past couple of years, she had run into a problem.

"But then as you know," her report said and she repeated it to me verbatim, "I wanted to ask the Travel Agents about any overseas visits; and there's only the one Agency in town, and no others any closer than Shrewsbury or Wolverhampton. So I walked in, asked for the Manager, told him roughly why I was there... And he pushed a button, and in came – Marina!

"You can imagine, I had to think pretty fast. The Manager began to say to her that I needed to look through their files, to check on the movements of – I quickly interrupted by saying, well, nothing sinister, but I'm acting for our depot newspaper

– oh, hello Marina how are you – and we want to get some travel experiences from members of the depot, now that travel is becoming possible again. I think I got away with it; but of course I backed off and said we'd be in touch at a later date."

I think "Struth!" or words to that effect, was my immediate reaction to this. "How did you wriggle out of it, and do you think she suspected anything?"

"I don't think so," said Bobbie with a worryingly confident shake of the head. "She doesn't seem to know much about her husband's affairs. It was nearly closing time and she invited me back to their place for a cup of tea. She's nice – I get on well with her. I think she's a bit lonely, left on her own so much."

"Why? I thought they were a happily married young couple?"

Bobbie was doubtful. "He's never there. Always fishing"

"Is she attractive? Is there something wrong with him?" You can imagine the counterbalancing arousal my questions provoked…

"Why not come and see for yourself, Mr Topps? I'm having lunch with her on Tuesday, she has a two-hour break and we're going on a new cosmetics hunt to Boots, they've got some new things coming in from the States, and there's a rumour of nylons too."

"Will the hubby be there? Remember, that's who we're after."

"I still haven't seen him. He was working overtime at Accounts, over in Building 12; but apparently he was then going off fishing again."

"Doesn't she ever go with him? Does she even know where he goes?"

"I don't think she's very interested – she is making a study of old ruins along the Welsh border, she's always been interested in the Normans, and of course they occupied the southern islands of Italy back in mediaeval days. I think that's her interest and the fish are his. I can only suppose they respect each other's interests and there's nothing wrong with that," Bobbie ended, just a trifle truculently. I briefly wondered whether my obsessive editing and story-writing were starting to get on her nerves.

★ ★ ★

The night-watch Sergeant of the Guard was indeed a Corporal, fresh and pleasant and too young to have been in the war, no ribbons on his uniform. He was expecting me.

"Yes, sir, last night you're asking about? It was very quiet."

"Did you have anyone coming in just before midnight?"

"Nobody unusual, just the normal routine, Duty Officer, Adjutant, what we get regularly."

"How about those going out?" I sensed that he was trying hard to be helpful, but couldn't find a way: he shook his head. Just the usual.

"But you see, sir," he added, "we don't bother to check them out. Not out," he added as if I was an idiot.

"Whyever not?"

He looked at me pityingly.

"Well, sir, if a car is outside, if it's gone out of the depot, it's not going to do us any harm, sir, is it?"

"So you don't stop them?"

"Well, no. We enter them in the book, that's all." But perhaps it was enough? I asked to look at 'the book'.

Only three vehicles had gone out between eleven and midnight on Sunday; two were no problem – the Duty Officer and the Adjutant, one occupant only; but there was also, at eleven-forty, a tilly, two occupants. No entry of the driver's name. I thanked the Corporal and walked thoughtfully back to the Mess.

133

Bobbie was still on CRS duty: I looked across the pond or whatever it was, and the glinting barbed-wire, but surrendered to the realities of a quiet night. I slumped into an armchair, adjusted my debonair hidden pistol so that it stopped digging into my ribs, and signalled to the ever-present Charles that his good services were needed: urgently, I told him; and I fell back on my early days of comparative innocence and ordered a gin-and-orange. "A large one, and go easy on the orange." Charles approved. There was no tutting. Indeed, he nodded.

People will tell you that alcohol clouds the mind: nonsense! There may be some long-term deterioration, but so there is with almost everything: just as small doses of arsenic have a gradual toxicity build-up, so – though rather less malignly – do small doses of red meat, coffee, nicotine of course, and probably parsnips. But short-term, that's another story. Stuffy people may mutter, but then, stuffy people always have done and always will. But tell me this: how many of our world-famous writers, whether novelists or thinking philosophers, have achieved their greatness without any recourse whatever to a drink?

Picking through my Complete Shakespeare in the school library, I used to enjoy looking for clues as to what the Bard might have kept on his writing-desk in a jar close to his lifting elbow. Would it have been the quart of ale "dish fit for a king", or that "good familiar creature", the wine which Cassio dipped into rather too much? On balance, I reckoned – after all, he was a country boy and a travelling actor – he must basically have been an earthy Falstaff rather than some effete Duke, a good strong ale would have been his preference. I must do more research on this... (Too much enthusing about rich imported juices, and Bacon might come muscling back into the debate).

I was drifting, as I sat there sipping my second Subaltern's Squash; but some tiny little truths began to filter through...

First: the break-in at Building 18 Printing & Pubs. If the window had been smashed from the inside, meaning the intruders were already in the building, why? And if the glass fell on top of the footprints, again, why? It must have been a cover-up job, clumsy indeed, and including the phoney opening of Chunk's files when they – whoever they were – knew they were after the Codonian files; and then the equally phoney stealing of the petty cash... And there was something odd about that missing Codonian file, if I could think what it was: something not quite right.

Then I had another thought. That tilly leaving the depot some time before yesterday midnight... It went out, OK. But when had it come in?

I got up, said goodnight to catering Kittie, and to Charles who was obviously glad to see me go and was only waiting for 'two poached eggs' to stagger up to bed; and – to my own amazement – I walked back to the Guardroom.

"Corporal," I said, as bleary-eyed as he was and far more dishevelled, "the tilly that went out before midnight yesterday–"

"Sir?"

"What time had it come in?"

He reached for the report book. After a bit of shuffling, he offered me a mug of coffee which I accepted gratefully: it was a good idea just then, and I took it without the milk.

Nursing my mug of the painfully-healing black stuff, I sat watching as the young corporal flipped his pages to and fro. Eventually he gave up.

"It was never checked in," he said. "Not for the past ten days anyway."

"Yet you checked it out last night?"

"Yes sir… It must have been in the Depot already, for a week or more."

This was getting interesting.

"And then," he went on, holding up the latest page, "it was booked in again early this morning – I remember that – about seven a.m. before I went off."

"Who was the driver?"

Looking down: "Doesn't say. But," he added brightly, "no passenger."

I echoed, as a question: "Doesn't say?"

"When it's one of our regulars, we don't write it down, sir. No point, you see, if it's someone we have on strength anyway, somebody from the motor pool, because they're coming and going all the time."

"You mean like – what's his name – Robert – "

"Bob Blackmore, yes sir, come to think of it, might well have been."

I thanked him, and swallowed my coffee which was far too hot, and panted with watering eyes back to House Four. I set my alarm at an obscenely early hour for the coming Sunday morning; but as I dozed off I still had the hazy self-editorial thought-processes to admonish myself – early hours on a Sunday cannot be described as 'obscene', they are the opposite, they are monkish, profoundly Christian surely, whereas the obscene are still abed?

XI

I was up with the monks.

It promised to be a lovely day, and we had to go and visit Bobbie's heart-throb Robert Blackmore, MC, the up-market driver at the motor pool, a regular, coming and going, no need to check in or out, vehicles at his disposal, the mystery man with charm, who had driven with a companion out of the gate, half an hour after the break-in. Check his boots.

I rang the CRS. It was five-thirty.

"Yes," said the voice. "Emergency. Name and location please."

I told her.

"For Christ's sake," she began…

"You and I," I said, "as soon as you're off duty – at eight, yes? – have to go for a bike-ride." Then she listened, and I spelt out my new suspicions.

"I thought our man was the Vulgar Bloatman?."

"I don't think so. I'll tell you all about it on the way to Blackmore."

"On the way? Are you saying we're going to cycle all the way to Bob in ruddy Newport? It's miles. I've done it, you know."

"Less than ten. No traffic hardly. But what's all this 'Bob' business?" I wanted to know.

She giggled,

"Perhaps he'll let me play with his medal."

"Very likely. But listen, I have to talk first to the DC, over in the Mess –"

"At eight on a Sunday? He'll still be in his jimjams."

"I must take that risk. I'll call for you at ten o'clock, Corporal."

"Sir," and she hung up.

★ ★ ★

As it happened, both the DC and Major Parrott were up and dressed, about to have breakfast; in fact, thoroughly dressed, in their best uniforms, gleaming and clutching their Sam Brownes because they had to attend some important function at the Garrison Church. It was one of those extravagantly pompous events that were far too often engineered, usually by the Adjutant, as a means of convincing all concerned about how important they were. I caught a glimpse of Bart Dixon himself, fussing about in his shining leather, row of clanking medals, and that pale blue beret, which signified something or other unique to his regiment, whichever it was.

The DC saw that I had some news to impart, and signalled me to join them for breakfast: over on a long side-table, like the Edwardian country-house weekends you see at the pictures, I loaded my plate with half-a-dozen modest bits and pieces: I had some cycling to do.

I told them about the suspicious tilly. Taken from the pool and returned. Just at the right time. Two occupants. No driver named. Known regular, no checks.

"That's our man, by George," said the Major. "Thought so all along." We arranged that he would ship a couple of his best men over to Newport, to give us cover at midday. "Worst possible," he was muttering as I left them.

"Be careful," said the DC, "and look after that girl of yours – she's good. Did my billet-doux help her in Wellington yesterday?"

I told him about Bobbie's bank visits, and that only Our Ivan had obtained foreign currency recently – at least locally.

The Major made a sensible comment. "So we can probably eliminate him, as he has nothing to hide. A foreign agent would never go and get his marks or roubles over the counter."

The DC nodded. "He likes to show off his Leftie credentials. I reckon he's in the clear, Bill." He turned his attention to the marmalade bowl.

"Unless it's a double bluff," I said, just to ruin their complacent Sunday morning; and went to find my bike.

★ ★ ★

"Are you sure it's only ten miles," Bobbie asked as we pushed our bikes up yet another slope. I looked at her disapprovingly.

"You're getting out of condition," I told her. "You weren't puffed tramping along the Teme a couple of months ago."

"I was much younger then," she said, "And anyway, I didn't have my rest interrupted at half-past bloody five –"

"Are you quite sure about that?" I asked innocently. "Thinking back, I seem to –" But she changed the subject.

"Tell me, why do you suspect Bob?"

I explained the report from the guardroom, the tilly taken from the pool, the two occupants –

"Ah," That reminded her. "Your nice Private chap – Brown? – rang me to ask if I had any plaster. You know, at the CRS, for broken limbs, plaster of paris or some such thing."

"Brown's hurt himself? Always was so clumsy…"

"No, silly. But he had this bright idea of making a proper cast of those footprints. They didn't photo very well. So we got all the glass shards out and made a pretty good cast –"

"We? You went over and helped?"

"Well, he hadn't a clue how to use the stuff. Yes, it worked. Then he took me for lunch to the NAAFI." She didn't look at me but I knew she could sense my eyebrows.

"What did you have?" I asked with enormous disinterest, bending down to look at some dead furry thing.

"I had sausage-and-mash with thick onion gravy, it was lovely, and he – "

I told her it didn't matter what he had.

"He was most interesting," she went on (and on) "He's been vegetarian ever since school –"

"When does he get to grow the beard?" – I had a vision of Bernard Shaw with that irritating superior quizzical smile.

"– So he went for the special salad they do at weekends, gorgeous it looked, with not just lettuce and tomatoes and spring onions and radishes, but slices of apple and orange and –"

"Nuts."

That pricked the balloon a bit, as we saw Newport coming up, and could freewheel down between a cluster of dark-red-brick workmen's cottages happily rusting in the sunshine, and went over the hump of the canal.

"I don't know how he'll manage when he's working in Fleet Street," she worried.

"I shouldn't fret too much about Private Brown," I told her, following her lead towards Blackmore's street. "He won't be more than a peachstone away from Covent Garden, and if – " as we dismounted, " – if he gets up at five-thirty in the morning he can pick up a few discarded apples and grapes; tell him that, why don't you, and maybe he'll find some discarded flowers to send you."

I don't know whether Blackmore heard us laughing when he answered Bobbie's call on the intercom; probably not because he came eagerly to the door, but his face fell a little on seeing me beside her. I was introduced: The Editor.

"Well, come in anyway."

It couldn't have been far short of midday and I saw two of the Major's bruisers in a small black saloon across the road. Security, knowing of our suspect's base at our motor pool, had sensibly used a private car that was unconnected with the Depot.

I followed Bobbie diffidently into the flat as she hurried after 'Bob'; at once I could see what she had meant in her earlier thumbnail sketch of the man, written before this unhealthy interest in him had developed. All his furnishings had been carefully chosen to make an expensive impression at the least possible cost. I don't mean this unkindly (as people always say), no, really, I don't think I do; but it was all just that little bit too obvious. There were half-a-dozen of those 'cut-glass' sherry glasses that used to be given away at petrol stations before the war. On a coffee-table with screw-in legs there were several outdated 'Field' and 'Tatler' magazines, and looking closely one could almost certainly detect the names of doctors' waiting-rooms at the top of the cover page. Along the mantelpiece, true enough as Bobbie had spotted, one saw and admired a range of old greetings-cards, slightly curling above the electric log-fire, but still displaying the crest of a London club, a Cambridge college and another from a top cavalry regiment signed "… (illegible), Colonel". Also an old Christmas card from the local MP who was notorious for sending them to everybody who had ever written to him…

"To what do I owe – ," Blackmore began.

"You'll remember," said Bobbie, "when I visited you last week, you very kindly invited us at the Codonian to call back. Well –"

"Well," I took over, "we are planning a series of articles on the war experiences of interesting members at the Depot, so my job now is to seek out likely people and," I looked at him enthusiastically, "write about them."

Already he was shifting a little bit in his chair, but he gave me a deprecating laugh.

"Oh, well now, I don't know. There were things one doesn't –"

"Of course," I went on, "the place is full of military folk who naturally had experiences both exciting and horrific; but the Codonian is interested in our civilian readers, many of them now modestly back in their routine jobs, but they must also be bursting with –"

"Other people," said Blackmore, re-crossing his legs again, "There must be so many who –"

Bobbie then, trying to do her best, brought things to a head.

"But Burma," she prompted him. "The forgotten Fourteenth Army, you told me? Not many of our readers will know about that."

"Er –"

I homed in on this.

"This would be fascinating," I said. "Were you with the Chindits?"

"Not entirely. Can I offer you both a drink?"

We both agreed that, since it was Sunday lunchtime, a sherry would be nice. As he was pouring them, quite pleasant but a little on the dark side, I felt I ought to get a move on. I caught Bobbie's eye and winked to indicate I was up to something.

"Robert," I said, "Oh, it is Robert, isn't it? We haven't got much time because we have to get the train back to Donnington."

Blackmore looked at his watch.

"It's not for forty minutes yet."

"Oh, good. You always use the train, to and fro, do you, every day?"

"Yes," he nodded. "It's by far the best way."

"Even though you're based at the motor pool, and you could so easily buzz here and back in one of the tillies?"

"That wouldn't be allowed. Why do you ask?" He was beginning to get ruffled. I switched the conversation back to the war.

"This Burma business – we really would like to write about it, all your experiences –"

"I wasn't with the Chindits, I was on special duties…"

"What, you mean behind the lines?"

He seized on this.

"Yes, yes, behind the Jap lines, I was down in Mandalay, on the bay."

Bobbie said: "Show him your medal."

"Oh, well, that…" He shrugged. "We don't like to –"

Bobbie again: "Oh Bob, go on. You showed me, didn't you? Show Tim your MC."

"All in the past," he mumbled, "Pretty nasty times there, Japs you know, down there in Mandalay. We don't like –"

"Of course," I said, just a bit abruptly. "Not if you prefer to hide it. Of course, so many were awarded in the last war, thousands and thousands –"

At this, Blackmore bristled.

"Hide it!" he exclaimed, and strode across the room so that we nearly spilt our sherries. He opened the bureau, a modern copy of old oak, and quite well done though the carvings had been exaggerated and from the wrong century in my opinion.

He stalked back to us, and handed Bobbie the Military Cross, that masterly piece of elegant design with its splendidly simple ribbon, the stiff-upper-lip white-and-purple almost as Englishly understated as the crimson VC itself.

I took it from her, the beautifully-worked front, and the plain reverse where the name was engraved right across the centre: "Captain R Blackmore Burma 1944."

"Beautiful," I murmured in awe. "Well done."

Blackmore was visibly relaxing after having finally produced the evidence of his career in the jungle.

"It must have been hell," I said, "in Burma?"

As he put the medal away, he turned to me. "Yes, hell. But you know, there are things I can't reveal. I signed the Official Secrets Act, you know."

"So did I," I told him, "So we can exchange notes, can't we?"

"Well," he said weakly, "I suppose so, but many things are still –"

"Secret, yes. But tell me about Mandalay. How was it there under the Japs – "

"Oh, you know –"

"But just now you said you were down there behind Jap lines – "

"Yes, of course. I can't remember everything –"

"It will so much interest our readers."

I turned to Bobbie.

"Pass me your pad, I'll make a few notes for our article. But for now," I added with another twitch of the eye, "can you leave us? It's all secret stuff and we'll need to discuss it in private. Tell you what," I ended, "I'll see you in the station buffet in half-an-hour."

She got up and went to the door. I called after her: "You can tell the security crowd to go home."

Blackmore had uncrossed his legs again, and gone rather white. "What security crowd?" He was a bit out of breath. "What is this?"

"Do you know, Robert, I'm going to need another drink; and pour yourself a double, please. It'll help us both."

We sat for a little while with our glasses without speaking. But I had to get on with this, I would have to punch above my weight: this likeable man was a good twenty years older than I was, but I was stuck with a nasty job, just because of the uniform I was wearing. I was glad I'd invented the railway excuse for getting away soon…

"When admiring your MC," I said, "I made the comment 'well done'. That was nothing to do with exploits in the jungle, Robert. It was just praising the workmanship of that elegant engraving on the back."

"I don't know what –"

"Oh, come on. Where did you get it done?"

He still clung on. "How dare you suggest –"

"Robert, an MC doesn't have the recipient's name across the back. That's often been suggested, but never yet introduced: I got the information last week from the War Office, and they said they had no record of you anyway –" I was lying, of course.

"Well, damn them, they've made a mistake. I was awarded it in the field by Wavell himself –"

Luckily, this was something I could put him right on, as I knew a bit about Wavell. "In 1944? I think you'll find Wavell was replaced by Alexander back in 1942 – "

He wouldn't let go yet. "Ah, of course; yes, I mean Alexander –"

"Robert," I said, taking a deep breath first, "You're a phoney."

"Are you calling me –"

"I've got to. The man at the War Office ordered me to. As he put it: you never held the King's Commission. You're a sham."

He slumped, but looked up at me. "I wasn't even in the Forces, let alone an officer."

"Yes," I replied, "I've found that out too. But as I am, and as I have signed that Act, I can promise you your murky secrets are safe with me. Our records show that when you applied to work here, the good-conduct reference came from a London charity. Is that OK by you?"

He nodded.

"It's a charity, is it, that specialises in rehabilitating prisoners when they're released?"

"Yes, but only non-violent crimes," Robert insisted.

"Like fraud, false pretences, mis-represent-."

"Yes, yes, all that."

"So, you went inside?"

"In 1940. Five years. Falsifying accounts, embezzlement, and so on. A lot of it." There was a flash of spirit: he said vehemently "I didn't hurt anybody – many others did, ruined people, and they got away with it. I was the fall guy."

For a moment I saw once again in my mind that painting of the Scapegoat. But there was still, I had to remind myself, the 'sleeper' suspicion to be cleared up.

"You told us just now," I said, "that you always commute by rail?"

"Of course."

"Was that entirely truthful?"

"What do you mean?"

I took a deep breath: I wasn't used to dealing with Communist spies, let alone threatening them with death. I clutched my hidden gun.

"Friday night," I said, "there was a break-in within the Depot. Broken window... Forced filing cabinets... And immediately afterwards a tilly was taken from your motor pool. It was checked out, just before midnight, and back in at six a.m. Monday. Have you any comment on that?"

"Break-in?" Robert had gone even whiter. "My God, are you trying to –?"

"I just have to follow up all the leads we've got. Did you drive that tilly out of the depot?"

"Am I going to be sacked because I borrowed a tilly overnight? I drive the bloody things, and tanks and ambulances and Humbers, day and night, so what's so terrible if I borrow a little tilly?"

"But this was a special night. A break-in; and then you drove off."

Blackmore took a deep breath again, to calm himself, but he was quite steady and his hand was firm and unshaking – I could visualise him signing the false signatures on all those greetings cards on the mantelpiece.

"OK," he gave in, "It's no big deal. I went to the Garrison Theatre. It was a good show, with that Shelton girl; and I got chatting to one of the chorus-girls – it was only the once for God's sake, your people can check it out – and I missed the last train. So, I thought I could show off a bit and we went through the back gate by the motor pool, I've got a key of course as I'm driving in and out at all hours, so in the end I just drove home through the main gate, but I didn't see any break-ins or any other stuff going on, at Building Eighteen, or anywhere else."

I was quite relieved, I must admit, that Robert Blackmore seemed to be innocent of our 'sleeper' suspicions: he was – what do they always say about such artificial braggadocios? – he was 'a character', he had charisma. After spending the whole war in prison, what was he left with, apart from his charm and his vivid imagination? I told him that his true background was safe with me.

"But," I added, taking a wild guess, "you must stop relying on poets."

"Poets?"

"Kipling."

His eyes lit up, though he was still puzzled.

"I love Kipling. I studied him when I was inside, along with

147

all the others from that era – we had a visiting teacher, she really brought it all to life."

"Yes, but –"

"She was lovely. All about Chesterton… Housman…"

"Robert – ," but I couldn't stop him just yet. He went on, telling me how his bewhiskered hero Kipling had set the scene for Masefield with 'The Merchantmen', ("apes and peacocks and all that, years earlier"); for Chesterton with 'Hymn Before Action' ("anger and holy swords and altars, well before GKC's 'God of Earth and Altar', splendid though that is"); and even showing the way for young Rupert Brooke's 'Heaven' with his 'Last Chantey' the same humorous take on the Book of Revelation's un-fish-friendly "there was no more sea". Kipling wrote that – he pointed out – when Brooke was five…

This was getting strangely difficult for me. What he was telling me was fascinating and I, too, had deeply enjoyed the same writers a couple of years ago, as part of my final exams. I had never seen old Kipling as such a trail-blazer. Moreover, this man was so much my senior, did I have any right to be both grilling and lecturing him? I had to keep reminding myself of the importance of the uniform I was wearing, and the lonely pip on the shoulder. But Blackmore would understand that. Not only had he pretended to that same authority himself, but he must have encountered a good few younger officers, and a good deal fiercer than I, in those five years. I pulled myself together…

"Robert," I said. "I'm hardly the man to give you advice, but you must be more careful."

He had been reaching for a book which I suspected would be Kipling.

"How do you mean?"

"We mustn't let ourselves get carried away by the poets, or believe all they tell us. I wasn't taught a great deal in my English

Literature classes, but one thing was to beware of 'poetic licence'."

"What's –?"

"It's the same as 'dramatic licence', where the writer bends the rules for the sake of the story, or even to make a rhyme fit." I waved at the book in his hand. "Turn to 'Mandalay'," I suggested.

He found it quickly.

"When you were trying to impress us about your time in Burma, you went on about being down there 'on the bay'. Yes?"

"Yes, of course –"

"Where the old flotilla lay, and the dawn came up like thunder, and all that?"

"Out of China, yes, I know. Wonderful stuff. Especially with Peter Dawson –"

"Have you ever looked at the map?"

"Er – Not really."

"Mandalay is four hundred miles inland. The flotilla wasn't the British Royal Navy but a tired bunch of riverboats chugging up the Irrawaddy or whatever it is… When the dawn comes up, like whatever it really comes up like, China is off-stage to the right, best part of a thousand miles away, the other side of three other countries that wouldn't fit the verse."

He was pretending to be indignant. "You're spoiling it for me."

"No I'm not, the whole message is beautiful. The Burma girl a-sitting, by that old Moulmein pagoda –"

"Looking Eastward to the sea, yes, lovely. She really enthused us with that picture, the soldier longing to return –"

"She? Your teacher at the prison?"

"I owe her so much," he said.

"Why don't you write to her," I suggested, "and tell her that

149

at Moulmein, which is hundreds of miles south of the bay and a thousand miles from Mandalay, you have to look *westwards* to the sea…?"

I got up to go, but he sat there, thoughtful. Then he looked up.

"Do you know," he said, "I think I will."

"It's a lovely song though," as I headed to the door. "Full of the old feel of Empire… "

"Almost by Elgar."

"But set to music by an American, believe it or not."

"He must have been an Englishman reborn," said Robert.

"Or married to one of us," I suggested.

Robert's imagination was at full throttle. "I'll bet he married an English soldier's widow, I'll just bet he did –"

"Like in Housman's 'Is my team ploughing?', you mean?" I called back as I went down the stairs.

There came a shout from the room: "Kipling got in there before *him*, too," he said. "Read 'Soldier, soldier'."

I did when I next went to the library, and Robert was right. I do hope he wrote to his prison teacher-lady – I'm pretty sure he was in love with her.

★ ★ ★

The buffet at Newport station was in those days a little oasis of comfort and calm, and smelt of coffee and beans on toast. However, it seemed to be the only place open on Sunday morning and a crowd of locals had gathered there until the pubs opened. They had made a mass exit at that point, so Bobbie and I had the place practically to ourselves when I arrived soon after one, propping my bike against hers just outside the window.

"Have a sandwich," she said, pointing to some cheese-and-pickle assembly behind me on the counter. "And tell me all about Bob."

Here, suddenly, was another problem.

"Look, honeybun, I can't," I stumbled.

"But Tim –"

"Honestly, it's private."

"Surely," she asked reasonably, "I'm in on the whole of this spy sleeper thing? Don't I need to know?"

I took a big bite of my sandwich and nearly choked on the cheddar, which was in slices far too big: a good fault in those rationed days, but a fault nevertheless. I wiped my chin. She watched dubiously; but commonsense was filtering through.

"We're stuck in this together," I began, "but from time to time there's going to be things happening that I won't be allowed to explain to you."

"About Bob Blackmore?"

"Not just him," I said lamely, "other things may happen that I won't be able to talk about."

"OK," she said, draining her coffee cup and putting it down on the table rather too heavily, "but what if I get secretive too? Keep me in the dark, just don't blame me when the Russians come with snow on their boots and I go over to the other side." She got up and we went out to our bikes. A young man was hovering around them and looking shifty.

"Bugger off back to the bloody Kremlin," she told him, and we cycled off.

When we reached the hump-backed bridge over the canal, she drew up.

"Why don't we go the pretty way? You know where this comes out, just outside the Depot, then on to Preston? Let's go along the towpath," and she swung off to the right.

It was a nice idea for a sunny Sunday afternoon. This quiet remote canal stretch was at that time almost deserted but had

151

still not become choked by weeds or murderously restricted by the collapse of its untended banks. It was in some inexplicable way a romantic landscape, with that peculiar Wrekin always lurking in the distance, but meanwhile some strange little villages or (more like) hamlets rejoicing in unexpectedly pretentious names: the settlement that Bobbie called Preston was, officially, Preston-upon-the-weald-moors, so was the next place Eyton – equally weald-moorish. In the Depot we had got used to somewhat superior commuters from both villages, flashing their hyphenations at the more lowly from Hadley and Oakengates and Trench… I wonder whether our Crapular Celt could sort that out.

Alongside this sleepy canal we cycled, lazily, as was right for such a sunny Sunday, when suddenly Bobbie stopped. I drew up by her.

"I realise now," she said, "that I'm only a subordinate and second-rate cog in your goldbraid machinations; do you need to check back with your Top Bloody Brass first, or shall we – right now – interrogate the fourth of your suspects?"

It had already, five minutes earlier, occurred to me that we may well encounter the fishing-obsessed Henry Colman somewhere along our route; but I had to pretend the idea was new to me.

"Brilliant!" I must have said; because indeed we did spot this innocuous little man holding one rod and keeping his eye on another, a mile or so before our Donnington path led away from the canal and pointed towards home, afternoon tea, and perhaps even cucumber sandwiches, being so close to those weald moors.

We stacked the bikes into the hedge, where they disappeared among the nettles and the heavy clumps of white whatever-it-is: there are so many ugly green stalks with a white cluster at the top, all claiming to be something special for our environment and many of them either poisonous, anti-social, or just a waste of space along the roadside. I think some come from Japan and I wouldn't be surprised...

"Hello," said Bobbie, the subtle undercover agent. "Are you Henry Colman?"

"Yes?" What else could he say, under the circumstances. But what the hell was Bobbie going to say next, I wondered as I stood there.

XII

Are you a Russian spy? Where were you on Friday night? What size are your boots? All or any of this I half-expected from Bobbie in her present state of mind; but no – she merely chatted to our suspect innocently, which enabled me to extract small bits of information, helpful I was pretty sure, while I hovered in the background.

"I'm Bobbie Roberts, I'm a friend of Marina," she began. "Perhaps she's told you about our meeting?"

"No, I don't think so, but hello."

"I called at your place a little while ago, when we were looking for accommodation for some Radar experts."

"Oh yes, now I remember – you're from the Codonian, is that right?"

"Yes, and this is Tim Topps, he's the editor – Lieutenant Topps, actually."

I smiled at him, apologetic for the 'actually'.

"How do. I buy the paper most weeks," said Colman, "but I don't get much time to read it."

"You keep busy?" I prompted.

"Oh indeed," he looked up at the sky. "These days especially – ideal."

He glanced down at his rods.

"Yes," Bobbie chimed in, "Marina has been telling me. What do you catch, mainly, here on the canal?"

My God, I thought, we're going to be here for hours.

"Roach… Perch… Sometimes there isn't a bite for a long time, but that often means there's a pike about, and he's worth waiting for."

"What about chub?" I put in blindly.

Harry Colman shook his head. "Not around here; but I get them on the Thames a lot if I can find the right hole –" He saw us looking puzzled. "You know, a deep pool, they seem to gather there."

But it wasn't that, that was intriguing me.

"Did you live down South, then?" I knew he was supposed to have come to Donnington straight after his military service, up through Italy and landing in the South of France, where he had picked up Marina.

"No, no, but I go there on my fishing holidays quite a lot."

"Lordy!" said Bobbie. "What does Marina think about that?"

"Oh, she puts up with it," he laughed. "Anglers' wives are a tolerant lot. She's at a travel agent's anyway, so she can make all the bookings."

"Whereabouts do you fish, down there?" I asked. "When I was a kid, my Grandad used to take me to Hampton Court, just at the mouth of the Mole a few yards before it runs into the Thames – I just got tiddlers most of the time."

"Yes, you would." He grinned at me, I felt he was a nice chap. "Further upstream, it's cleaner, so the bigger and more sensible fish go up. Simple, eh?"

He swung round suddenly, at a sound which he recognised though I had quite missed it. One of his rods was trembling and the float bouncing about.

"I've got to get on," he said.

So we retrieved our bikes from their jungle, waved to him, and headed home.

There really were cucumber sandwiches with the tea in the Mess, but I couldn't take Bobbie there of course. So I wrapped a handful of them into a napkin and took them across to the

CRS, where I was becoming fairly well-known, and almost as acceptable among their NCO staff as were the junior RAMC medics – officers, as was I, but implicitly free to fraternise (if that was the word for it) with their ATS nurses. Nobody made any adverse criticism of this, so far as I ever heard. As always, I found myself existing happily on the fringe of other people's established liberties...

"Let's size up and take stock," I said, and it's not easy to say with your mouth full.

"Well now, who d'you reckon our sleeper is?" asked Bobbie as she put the milk in the teas. "My guess is still the man with the hairy stomach."

"You mustn't be swayed by physical repulsiveness," I told her and hurried on, "At first glance at Ivor, I'm sure everybody would agree with you, but – "

"Major Parrott said he was sure of it all along."

"The good Major is always sure – he has said exactly the same thing about all of them, one after the other. But he seems to be losing heart – only two security men in Newport today."

"Perhaps Major Parrott himself is the spy – how about that?" she said. I told her it was sacrilege.

"What about that little Pole? Is he really amnesiac?"

Unexpectedly, at that moment a young Irish RAMC officer walked in, in search of refreshment after doing his rounds.

"Who's an amnesiac?" he asked. "And who are you?"

I remembered him from that epochal carol-singing excursion at Christmas, so recent but so long ago, and explained my presence in the off-limits CRS, by the need to research my forthcoming feature on the place, to appear in the Codonian –

"Of which," said Corporal Bobbie, "he is the editor – actually."

The officer, whose name still may well have been O'Hara

but I've not had time to research it, spent a few minutes giving me stories from the past: the belated American invasion which led to the barbed-wire defences; the casualties when the railway was bombed by a stray Dornier trying to win an Iron Cross; the long-remembered halcyon days of Major Hallam; and O'Hara's enjoyment of being posted by his Medical Corps to this large Depot where he could pursue his medical interests without being governed or dominated by the local bigwigs and military bureaucrats.

I was, of course, ostentatiously making editorial notes on all this, while wishing he would go back to Armaments Mess or somewhere and get on with his Guinness.

"You mean," I tried to show interest, "you RAMC people don't come under local orders?"

"Bejasus, no" he might have said, or certainly something that sounded like it, "We're controlled from our own HQ. We come and go and do as we like."

At which, thankfully, having come, he was gone, and I suppose he did indeed do what he liked, judging by later noises down the corridor. Bobbie and I drank our tea and finished our sandwiches; and got back to the matters in hand.

"So, back to Klenov," I said. "Is his memory-loss a cover? We know he was brainwashed. He might have been programmed, and planted… And he's there at a desk in the HQ building…"

Bobbie thought about it, but shook her head. "It doesn't add up," she decided. "It would be too obvious a cover, surely? Amnesia, I mean, it would be pure Hollywood, and it would simply invite all sorts of lie-detectors and truth machines and God knows what… It would make him unreliable. Maybe OK for a quick spying job, but not for somebody they wanted to be a long-term sleeper."

"So, his furtive looks up and down the road, and the oddness of a cello but the case for a violin, aren't significant?"

"Tim," she said, "everything around us can be suspicious if that's what we're looking for."

"You mean, for example, a scruffy man with a hairy stomach?"

"But a declared Communist supporter?"

"No," I said, "he's just too obvious as well. He was simply looking after his members' interests. And anyway, he'd never have broken in – he knew where our desk was, and he'd have keys to all the Buildings. No need for smashed windows or faked break-ins, but –" I stopped as an entirely new thought hit me.

"What is it?"

"Blackmore."

"Oh, no," Bobbie waved me away. "Come off it, you're not going to drag Bob back into this. As we were going along by the canal you told me not just how well you'd got on, but how impressed you were with his British loyalty – all that Kipling Empire stuff. I thought Bob was in the clear?"

"So did I, at the time, but I've been thinking back and," I lied, "looking through my notes." It didn't work.

"Notes?" said Bobbie with her hand poised over the last of the sandwiches.

"Well anyway, listen. When I mentioned the Codonian break-in, and he was explaining why he'd taken out that tilly on Friday night to run his floozie home –"

"Floozie!" She bristled. "Bob was driving her back to *her* home –"

"Yes, well maybe, but –"

"A perfectly respectable –"

" – Con-man?"

"There are plenty of respectable con-men," she told me, "not just in spivs and doorstep sales but in government and in the bloody Army and probably the Church too –"

158

"Listen!" I said again. "When I spoke about our break-in, he said that when driving out of the depot that night, he'd seen no sign of it; but –"

"So? Why should he have?"

"He said 'in Building 18'; but I'd made sure I never once mentioned the name of where it happened."

The two minute silence that followed, I found very enjoyable; and I was able to seize that sandwich as her hand fell away deflatedly, and she saw her pal Bob back in the limelight.

"Next," I went on, munching, "let's look a bit more at little Harry Colman. Is he a phoney too?"

"Certainly a bit fishy," she laughed, "but leave it to me. Remember, I'm going shopping with Marina on Wednesday and I'll see what more information I can get from her. But you know?" she went on puzzled, "I wonder how much they really know one another, they seem to lead such separate lives, don't they?"

I said I didn't think it was all that strange, considering the background. With her bullied into forced labour under the Nazis, and him suffering a pretty brutal war up through Italy where things had been especially vicious, it was the most natural thing in the world for each of them to seek peace and quiet in their own chosen way… Look around, I said: the people here are all full of stresses. Look at the DC even, so laid-back on the surface, but he still has his office bottle like so many of the others."

"God!" I ended, "I'm hitting the scotch myself and I wasn't even *in* the war."

So we adjourned. Bobbie had to go on an ambulance trip tomorrow to the military hospital in Chester and back on Tuesday; so we agreed to meet up after her Marina chat midweek…

★ ★ ★

It may or may not have been stimulated by the pervasive smell of my neighbour's socks (it was rumoured that he had avoided a posting to the tropics because the scent is irresistible to a vicious type of mosquito), but my night at House Four involved a long dream about boots of all shapes and sizes; so it was no great surprise in the morning to be handed by my fractional batman a bulky brown paper parcel, which contained the plaster-cast achieved by Bobbie and Brown. Edwards had evidently looked inside, but as usual he kept his bewilderment to himself.

"The lady brought you this," was his sole laconic comment, "in an ambulance." So she had dropped it off on her way to Chester. I carried it to breakfast in the mess, gobbled the food down and sneaked a couple of rounds of toast for later, into my bicycle basket; then balanced the parcel somehow on top of everything and wobbled towards Building Five.

The sergeant of the guard was my informative friend from the weekend. Quite unusually, and I suspect mischievously, he threw me a surprise salute... As he guessed, it was quite impossible for me to acknowledge it and I'm sure he was hoping I would fall off; but I have always been quite good at cycling hands-free and I threw him a small piece of toast.

As I walked through Building Five and passed Mac's window I showed her the contents of the bag, just to confuse her.

"Don't tell me," she said, "You got plastered in Paris?"

"Put my foot in it there, too."

There was a note on my desk, taken by Mr Stanworth, from Brown. Would I please come over, there had been a development.

I walked back through the building, passing Ivor the Ap, and we smiled bleakly at each other. I checked his boots: medium...

Brown was waiting for me at the door of Building 18 and I was keen to satisfy his undoubted eagerness to know how my weekend investigations had gone.

"I've visited most of our suspects," I began breathlessly, "but no sign of the missing file so far. But never fear, no doubt I –"

Brown looked at me sadly.

"I've found it," he said, treading out his cigarette-butt.

"You've what?"

"It was in the cabinet all the time, sir –"

"For God's sake, Brown! What's the matter with –"

He was much calmer than I was, waving my brown paper parcel.

"It had been misfiled, sir."

Oh Lord, that built-in weakness of every office system, human error.

"But not by me." He let this sink into my subalternine skull, then went on in that patient tone one uses… "I had it filed under 'P' for 'Paper Caper'."

"Where else?"

"But you see, sir," and I did so wish he'd leave out that 'Sir' sometimes when scoring points off me, "it had been put back under 'C'."

"Ah," I must have said, as we strolled back into the building and settled at the Codonian desk.

"This suggests, doesn't it sir, that of the two intruders, one found the file and afterwards the other one put it back?"

Even I could see that – and, in our part of the Army, its implications.

"The storeman's mind!" I volunteered.

Of course we both knew what were talking about: we'd both been through RAOC training in the management of stores, and in the exact routine required for ordering them on those flimsy coloured requisition slips.

"Cups coffee," I said, "and cups tea".

"Glasses beer…"

"Glasses whisky…"

"Boots, wellington," said Brown, "Caper, paper" and we sat and looked at each other.

Then: "A storeman," we said, and I added: "We're back to Appy-Ivan, are we?"

"But we don't know for sure; and we don't know who the other one is."

So then I unwrapped the plaster-cast and examined it closely for the first time: it still told me nothing, and I put it away on top of the cabinets, turning my attention to the file.

"Have any papers been taken?"

"I don't think so, but there wasn't much in it, just the drafts of our stuff for last week –"

"Yes, but remember, this was the issue setting the DC's trap, and it must have been the reason for the break-in." Then I began to pull myself together: all this spycatching had been distracting me from everyday life. "Good God, Brown, we've got to get this week's issue put together –"

His whole manner was telling me to calm down – everything was well under control.

"Yes, but I have to write the follow-up piece about the Radar research not being at Donnington after all, just at a sub-depot. You know, the DC sent a letter about it?"

"Yes, but it's not here, sir. Did you take it away ready to write the article?"

"Oh, probably" I told him, heading for the door because I must go and talk to the DC and Security about our friend from the Essex Valleys, Official, Union, Communist…

★ ★ ★

Major Parrott had known all along that Ivor the Unreadable was our man: worst possible kind. The DC and I glanced at each other; but we agreed that the man should be watched. It was, as always, vital to stay covert: we were ultimately seeking the Big Shit with the little splash. The Major said he would at once put a good chap on to following him wherever he went, and another good chap to sit outside his flat all night.

I suggested it should be two chaps on the night shift, one of them to follow home the girls who might visit; this was agreed with a certain amount of ribald comment.

As the Major left the room, I saw the DC's eye stray towards the bureau in the corner; but no matter what time it was in Cairo, I had other things to do: other fish, one might say, to fry? I went back to the house, then cycled into Wellington, somewhat ostentatiously I must admit with hindsight, since I had changed into my formal service uniform – yes, Sam Browne and all – the better to impress people in local offices and get to the Man In Charge instead of being fobbed off by some self-important secretary. It was easy to find the travel agency on the square; easy, also, to spot Marina and avoid her. The other staff were excruciatingly obvious Salopian matrons; she, in contrast, was delicious. Bobbie hadn't told me that.

"Good morning," I said to a frayed-looking sixty-something behind the counter furthest away from Marina.

"Good afternoon," she replied coldly, looking at her watch. I did, too, it was three minutes past twelve.

I told her, sticking out my leather-belted chest, that it was vitally important for me to speak in confidence to the Manager. This worked, and I was soon shown into an airy room with posters and timetables around the walls. The Manager seemed OK – Major Parrott would have labelled him a good chap. Fair-haired, slimmish, fiftyish… But there was a walking-stick in the corner near his desk and I guessed that, like so many people happy to be alive, he was 'back from the war'. As we went through the initial counter-chat, he confirmed this. He even showed me the three machine-gun holes he had in the leg from St. Nazaire.

"But surely," I asked, "there isn't enough overseas travel yet, to run a place like this?"

"Hell, no," he laughed. "All these posters are pre-war, just for show. We make our living nowadays mainly from run-of-the-mill bus and train tickets and things that spin off from that: hotel bookings here in the UK, you know... But sometimes people have special contacts overseas, so they can travel because they don't need to apply for foreign exchange. You know, if somebody at the other end will support them, it's just the travel cost, maybe not even that."

"As a matter of fact," I said, leaning forward to light our cigarettes, "That's what I'm here for."

"Tell me more."

"At the depot," I confided, "we are rather neurotic about espionage –"

"Understandable."

"And among the civilians we've a few – well, of course a lot of Lefties – but a few whom we suspect of having actual Communist affiliations –"

"Ah." Was he going to be helpful and accommodating, or was he going to tell me that Karl Marx was his bedroom pin-up since childhood? Or, in fact, tell me nothing at all? I needn't have worried.

"I can open our files to you, willingly," he said with a wave towards a row of cabinets that made the Codonian look like a fifth-former's butterfly collection. "Tell me the name."

"Something like this" I said, passing him a bit of paper

164

which made the best of it; and watched but there was no reaction that I could see.

He went across, dug around for a while; then he came back to his desk empty-handed.

"We have a close match," he nodded, "and he's a Union official with you; but he's only been abroad twice and that was to attend rallies, Trade Union stuff I suppose, once in Turin and once in Berlin, and he didn't ask for any currency."

"So it seems he's –"

"OK," said the Manager with a half-smile "but unmentionable".

"Unspeakable, indeed," I added with feeling. "Well, thanks anyway," as I got up and headed for the door. "Oh, by the way, please keep this between the two of us?"

"Of course. We've both signed The Act, I'm sure." He smiled me out. "And any time," he added.

★ ★ ★

I was halfway across the square when I felt a tap on the shoulder. I turned, and was met by two glowingly brown eyes set in a dream of a face, glorious high cheekbones, pale chestnut hair you would long to wrap yourself in, echoes of the best of Botticelli… The lips… Oh, the lips… That excruciating open-ness… The whole of the square seemed to sway idiotically around me. It was Marina.

"Can we talk?" it said. The voice was sweet bells across an elysian meadow, the accent must have come from some whispering spring on Parnassus.

I don't think I actually said anything in reply to this, but just took her elbow and headed for the decent-looking pub on the corner.

As we passed the windows of Timothy White's, I looked at

the reflection and noted how terrific her legs were… I knew I must stop this.

We settled in to a cosy corner and she insisted on ordering the drinks.

"Well, just the first round," I said gallantly, adjusting my seat so that I could see her properly when she stood at the bar. Oh dear, those legs.

"Now then," Marina began, with that accent, "tell me. You are the friend of Bobbie, no?" I couldn't deny it. "So," she went on, "why are you asking so many questions about my Harold?"

I used the age-old excuse of sipping my pint to play for time; she was already halfway through her cider before I had come up with a reply.

"Well," I said, flourishing my important uniform as best I could when stuck in a tight corner-seat with the Sam Browne killing me as usual, "we at the Depot have to be always on the alert. We are vulnerable – you know the word?" I ended full of empathy for these foreigners.

"I know the word," Marina answered drily. "I know most words."

"So. We want to be sure that depot employees who are new to us, have come in from 'recognised' – You know the –?"

"I know the."

"Recognised and approved sources. And your husband Harold came to us with no previous connection."

"So, is suspicious?" Those cheekbones were fantastic.

"Well," I melted, "No, not really, not now. But we have to –"

"Was in Army, right up through Italy. Was very very loyal, no?"

"Yes, of course Mrs Colman –"

"I, Marina, please. You Tom?"

"Yes, Tom. Er, No, Tim. So all we are doing –"

"You are doing things to worry my Harold. You talk to him by the canal, Tom, and he come home very worried."

I was going to have to sort this out – we couldn't go on upsetting honest people, and our search for sleepers was clearly beginning to do that.

"Mrs – Marina – I want you to know, we are just exploring all possible clues and leads that might identify somebody inside the depot who is planning to harm us. We now know Harold's innocent reason for coming here, and not least his equally innocent activities –"

"Fish!" she cried. "He is a mad fish-man."

I felt inclined to tell her that we all have our weird English obsessions, from crosswords to polo; but she was ahead of me.

"Always fishing," she lamented. "His always hang-up." She looked at me temptingly across the cider-glass I had just refilled. "What your hang-up?"

At this point I had to pull myself together. I sought an answer...

"Tom?"

At this short notice, I found I couldn't really think of any hang-up that was worth reporting; but I mumbled my interest in local history. This turned out to be rewarding, eventually, but in a way that wasn't at all clear-cut.

"Ah," said Marina, "You like old history. I like very much the ruins."

Yes, I told her, I knew she had mentioned this to Bobbie.

"The castles," she went on. "The Norman castles. How clever, those Normans. You know? They came from up North – the Northmen?"

"Yes," I knew this. And settled in what is now called Normandy. And then in came William the Bastard, and we were conquered.

"But before, earlier," Marina told me excitedly, "the

Normans come round into the Mediterranean, and they conquer Sicily and then the bottom part of my Italy too…"

I hadn't known that.

"Castles," she said. "Those castles, all up through the Mezzogiorno –"

"The what?"

"The bottom part – we in Italy call it the Mid-day because we think that nobody gets out of their bed till then. It's a joke."

I remembered a bit about this well-known slander on Southern Italy, and had my own name for it. "Italian Domaniland, my father used to call it," I told her.

"Yes, very good." What a lovely smile she had. "I am from the North."

"Milano?"

"Close to. But I first went with a school group to see the castles down past Napoli, and I found them so –" spreading her hands, " – so magic…"

"And you made a study of them?"

She nodded. While waiting to go to college. But then, the war…

"And then, when the Germans marched us to France – horrible – work-parties making defences – all that, I can't talk about it – I was young, you know, and the soldiers, they thought me quite – ," she shuddered and I waved the subject away. "But at last, when the liberation came, I was shown some fine castle ruins, he was an old officer, British, he liked them as I did, we explored a lot…

"So, next," she ended, "I found Harold. Now, here I am."

"And still exploring our castles?"

"So. This Walesish border is very full, very interesting."

"Does Harold drive you to see them?"

"Harold cannot drive – he already tell you that, why you –?"

"Oh yes, of course," I said hurriedly. "I forgot."

"Harold fish."

Harold crazy, I thought to myself.

"Do you like old castles, Tom?" Dear God, her hand was on my knee.

"Oh, er, yes," I muttered, "all old history; but I don't have much time for that nowadays. In fact," I went on, struggling to get out of the corner, "I've really got to hurry back now, must go and find my bike –"

This amused her a lot.

"You bike! In a lovely uniform and the Sam belt? You don't drive a nice Army motor car?"

Not just yet, I told her, though in fact I was almost ready to pass my test after half-a-dozen lessons around the camp.

"Hurry to pass," she laughed, "then you will drive me in a big Hummer to castles, no?"

We walked together across the square and she went back into the agency, blowing me a kiss. I forget whether I returned it, but I wouldn't be surprised.

★ ★ ★

Back at the Mess I went down to the unfashionable end, to be alone so that I could think: it had been difficult, all the way home, to keep the wheel straight after that mesmerism induced by Marina, but luckily a heavy drizzle dampened me down – I had seen the Wrekin very clearly that morning and this ought to have warned me – and I went first to my House to peel off the service dress and dump it on Edward's ironing-board. My "Sam Belt", as she had called it, hardly suffered at all. Her English was so delightfully fractured…

So, what had I learnt from the unexpected encounter? Even after discounting the flirtation (and how genuine was that?) it seemed pretty clear that Marina was sure of her husband, was

169

either amused by or tolerant of his dreary hobby, or obsession more like it; and after all her unpleasant wartime experiences, simply very glad indeed to have been rescued by Harold and brought to this haven, England, where she too could indulge her interest and researches.

It would be sensible to double-check, I supposed, and Bobbie could do that when they went shopping on Wednesday. Meanwhile, this was Monday still, and I had an article to write for the Codonian. I did it from memory: sorry about the faux-pas; the Radar secrets are well away from the depot; no further need for accommodating the boffins; subject closed; on with the motley… Perhaps it would fit as an Editorial – one of mine, with the capital 'E'?

I saw Major Parrott come strutting into the common-room, and decided not to tell him about my Wellington visit. All in good time, but presumably his men wouldn't be too long in rounding-up that unpleasant little man with the loose shirt and the hairy stomach? Must keep an open shirt… No, no, must keep an open mind… Must go and lie down for an hour…

As I wandered back through the armchairs, the Major called me over.

"Topps," he said, "I want you to be on call tonight."

Oh God, I thought; one of the banes of commissioned life is to be Duty Officer, having to stay awake all night, or at best lie nervously on a hard mattress beside the telephone, with a tilly sitting outside the door, with nothing happening but no release until breakfast. On a fairly decent rota basis, this would hit me less than once a month; but apparently the scheduled victim for tonight – my neighbour Lt. Smith no less – had succumbed to some bug or other (malaria, after all, I wondered?), and a replacement was needed. "And anyway," the Major went on, "we've had reports of a bit of snooping activity around the sub-depots, so perhaps you're the man to remember to keep everything low-key, don't you know?"

I supposed so.

"Oh, and Topps, you do have a gun, don't you?"

I lay on the bed in House Four, ridiculously cleaning my pistol and fiddling with the bullets. It was only mid-afternoon but I had to be awake on that awful mess mattress all night. I wondered when Bobbie would be back from Chester tomorrow... I wondered how much I should tell her about my Marina meeting... I found myself effortlessly driving a "big Hummer" around a ruined castle while some little man was fishing from the back seat, and a nice girl sat beside me, with a hand on my knee and I couldn't quite tell whether her accent was Milanese or Lake District...

XIII

The Duty Officer telephone in my cubbyhole under the stairs suddenly shrieked at about three in the morning. The small hours, in the mess, were bad enough without that; but I groped in the dark and answered.

The voice was Major Parrott's.

"Topps, get over here quickly, there's an intruder."

"Where are you, sir?"

"Wem, man, Wem."

I was dressed of course, so that I was outside in a minute, climbing into the Duty Tilly where Helen sat half-asleep. She was alert, though, at once.

"Where to?"

"Wem," I said, and we slid off at once, it was about twenty miles away to the North, a rather boring sub-depot... But that gave me time to think...

Was there any connection between the two incidents? The Codonian's apology article about the Radar base hadn't even appeared yet... Then it struck me: I don't even mention Wem in that article... The name only cropped up in the private note I received from the DC... And it had been in that 'missing' file, but no longer.

Helen was driving skillfully along narrow minor roads, very picturesque if one could see anything in the small hours. I had done this trip with Bobbie by bike a few weeks before, on a Sunday picnic; and we now sped through little villages with wildly important names – Long Waste... High Ercall... Moreton Corbett... Preston Brockhurst... After which, one wondered about the simple three letters of Wem.. Earlier in the year I had written about this in one of my local history articles. Nobody seemed to know where the name came from: in the reference books there was unusual bewilderment. 'Marshy ground'? 'Holy'? 'A Gothic king' for heaven's sake? Or maybe just the age-old memory of a chap who owned the place a thousand years ago.

"What's all this about?" Helen asked, hurling us round a village green.

"I can't tell you," I croaked. "I don't know yet, myself, but apparently there's something fishy going on."

At once, of course, I was back with my four suspects. But how could any of them get out to this remote camp in the middle of the night? I knew that fishy Harry Colman had no car, nor did Klenov. Ivor was under observation by the Major's men, one hoped. The only one with access to a vehicle, evidently, was glamour-conman Bob – but having been found out once, surely, if he *was* our spy, he wouldn't risk it?

And then, I reminded myself, judging by those footprints we were looking for two people, not a loner. An unknown, with very big or rather small feet, who was driving our suspect around? And if it wasn't the glamour-boy, it must have been one of the two staff cars that were checked out of the depot last Friday night.

Helen was chattering away about something, but I just grunted Yes or No or Good Heavens, while I gathered together impossible thoughts. Never mind the DC's letter in the Paper Caper file, who else knew about the Radar research being at Wem? Who had regular access to a staff car, without having to get permission? Who, come to think of it, was actively stirring up suspicions of other people, was shifting his security men around them all, and – Great Scott! – had contrived to put me on Night Duty so that nobody else would be involved in this Wem intrusion, whatever it was?

Dawn was just beginning to come up as we sped through the outskirts of Wem and clearly something important had been happening because a big Army Humber swept past us in the opposite direction.

Helen took us into the grounds of the sub-depot, bleakly uninteresting Nissen huts surrounded by decrepit old vehicles; she stopped by the flimsy HQ building, alongside another tilly, and went over to sit with its driver.

I walked towards the wooden hut which I guessed would harbour the Radar boffins' unit. I saw a couple of shadowy figures a few yards ahead of me...

The gigantic red-and-yellow flash of the explosion threw me into the bushes and that soft landing saved me.

★ ★ ★

As Helen and the other driver came running, I dragged myself up and headed for the shattered hut. I saw something spread out on the ground, arms and legs at strange angles everywhere. It was evident that Major Parrott had not been our suspect.

Across to my left, half-propped against a Nissen hut, was another uniformed figure. I knelt beside it: the three stripes had blood on them.

Mac was bleeding from various places. She looked up at me, only half-focussed.

"That was a bloody silly joke," she said; then her eyes sort of slid up, and her head went over sideways. But wait a minute: three stripes, yes, but no crown above them. I looked more closely, and it wasn't Mac after all This was the Sergeant Sheila Something in HQ Building The Major was dating another

NCO, and Mac must have told her the Lambert joke in their Mess. How easy it is to be wrong about people! I wondered whether the DC knew.

★ ★ ★

Helen and her friend had the immense presence of mind to break into the HQ building and ring for an ambulance; and not just that easy option, but for an Army ambulance from Donnington, so that we could preserve confidentiality. They were a splendid lot, those ATS drivers.

Then between us, we did our best to patch up Sheila and the Major, both now unconscious. None of us was qualified to judge whether they would live or die, but it seemed that although they had been peppered with bits of flying splinter, there was no life-threatening deep shrapnel wounding: no embedded metal so far as we could see in the half-light…

After the ambulance had taken them away and more security people arrived to take over, I got back into Helen's tilly and we headed for home.

"Quite a night," she said, shifting into top as we reached the main road. "I suppose I have to keep quiet about it?"

"For the time being," I told her, "but all in good time, I'll feature you in the paper, when I can get round to it," I had a bit of a headache.

"Ah, yes. The Codonian – I know what it is now," remembering our visit months ago to the Mytton and Mermaid with Private Brown.

"Turn right at Shawbury," I said. "Let's go to the Mytton for breakfast, we've earned it."

★ ★ ★

175

After any nervewracking experience, it does good to keep completely off the subject for a short period; and Helen knew this instinctively. Our sausage, bacon, eggs and potato-cake went down comfortingly with small-talk about our backgrounds and how they had led us, immediately post-war, into the Army. It was only as she dropped me off at the HQ building in Donnington, that I got back to the business in hand, while my aching head was still clear.

"Helen," I asked, "I know it all happened so fast, but if you are able to recollect any little thing that might help, from last night, do please get in touch."

"Only if I get my photo in the paper," she said as she drove away.

★ ★ ★

As you can imagine, I went straight to the DC., who was in conference with the Brigadier. They called me in.

The Brigadier was confused, and in mid-sentence.

"This ATS girl, this Sergeant, whatever was she doing out there?"

The DC looked at me helplessly.

"Oh yes, sir," I said as innocently as possible, "she has been on special duties with Security for some time."

"Terrible thing to happen." He turned back to the DC. "Accident? Or sabotage?"

"Well, Bill Parrott had been looking into our suspicions together with Topps here, hadn't he Topps?"

I told them how the Major had telephoned me about a suspected intruder; how our quiet researches had produced the four prime suspects; and how we were still working on them. I sensed that if I didn't make all this sound as though the Major had it under control, the Brigadier would call in a team of out-of-town up-market boffins from the War Office; and I was sure the DC didn't want that, mainly because we wanted to identify our own small-time sleeper covertly, as a way to eventually close in on the Big Shit with the small splash…

"Well well," as he left us, "Keep up the good work," said the Brigadier, probably off to the pictures. I watched both Brigadiers go: I was seeing double.

It had already been a long day, after that long explosive night, no matter what my watch was saying. I looked at it disbelievingly… It wasn't saying anything.

"Sir," I pleaded to the DC, "what's the time in Cairo?"

★ ★ ★

I then went to the guardroom, head swimming still, and asked what traffic they had recorded last night. Nothing out of the ordinary, just the usual official ins-and-outs. But there had, come to think of it, been an irregular exit of a small car, a tilly, after midnight, which came back in after breakfast… Suspicious?

That description was enough, and I walked out.

"That was me," I hazily remembered. "And the potato-cake was lovely."

So, it seemed we could rule out Bob the highly-decorated Blackmore.

★ ★ ★

Next, I contacted Major Parrott's office. The Major was in hospital, but mending. Yes, his spooks had indeed watched Ivor all night: a rather attractive girl had visited around ten p.m. and not left till morning. What did she look like, I asked, for no genuine reason except disbelief that anybody could fancy that man. Non-commital.

So, it equally seemed we could rule out Innocent Ivor from last night's Wem entertainment.

★ ★ ★

I dropped into the HQ building to ask Klenov a few questions, but our amnesiac Polish friend was away on leave. Nobody could tell me where he had gone – nobody seemed to know him well, nor much about him – but he had been seen catching a train at Stafford last Saturday. He wouldn't be back for a week.

★ ★ ★

By now I was seriously in need of some sleep, but I must check in with Brown at the Codonian, mustn't I?

"Good afternoon," I said to Gloria Goodbody, then to The Chunk, and lastly to Private Brown as I walked through the building... Why were they all looking at their watches? I slumped into the Codonian's hard visitors' chair, and Brown picked up the Nescafe bottle.

"There's been an incident," I told him, "at Wem."

He put the coffee down again. Wem? I could see his mind flipping through the papers in that file.

"Did you find, anywhere, that note you had from the DC last week? You know, sir, the one about –?" I shook my head, it was swimming through a mist.

"Then –"

"We've got to assume," I began, "that the DC's informative memo was seen, at least, and probably actually taken, by the two intruders last Friday night; and that they are our sleepers, and that they are also the people who followed-up by going to Wem last night and blowing up the Radar research hut –"

Brown was scribbling away frantically, but I quickly stopped him.

"Yes, it's the start of a great story," I said, "but not yet. We mustn't report this, not anything, not at all." Security, don't you know.

"It was blown up?"

"Out of all proportion," I answered nonsensically but in good journalese. "Two people from here quite badly hurt, and one slightly." I pulled up my sleeve to show him the nasty wound I had received from a flying splinter of wood. I had some difficulty in finding it and Brown very nearly reached for a magnifying glass, but then thought twice.

"So," I ended, "we now have a sleeper who has been coaxed out the of woodwork. Why, we're not sure. But according to the DC, this might turn out to be a key development – so long as we continue to act and react very very calmly."

Brown got up and took my brown paper parcel down from the top of the cabinet.

"I've been studying this plaster-cast a bit more," he told me. "Look."

Oh, blast a plaster cast, I remember thinking: I might even have said it out loud. A wind was blowing and it was raining inside my head.

"Not now, Brown," I pleaded, "Tell me tomorrow."

He was saying something incomprehensible about nouns and adjectives. I told him Good Afternoon, said it again to everybody I passed on the way out, and cycled erratically to the ATS CRS.

I propped the bike against an entirely insufficient lavender bush, so that it sank at once to the ground. I stood and looked at it for a while. I was very tired.

Inside, I learned that Bobbie was still not back from

179

Chester, but then, as I found to my astonishment, it was still only eleven in the morning.

It was Tuesday, somebody pointed out, and I ought to go to bed.

I scribbled a note for Bobbie to come and find me on her return, we needed to talk before her visit to Marina tomorrow. I had to warn her that of our four suspects, little Harold now seemed to be the most likely, but somebody unknown must be driving him. Be careful, my note ended.

I left the note in the letter-rack in the hall (right next to the carol-singing site from last Christmas); and then I wobbled back to House Four, and kicked off my shoes before falling happily on to the beckoning mattress...

XIV

Groggily – that's the only word for it. I woke up groggily. I came to, still with the swimming headache, but it had somehow faded away into a less aggressive background effect, a sort of 'noises-off'. I could cope with that; but then I got up and found my legs were both shaking, and I had to squeeze them to make it stop while I searched for my shoes, then clumsily put them on. Doing the laces was most tricky of all…

This was disturbing, but alarm really struck home when I looked at the time: it was ten in the morning – Wednesday – and I had slept for – Good God – I couldn't even add it up!

I was still fully dressed in the clothes from, from when? Yesterday? No, from the previous night when I had been Duty Officer over at the Mess…

Heavens – Wem! A bomb! Mac… The Major… (Even in my confusion I remember drily noting the order in which those last thoughts came).

And what about Bobbie? Why hadn't she come to the House to wake me – or had she done and I couldn't remember? I must get across to the CRS…

Managing the stairs, and then wobbling down to the mess using my bike as a swaying crutch, served to pull me together a little, though my legs seemed to be made of rubber. I said "Good afternoon" to an orderly in the emptying diningroom, grabbed some toast, which seemed to be becoming a hasty habit, and zigzagged towards that useless lavender bush and around it, into the sanctuary.

Yes, said the girl in charge, Bobbie got back yesterday about teatime, had an early night, and then left half-an-hour ago; going into Wellington, she thought.

Had she got my note? What note?

No, said the girl in charge, there hadn't been any note in the rack yesterday lunchtime, just that sealed envelope up there now, for the SMO, who wouldn't be calling here until the end of the –

I turned to run out of the hall, but bumped into Captain O'Hara who took one look and told me I should be back in bed. Had I been at Wem?

"Shh!" I said. "Musn't talk about Wem."

I peered in front of my nose and saw that my finger was wagging at O'Hara accusingly. He sat me down on the same seat I had been on at Christmas. I gave him a great big smile.

He called to somebody dressed in white.

"I reckon it's delayed concussion," he said. "No visible injury, just the blast."

They started to manhandle me – gently enough, but the very idea of being interrupted made me angry, and they stopped. After all, this was an ATS outfit and I wasn't their responsibility.

"There's something I have to do," I said to O'Hara, "You Irish idiot."

I heard a couple of quiet giggles behind me; so did he.

"It's working its way out," he told them clinically.

"Please, Doctor," I pleaded. "I promise I'll come back for some of your lovely girls – er, lovely treatment, soon; but I have to report to the DC about –" and I whispered loudly, wild-eyed, "Wem!"

"We know all about Wem," O'Hara told me, "we've got the Sergeant here, so –"

That, more than anything, pulled me together.

"Mac!" I cried. "How is she? Will she pull through? I was there and helped with the bandaging. All that blood –"

The Captain turned to the assembled nurses. "This," he announced, "is the man who put on those first dressings." There were one or two murmurs of subdued admiration. "Thank God above," he went on, "the ambulance men got there in time to change them all and save the poor woman from blood-poisoning."

He paid attention to me again.

"Sheila will be fine," he assured me. "Lots of small surface wounds, as no doubt you know, but she'll be up and about in a couple of days. But as for you," he sucked his cheek, "All right, I'll give you a quick jab to get you through the day, but then you must rest up, think nice calm thoughts; and no alcohol.

"Not even – ?"

"Not even," he said sternly.

★ ★ ★

I don't know what was in that hypodermic, but I was in control of myself almost at once. The army of the late forties was amazing like that: it must have been stuff they developed during the war? And even for run-of-the-mill indispositions they seemed to have the answers, too. Not just the universal 'two-codeines-and-two-Dovers' for colds and flu; there was the instant cure for tummy trouble: bismuth-and-chlorodyne... kaolin-and-morphine, too.

Never mind the DC for the moment; I'd lied to O'Hara. My chief concern was for Bobbie. If she hadn't seen my note, she wouldn't know that Harold was our big danger – nor, probably, that we were now dealing with violence.

But did her friend Marina – Hell, my friend too, now, by

the look of it! – did that cute little thing know what her husband was up to? Perhaps she was completely unaware, thought he really was fishing all the time? And, it now seemed clear, he was encouraging her to get absorbed in her castle hobbies, as the best way to stop her getting too inquisitive? And anyway, her gratitude for being rescued and brought to England, that was probably sufficient to keep her loyal to her Harold, whatever he got up to?

As for the way she had chatted me up the other day... The other day? God, it was only the day before yesterday: seemed weeks ago... Was it a joke, completely harmless? Or possibly she really was being neglected, and looking for some consolation, especially if it was fairly presentable and came in uniform? She was evidently impressed by the 'Sam belt', after all. Ought I to tell Bobbie about the drink in the pub? Er – not just yet.

I was cycling quite normally by now, and reached HQ. The DC beckoned me in.

"You look terrible," he said.

I thanked him.

"I'm not sure whether I explained to you yesterday –" I began. He shook his head.

"Whatever you were trying to tell us yesterday, made very little sense," he said. "You were obviously off your rocker, Topps."

"Yes, sir. I'm told I have concussion. Delayed, you see."

"Well, luckily Major Parrott can still talk coherently, even though he is in several pieces."

I enquired into the Major's health.

"I think he'll be back in a few days. The main injury was to his pride, you know?"

I said I knew. I was sorry he had been hurt, but I was also sorry to have been concussed.

"Who diagnosed that?"

"The Irish Captain, O'Hara."

"Good God, that chap's concussed permanently."

"He said I mustn't drink."

"They told us that at Alamein." The DC got up, and I didn't even look at my watch, which had stopped anyway, at ten to four two nights ago.

"While I am still articulate," I told him, "I must tell you I think we know who our man is." He raised his eyebrows into two question marks.

"If," I emphasised, "it is indeed one of the people we've short-listed, it seems now that it must be little Harold Colman." I explained how all the others appeared to be ruled out, and that Innocuous Ivor, in particular, had been under all-night observation at the time of Wem.

"But," I ended, "this raises a quite different problem. Somebody else must be driving him around: someone with big feet, with easy entry into our buildings, and possibly –" I paused for effect, "driving a staff car."

I left him with this interesting thought, and walked, perfectly steadily, but pushing my bike just in case, to the Codonian offices.

★ ★ ★

The Chunk and her sidekick both looked at me nervously as I strode past; but my head was clear, the throbbing had stopped miraculously, and I knew it wasn't afternoon yet. I remember telling myself I must smuggle some of that Irishman's mixture out into civilian life: what a cure it would be for my coming Oxford hangovers!

Brown got up as soon as he saw me coming, and reached yet again for the wretched brown paper parcel. Just as he did so, his telephone rang...

He passed it to me. "It's Bobbie Roberts for you," he said. I gave a sigh of relief.

"Where are you?"

"Are you all right?" she asked.

"Yes, yes, I'm OK. But why didn't you come and wake me, as I said in the note?"

"What note? I thought I ought to let you rest, after the Wem thing, but listen –"

"I left you a note. Anyway, where –?"

"I'm in Wellington, but listen, about Wem –" She sounded very keyed up.

"Be very careful of Harold," I began " I'm pretty sure –"

"Yes, love, I know. Do listen. I went to Marina's, and checked with her about our shopping trip this afternoon, it's her day off you know? But this is the point – you must be right about Harold, because on the table – you know that Ordnance Survey map I told you about, spread out? Well, there was a new mark on it, it wasn't there before, but there was a ring around Wem. I thought I ought to tell you right away, but I've got to pop back now."

"Is Harold there?"

"No, I suppose he's at work. I'll see if I can sound Marina out, I wonder whether she even knows about him, she must think he's just fishing all the time?"

"At three in the morning?"

Brown nodded to me across the table. "They do, you know. I had an uncle –"

Bobbie was also nodding, I sensed, down the phone. " I know, I had an uncle –"

"Christ! What sort of families do you two come from?"

"I'll call you later. Bye." The line made that purring noise.

★ ★ ★

186

Brown was looking a bit worried as he sat opposite me. I asked him what was the matter.

"This person, Marina, I haven't heard about her before. Is she –?"

"She's Harold Colman's wife, she's Italian."

"Oh," said Brown. "Oh dear," he said.

"She's crazy about Norman castles," I told him, "she's rather a nice…" Then I petered out. "What do you mean, oh dear?"

He handed me the brown parcel.

"Do please look at it."

He pointed to the instep of the smaller footprint. Faint but quite unmistakeable, there was a number inside a circle. The size: either 36 or 38…

"Continental," said Brown, without looking at me.

I sat and gazed at it.

"And," he added, waving a hand at the filing cabinet, "they tend to put the adjective after the noun, don't they?"

I was still gazing at it.

"It's a small continental woman's boot and –"

I told him I knew, I knew, yes, yes. Let me think…

That map on the table was all about Norman castles, so it was hers, not his. We must round up Harold and find out where he was on Monday night, and where Marina was, too. Who was in that big staff car we met just before Wem?

And meanwhile, I must get over to Wellington fast and rescue Bobbie. Things had got serious, it was no longer funny.

★ ★ ★

This was no time to go anywhere by bicycle, and I rang for a tilly, but none was available on a busy midweek midday. I then had a brainwave: I was due for my final driving lesson, if only I could find a qualified person to accompany me…

187

I biked furiously across to the motor park and, amid all the tired PCVs and bullet-holed ambulances, I found Bob Blackmore, on his back with an oilcan. I dragged him out by the legs.

"I've got to get into Wellington very fast," I said.

"And you want me to drive you?" pointing to the nearest roadworthy car.

"Far from it," I told him, and climbed into the driving seat. "I need you as a chaperone."

I suppose I was lucky that – being lunchtime – the roads were fairly clear; and with Bob quivering beside me and pointing out with a shaking hand every cyclist and several of the lamp-posts, we reached the main square in what must have been record time for an unlicensed tyro. I told Bob to wait and ran across to the flat. Nobody was there, or at any rate, nobody answered my ring.

I thought for a moment – they must have gone into Wolverhampton as planned for their shopping trip – and then I went into the nearby Travel Agency, where my friend the manager was luckily not yet at lunch.

"I'm sorry, but I haven't any time to explain," I began –

"Is this about the Secrets Act?" I nodded. "Fire away."

I told him that I needed to see the files for all bookings his firm had made for Harold on his so-called 'fishing trips'. I didn't mention Marina just yet, as it had to be one thing at a time, and besides… Well, you know, she really was… Maybe, I was telling myself, just maybe, he had borrowed her boots that night? But then, he wouldn't file under 'c', would he?

By now, the manager had a bundle of papers on the desk. Harold had made two bookings at a small hotel in Kidlington just North of Oxford, each time for three nights; and three bookings, also for three nights, at a similar small hotel in a village just outside Wallingford, on the Thames between

Oxford and Reading. So those were his upriver fishing places he had told us about. But what was he really up to?

"And each time," said the manager, turning pages, "the train tickets were to Oxford, and he hired bicycles from a shop near the Covered Market."

"Bicycles, in the plural?"

"Oh yes, of course, Marina always goes with him."

I got back in the car, but Bob had moved himself into the driving seat and I didn't argue, I was too busy thinking. After a couple of hundred yards though, I stopped the car, went into W H Smith's and came out with the Ordnance Survey map of the Oxford area.

It was too big to spread out in the little Hillman Minx, but I still wasn't quite ready to make small talk, and Bob, to his credit, understood this. As we drove back through the depot gates, I thanked him.

"Only too pleased," he said.

"Listen, Bob, I may need to call upon you again. But it will always be highly unofficial and probably at short notice."

"Only too –"

"And very, very confidential."

"Will the dawn be coming up – ?"

" – Like thunder, I wouldn't be surprised," and I cycled off with my map.

★ ★ ★

The Codonian was supposed to go to bed midday Wednesday, so I dropped in rather guiltily at about one-fortyfive to find Brown a bit irritable: what did I want to say about the event at Wem? He had held a couple of column-inches on the front page...

"Nothing?" I suggested; but that wouldn't do, because of

course the news had filtered back to everybody from the permanent skeleton staff out there. So I quickly drafted a couple of sentences to the effect that the explosion, in a small storage unit, was from a cause at present unknown but possibly an electrical short-circuit. None of the Wem staff hurt, no reported injuries. I took it over to the DC for approval.

"Yes," he said. "The fragmented Major and the perforated Staff Sergeant can come in our autobiographies."

I then brought him up to date.

"We have to assume, surely," he thought out loud after a while, "that both this Harold chap and his wife are involved? But if neither of them is a driver with big feet, there has to be a third person." He looked up. "Could that actually be the Big Shit?"

"I don't think so, sir. The Big Shit wouldn't have let himself get involved in petty activities, would he?"

"Unless he had to for some very important reason, like – say – ultimate self-protection. No, as you say Topps, it's unlikely. I think Bigfoot isn't Big Shit… Middling Shit maybe – a sort of in-between, or just another member of the network?"

"We ought to talk to Harold Colman," I said nervously, "but however on earth do I start?"

"Let me sit in on it," the DC offered, to my great relief. "We'll have to tread very gently. If he's our sleeper, somehow we mustn't alarm him or he'll tip off the Big Shit at once and we've all been wasting our time –"

"And our life and limb."

"But if his wife is the sleeper, either he knows it or he doesn't. If he doesn't, it's going to be the biggest shock and disaster of his life. Can you and I handle that?"

The DC's eye had wandered across to the corner cabinet again, and I got up.

"Let's wait a bit longer before rounding up Harold," I

suggested. "At least until Bobbie gets back and reports on her time today, sounding out Marina?"

"The sun is setting across the Nile," said the DC dreamily. I sat down again.

★ ★ ★

Nevertheless, I told myself half an hour later, it might be an idea just to exchange a few words with Harold if I could do so in an inconsequential way; so I sauntered past his part of the depot and made myself "pleasantly surprised" to stumble across his desk.

"Why, hello!" I said brightly. "How are things at the canal?"

He smiled but pulled a face.

"Nothing's biting at the moment."

"Have you tried at night-time – somebody told me they feed well when there's a good moon."

He brightened at once.

"Oh yes, indeed. I often take a thermos, a torch, a sandwich and a good thick blanket. I love just sitting there, in the absolute quiet, you know?"

I liked this little man, couldn't help it.

"And then, suddenly," he went on, "there'll be a gentle splash, and a water-rat goes across like a motorboat…"

"Going to see Mole?" I suggested tritely, but he warmed to it.

"Oh, yes, not half! Oh my! But he'd forgotten the hamper, hadn't he, with the cold chicken –"

"Cold tongue cold ham cold, I forget the rest of it."

"I love that book," sighed Harold. Of course he did. So did I.

"I think the best bit is when Mole gets homesick and Ratty takes him back and the carol-singers come…"

"No." He shook his head. "The best of all is the baby Otter

191

bit. After all, it gives its name to the whole book, doesn't it – that's where we get the wind – in the willows, you know?"

"Ah," I remembered. "The Piper At The Gates... Do you know," I found myself confessing for the first time in my life, "When I read the book as a youngster, I used to skip that chapter because I didn't understand it. Only some years later..."

He was nodding, delighted to agree. I really did like the chap. But I had a job to do.

"When you're fishing in the Thames, as you were telling us on Sunday, do you see more of that wildlife than just out here on a canal?"

He thought for a moment.

"Difficult to compare really. Funnily enough though, despite the canal being a purely man-made ditch, nowadays a less-used one out in the country seems far more natural than a river – especially comparing a really rural stretch of canal like we've got here, and a great bustling river like the Thames is."

"But," I asked him carefully, "you said you had quiet places down there too?"

"Oh yes, but you have to be choosey. Look at the map, then explore."

"What do you look for – "

"Well," he shrugged, "I leave that chiefly to Marina – she's the one who finds good places for me to fish. Upstream of course, or on the tributaries."

"Really?" I was egging him on.

"And of course there's usually a Norman castle somewhere near, so she can cycle to it and keep herself happy too. She's just as mad as I am."

We both laughed and I went back to the Mess with my map.

★ ★ ★

First of all though, I asked an orderly to ferret out the last few days' copies of The Times, my illustrious contemporary. My hunch was correct: last Sunday had been full moon.

I spread out the Oxford area map and put my coffee cup and a sandwich on the far corners of the damn thing to hold it down. I found Wallingford and its very old and important Norman castle ruins alongside the river: no problems there, Marina would well occupy her time: the entire little town had an earthen wall around it, too, and even the town's charter apparently dated way back to Norman days, or nearly.

Then I looked at Kidlington and it was nowhere near the actual Thames; however, it sat on a flourishing tributary, the Cherwell, which wove its way literally alongside the Oxford Canal; so, an easy choice of where to sling your hook. But where in that area would Marina's castle researches be?

I crisscrossed the map, first at random and then earnestly and with a methodical purposefulness that surprised me. Apart from Oxford Castle itself, which I knew to be in use as a gaol and therefore out of the running anyway, I couldn't find any castle, large or small, that would be within easy distance by bike and merit the study-time and study-material justifying two or three days' at a hotel. Whyever had Marina made this choice?

I used the saucer from my coffee to draw a circle around Kidlington, and it gave me a radius of about eight miles. Across to the west there was Blenheim, of course, but that was five hundred years outside her period of history; then, just past Blenheim, there was certainly a round thing called "Round Castle" in the OS's slightly patronising antique font, but clearly that would be a simple manmade mound, five hundred years in the other direction; but then, swivelling slowly clockwise, and stumbling over a thick scatter of antiquities: a Roman road; a place on it called a 'castle' but really a country pub; a series of 'fish-ponds' dating back to some mediaeval Harold (I had a horrid vision of an angler with an arrow in his eye); and a 'mill-mound' which I had never come across on a map before… After all that, and crossing a long prehistoric 'boundary-ditch', I found another mound which was given the dignity of 'motte and bailey'.

Now, I remembered an old joke at school which made the form laugh, when I asked the master about Mott & Bailey, that famous firm of Norman builders. So, now we had our evident target for Marina's studies, just across the fields from that famous old Roman centre, Bicester…

Wait a minute.

Apart from our own depot here at Donnington, the two most important Army Ordnance depots were at Bicester and Didcot…

And Didcot (I looked again at the map, its lower section) is just across the fields from Wallingford.

I went back to see the DC again and I took the map with me. I was halfway there when I realised I was still carrying the saucer.

★ ★ ★

"Is your friend Bobbie back from Wellington yet?" asked the DC.

"No sir, but she shouldn't be long now. I'll get her to report direct to you in the morning, if that's all right?"

"Well…" He shifted awkwardly in his chair. "Er – Topps… Tim –"

This was suddenly alarming. Not only had I never seen him embarrassed before, but he was using my first name again.

"Something has cropped up." He wouldn't look at me at first; then he handed me a sheet of paper off the desk, but I looked at him rather than it.

"Sir?"

"That RAMC Captain – O'Something –"

"Hara."

"Yes. Well, he came over to me about half-an-hour ago with that paper. It was waiting at the ATS CRS addressed to the SMO, but we don't have a proper SMO at present, still hanging about for them to send us a replacement, so O'Hara had opened it."

Now, I read it. A single sentence typed on to official RAMC letterhead, "To whom it may concern, ATS, Donnington."

"Please be advised that Corporal Roberts B. is on immediate posting to Military Hospital, Catterick, Yorkshire; instructions for forwarding or disposal of equipment and personal belongings will follow."

"Can this happen?" I asked, in a voice that seemed to echo hollowly inside me where my stomach had fallen through.

The DC wasn't far from the corner cabinet, but I waved away the offering, I had to think clearly now.

"Technically," he said, "Yes, it can, because not only does the ATS run its own show, postings, pay transfers and all that, you know; but within that, the RAMC are also aloof and make their own arrangements. So, there's a duplicated muddling of the issues. If your Bobbie has been officially posted, there's not a thing I can do."

"But –" I began, but he held a hand up, with the glass in it.

"But," he repeated, "I smell a fish, and I don't think its name is Harold."

He pointed to the letter.

"Quite a few fish, in fact. I've been sniffing them out. First of all, the wording is all a little bit wrong. It doesn't quote her Army Number, which one always must in official letters."

I was trying to convince myself that the letter was genuine:

it would be bad news, a distant posting, but at least it wouldn't imply danger…

"And then," he went on, pointing again, "they give her initial as 'B', but that is surely a nickname?"

I had to agree: Bobbie's real names were quite different, as I had once seen on her paybook.

"And finally, Tim – " There, he'd said it again. "Finally, sending her up to Catterick would be quite out of the question. That's in Northern Command. All personnel are always shifted around within their own Command: us, ATS, RAMC, everyone, except when there's some great upheaval. So –" He thought for a minute while the situation soaked into me. "And you're sure she hasn't come back? Mind you," looking at his watch, "it's not even teatime yet, and she could just be chatting with Marina perfectly innocently."

"In that case," I pondered, "this curious letter could be simply out of the blue, some sort of joke and nothing to do with any of our suspects?"

"That's true, we mustn't jump to conclusions."

"Although, it seems to have been put on the CRS noticeboard and my note to her removed… My note was asking her to contact me, at all costs, before she called on Marina…"

The DC again sat pensive, while I grasped at the only straw left.

"Could you please, do you think, ring the RAMC," I pointed to the letterhead, "just to make sure? It could be some sort of clerical – ," but he was shaking his head.

"I did."

"And it wasn't …?"

"It wasn't even the right number. This is an old letterhead, God knows where they got it from, whoever they are." He looked across at me grimly, fiddling with his glass. "We must just wait, and see if she comes back. Catch me in the Mess at breakfast if she hasn't."

I got up and went out. I did remember to salute, but the DC just watched me go in silence.

XV

Down at the far end of the Mess common-room, turning left into the more shabby section and pressing on to the furthest window, I found a chair from which I could keep an eye on the approach to the CRS. Charles, with just the slightest glance, could tell that I was in no state to attend this week's full-dress Mess night dinner; and delivering my second Scotch he hovered over me with quite a big tray of assorted sandwiches. I thanked him profusely and he shimmered away. I sat looking at them miserably, then back through the window at the sinister CRS, and this continued for a couple of hours...

I slowly managed to marshal what few intelligent thoughts I had. First: so far as I knew (and surely I would know?), Bobbie had no personal enemies wishing her harm in any way, so I had to assume that this mysterious "RAMC" letter did have a connection with our search for the 'sleeper'...

Second: it must imply that we have stumbled somehow upon that person, or those persons. So, somewhere along the line, we were on the right track.

Third: since my unsealed note, warning about Harold, had been taken by the courier when he – or she – put the RAMC letter into the rack, this seemed very likely to link Harold or Marina into the scheme of things. But why on earth would they want to come out into the open in this way? Surely their whole purpose is to keep under cover? Far more sensible, from their own 'sleeping' point of view, to maintain the chatty friendship with Bobbie; as, let's remember, Marina had been doing successfully with me. I could still feel that hand on my knee and see the shared-secret glow in those lustrous – Good God, I told myself reproachfully, and ate two whole ham sandwiches very quickly.

Something must have gone very wrong within that spy network, to bring Marina into the open. Strangely, though, despite my obvious concern for Bobbie, I found it impossible to fear for her actual life and wellbeing: whoever it was, they either just wanted her out of the way because she was getting too close, or they planned to use her for bargaining? I remembered, again, that the RAMC letter had been written and delivered before she went to Wellington, therefore it couldn't be referring to any nasty 'accident' which – please God not – might have occurred since.

What was more: whoever wrote the letter, must surely have known we would be following it up, would soon discover that it was a fake on out-of-date paper, and – wait a minute! – would also know that a posting outside the Command was not feasible?

That RAMC letter was intended to be exposed…?

Nevertheless, Bobbie had not come back from Wellington.

I walked across to check on this, but only three times, struggling to subdue my anxiety so that the CRS staff wouldn't begin to suspect a problem. Nor did I want them to start regarding me as a poor sap, a chinless cuckold whose girl was doubtless somewhere in the muscular arms of a gorgeous PE sergeant…

Then I went back to my House and spent a most unsettled night, half the time wide awake and worrying, the other half dozing amid fitful dreams of Tarzanian gymnasts with stripes on their sexy leotards…

I got up at dawn and went to the Mess for an early coffee, then one more time to make sure at the CRS that Bobbie had not returned.

So, the problem was real.

★ ★ ★

The DC was moodily slicing a sausage lengthways and spreading it with some special sort of mustard which deserved to say Fortnum on the label. I sat down opposite him and toyed with my cornflakes. We didn't say anything for a minute or two.

"I don't think," he then began slowly, "not really, you know, I can't somehow see that your friend is in any mortal danger. For some reason," he went on, turning his attention to the second half of the sausage, "this Marina woman has panicked, and broken her cover... Unless," he concluded in bewilderment, "she isn't our sleeper at all. We haven't any proof yet, that your girl's visit yesterday was directly linked to the phoney RAMC letter. Try that."

Try what? I had been gazing thoughtfully into the distance where waiters came and went, but guiltily switched back to the DC, who was holding out a fork carrying a piece of sausage heavy with a sinister layer of greyish-yellow. I took it cautiously.

"What we must do right away," he said and of course I knew this, "is round up the husband, the fisherman, this William chap –"

"Harold."

"Yes, that's right, on the losing side, I must remember that... Anyway, Tim, collar him, bring him in to me at – " he looked at his watch, shook it, "say nine-thirty, eh?" He was getting up. "What do you reckon to my mustard? Got it from a friend in France. Like it?"

I told him that I had acquired a strange taste at school for sausages with marmalade – nothing to touch it.

"My old mother," said the DC, "used to make apple jelly and we had it with everything." He stumped off. "Except fish," over his shoulder, at the door.

★ ★ ★

I seemed to be getting into the bad habit of taking the final slices of my breakfast into the depot on my long-suffering Khaki-issue bike; today was no exception. I fed myself from the handlebar basket as I went along, and decided to perpetuate a tradition by chucking a small piece of toast at the guard on the gate, provided that he was somebody I knew. Since it was Thursday, and the Codonian had now gone to bed, my basket was empty of the paperwork and scribbles which otherwise would have filled it.

A couple of hundred yards past the guardroom, as you may remember, was the grim and purposeful base of our ineffective Garrison Adjutant, that big decaying ginger lump to whom I had taken an instant – and reciprocated – dislike when I first came to Donnington. He was lumbering about by the self-important entrance to his maze of Nissen huts, wearing that silly beret. He looked at me, and stood stock-still as I cycled past, following me all the way disapprovingly. I very nearly threw him a piece of toast, but then didn't. Moron. "Bart Dixon," ha-ha.

Outside the Building where Harold sat at his desk, I hesitated. This was a crunch moment – it was, though in a quiet and unrecognised way, going to be an earth-shattering event, and I had had little training for such personally tragic things. My only experiences in the past – and even now I was barely 21 – had been back at school when, as Head of my House and in the absence of the Housemaster, I had twice had to break to junior boys the sad news that their parents had been killed in an air raid. I gritted my teeth and went in.

"Hello again, Harold. How are you?"

He looked up at me, forlorn. So he knew already. Confession time: I was so relieved.

"OK, I suppose," he shrugged. "But no, not really. It's Marina…"

I looked round and found a spare chair, typists, steel, stackable.

"Tell me?"

"I think," he heaved a semi-sob, "I'm pretty sure, she's left me."

"Good Lord," I managed.

"She's gone away with your Bobbie."

★ ★ ★

Have you ever overturned a chessboard mid-game and tried to replace all the pieces in the right place? Or, perhaps a better example, switched sides suddenly without warning? (I once won a prize from a magazine for suggesting this, every now and then, as a way to liven the game up).

What the hell should I say next? I had been brought up by sensible parents and wise schooling to give everyone their moment of explanation: always listen to the other side, "walk a mile in their shoes", see both sides, and all that crap.

Was this crisis nothing whatever to do with spies, politics, Cold War, all the overblown political nonsense the papers were spraying over us? Could it be simply that my desirable Bobbie had run off with the highly-fanciable Marina?

After all, let's face it, if I hadn't been sort-of-promised to the one, I would only too happily have gone off with the other! God, those eyes…

My immediate challenge was no longer to offer soft reassuring words to a man who had lost the affections, one assumed, of his wife. It was now more personal. It was to get to the bottom of these latest developments, and to try to remember we were searching covertly for a 'sleeper'; covertly, I kept telling myself. Whatever seems to be developing 'under the counter', as one said those days about everything at all

202

surreptitious like the concealment of the best tobaccos or the last half-pound of unrationed offal... Pull yourself together, Topps.

"Harold," I managed to say in a calm and comforting voice, "we really must talk to you, talk everything through, so that – I'm sure – we can get Marina back to you. The woman you love."

"Sod her." That was Harold, and he had snapped his Government-issue pencil in half.

★ ★ ★

I got him across to the DC's office, where he was understandably subdued by all the red tabs. To my astonishment, Major Parrott was there too, his jacket with the Eighth Army ribbons slung on top of a wealth of bandages. He was lodged in a bath-chair and there were wrappings and stuff down his legs, and he was unlikely to be moving much. I smiled at him and he nodded painfully.

The DC beckoned us towards a couple of upright but comfortable chairs.

"I've briefed the Major," he told me, then turned to Harold with what seemed to be a friendly-enough smile.

"So, William –" I caught his eye. "So, Harold, we need to have a little chat."

The poor man was clearly bewildered, and looked from one of us to another. Whatever business was it of ours, he was wondering, that his wife had run off with another woman? I felt that under the circumstances, it was my job to clear up that complication at once. The two senior officers, in any case, were intrigued and hung on my every word with their mouths open, as I endeavoured to get Harold back into the real world.

"What you are imagining," I told him, "just can't be true.

My girl Bobbie is firmly attached to me, we have an excellent, full-scale and satisfying sex life, daily, (both officers coughed) and she has never shown a single sign of being physically attracted to any female. When we go to see a film it's the men stars she gets excited about. And," I went on rather carefully, "your wife Marina, whom I've met, certainly gave me the impression – er – I sort of sensed, that she is a perfectly healthily normal young lady."

"Well, whatever you say," he retorted, "but she's been chatting up Marina and going around with her for weeks, all over the place, all those silly Norman castles, even in the middle of the night, and –"

"Hang on," I put in. It was my turn to be bewildered.

"Driving off at all hours –"

"No. Absolutely not." I had to stop this, with both hands raised against him. "You've got it wrong, Harold. Not only hasn't Bobbie got a car – she can't even drive. And she only met Marina a week or so ago."

The DC and the Major were now leaning forward at an almost dangerous angle; I glanced across in case they wanted to enter the conversation, but they both nodded for me to continue for the moment.

We had reached a crucial moment, and I took a deep breath.

"The reason we need to talk to you, Harold, is that we have to find out who it is, really, who has been driving Marina about. I can't tell you why – let's assume it's all to do with the Norman castles, but for an unlikely reason. That's all we can say just now; but to investigate the background to it, I really must ask you to let me have a good look around your flat."

"But she left me a message, on the kitchen table."

"What did it say?" asked Major Parrott through his bandages, quite sure that Harold was the worst possible kind…

"Just that she had gone away, with Bobbie, to see some castles, and she might ring me some time, but don't expect it."

"Ring you? You're on the telephone?" the DC put in sharply. It was quite unusual for small flat-dwellers to have a telephone.

"Oh, yes. Marina arranged it, she pays for it, so she can call her folks in Italy. Or rather, they call her."

"Are you sure? Who else rings her?"

"Nobody I know of." He looked around at us all wildly. "What is all this?"

Major Parrott, with a terrific effort and winces of pain, levered himself out of the bathchair and stood upright, swaying on two sticks. We all three made a nervous forward movement; but he was in control.

"Mr Colman. You have been in the British Army, I understand."

"Yes, sir. First Army, Tunis, then up through –"

The Major would have waved all this background away if he had a hand to spare. But Harold was evidently proud of his service record, and sketched in his months which ended gloriously after the landings along the Maures Riviera, east of Toulon and full of garlands and girls desperate to show their gratitude.

Major Parrott, probably a little envious of all this remembered triumph, at a time when he himself had been setting a good example to the troops, cut in at last.

"We need information from you, and we will also need more information as soon as you are in possession of it. As a serving soldier until recently, you must be reminded that you are still on the Emergency list and subject to recall.

But," he added pointedly, "as a serving member of His Majesty's Ordnance Offices, you are equally committed to the security and wellbeing of the State –"

This was pretty good, off the top of his head, I thought to myself.

" – So that I must now request, as Security Officer, indeed require," he paused dramatically, "that you sign the Official Secrets Act."

It was very largely a heap of pompous nonsense, but – my word! – it worked. Little Harold sat there profoundly impressed. Right through the war, he was unlikely to have exchanged a single word, except for shouted commands, with anybody with more than two pips, and now –

With a kindly smile the DC put in an encouraging word, so well chosen.

"We've all signed it." He scratched his neck, just where the red tabs were.

And then as I shall long remember, the Major's stage management achieved perfection: the door opened, and the Brigadier himself walked into the room, said absently: "Ah, Colman, good man," and went out again.

Harold had a look on his face that more or less cried out: "Where do I sign?" I left them to it and waited outside.

★ ★ ★

I had rung the motor pool and was lucky enough to get Helen and her tilly. I got into the back, letting Harold have the front seat, where he sat mostly in silence all the way to Wellington; I had warned him not to discuss our problems in front of the driver.

But I had equally warned Helen to say nothing of any importance, because as we got in, she had whispered: I've remembered something. "Tell me later," I'd said, "but for now, just hang about. Go for a cup of tea and a smoke, I'll be a good hour."

Harold led me into the flat, and went to make some coffee. I looked around, trying to remember Bobbie's report – good Lord, only a few days ago – after her first visit. There were the pictures of Italy on the walls: she was right about the Milan Duomo, and the other one certainly was Florence, with that double-decker bridge across the Arno, the only one the Germans had left, a good deed in a bad world... The books? Yes, boring economics... But the spread-open OS map had gone from the table... The other two, up on the shelf, were still in place and I took a quick look at them. On one, I could have put money: Oxfordshire. But the other posed a new problem: Stratford-upon-Avon and that part of Warwickshire.

Harold came in balancing two mugs and a plate of biscuits.

"Ever been to Stratford?" I asked chattily.

"Only the once." He sort of laughed. "Does anyone go there more than once, except they're Shakespeare addicts?" And in a shocked voice: "D'you know, you have to pay to go into the church!"

I told him how scandalous that was, and I had actually written a poem about it. What the hell, I thought, it may help to loosen him up.

"They bought their entry, led him in to see the sacred view. In awe they tiptoed through the shrine, Towards the altar, where recline Relations of the Bard in line... They paid the homage due. He noticed, as he raised his head, the Figure on the Cross. He said: 'Is that one Shakespeare too?'"

Modesty prevents me from placing on record the spectacular reaction this received. Modesty somewhat diluted by my awareness that poor Harold was desperate to home in upon anything, whatever, that would soothe his current personal worries: yes, he had responded well to his interview with the Top Brass, he had signed the Act, but he must still be in a state of complete upheaval about his relationship with Marina...

"I only asked because I saw this map," I explained, and he briefly laughed.

"That's her again… This castle obsession – she went to look at Warwick and Kenilworth, but came back saying she wasn't really interested because they were too well preserved." He shook his head affectionately. "She likes ruins. She even dismissed Ludlow, of all places, because it was too clean and tidy."

"She sounds like a true Romantic," I was silly enough to say. His eyes filled with tears.

"Oh, yes, she's romantic," he muttered, and I sat there wondering whether to explain what I had meant by the capital 'R'. It wouldn't have helped…

"Has she kept any records of all her researches," I asked cautiously, knowing that this could be a crucial question. "Not that it matters," I added as I nonchalantly sipped my coffee.

"Oh, no," he replied equally vaguely, at which my heart sank. Was all this a waste of time? "Well," he went on, "I think there are a few bits and pieces in her desk over there – I've never looked in it."

"Too busy with the fish?" I joked, and instantly regretted it.

He sadly agreed. "I suppose so."

I went across to Marina's bureau. It was one of those drop-front affairs, it was locked and the key had gone.

"Forgive me," I said, "but I'll have to open this."

Harold went into the kitchen and came back with a chisel. I saw him hesitate, and felt for him in this enforced intrusion into the mutually-shared privacy he and his wife had maintained… I was driving a cold steel blade into a loving relationship that had nothing to do with me.

After all that, there didn't seem to be much in the desk. Some scribbled family postcards from places around Milan, all with abbreviated family affection; a couple from the South of France; a letter from the secretary of Vittorio De Sica regretting Marina's non-success at a 1943 audition, and another, much longer and suggestively loquacious, from another Italian director with a virtual promise of a part in a forthcoming extravaganza "subject to further meetings between the two of us"…

Harold said he had never seen all this stuff before, it was hers, and it was all in Italian anyway. I asked him if there were any other bits and pieces.

"Just the castle files," and he indicated the top shelf of the bookcase. "She's very systematic," he assured me proudly, "They're all labelled, you know: A-one, B-one, and so on." He reached them down for me – only four of them though.

"Is that the lot?" as I skimmed through.

"Well, yes, I think so. I've never –"

But I wasn't listening any more. I was trying to bring some sense to the neat white labels in the top left hand corner of each of the blue folders. There was none labelled 'A-one'. There was a B-one; nothing for 'C'; then a D-one. The next folder was by far the fattest, but it was a 'D' again, though D-nought. The fourth folder was labelled 'LM', which broke the sequence, but it was empty, apart from one picture postcard, surely mis-filed?

I told Harold that I must take these files away, to search through. The poor man was still mentally numb, and I felt I really should do what I could to console him.

"You have a very lovely wife, Harold, and I've no doubt at all that she loves you as much as ever." He made a noise that was somehow half a whimper and half a snort. I ignored it, mainly because I couldn't for the life of me interpret, and anyway was anxious not to cause him offence or make matters even worse.

"It is beginning to look," I went on as gently as I could,

"that Marina has got herself involved in something tricky and political."

"She hasn't a clue about politics," Harold said indignantly. "Neither have I."

I told him I hadn't, either. But lots of funny things were going on, with the end of the war and the growing split between the Allies. I mentioned the United States' neurotic alarm about Russia and the mad scramble for superiority with the atom bomb, which the US had dropped on Japan only three years ago, and after which they now dreaded the Soviets' overtaking them with the vital research.

"What on earth," Harold asked, and I couldn't really answer except by using the waffles that one heard daily from Washington, "can this have to do with my Marina?"

"Did she, when she was in the south of France, have any contact with their very widespread Communists?"

He didn't know, not in the least; but the question was itself enough to plant some thoughts in his mind.

"You see," I went on, and I now confess that I was largely making it up as I went along, "those people are very strong along the south coast, like the Marseille dockers, and even in Northern Italy itself – the motor trade in Turin, you know?" I ended, as though I knew what I was talking about. "Has Marina ever given you any sort of hint – ?"

"Never," he told me loyally, or out of ignorance. "Not once. Not ever."

"So, she has never mentioned anyone she met in France, who might have –"

He shook his head, but it stopped midway.

"Take your time," I said.

He took his time, and it slowly came out, reluctantly, that when released from that time of Nazi bondage, during which many extremely unpleasant things must have been happening to thousand upon thousand of young girls, Marina in her initial sense of relief had formed an association – as Harold put it – with an English officer, now retired. This, he said, had been a heartwarming incident, and had led her to seek a life in England. She had met Harold soon afterwards, and the rest was perfectly straight-forward: an Army marriage, so normal, and setting up home here in Wellington to be close to his parents. I couldn't detect anything in the story worth pursuing at present, and had to get back to the more immediate business: where was she, where was Bobbie, and who had taken them to – wherever it was?

Harold was still shaking his head and muttering, which was understandable but didn't help.

"Now do try," I said, attempting to be firm. "If Marina can't drive –"

"No, she can't."

" – And Bobbie can't either, couldn't get petrol anyway, either of them. So then, who is it driving them?"

"Well," he conceded, "if it wasn't her at all, it can only be that chap Curly –"

I opened my mouth and shut it again: let him speak.

"You know," he looked across at me as though I ought to know all this, "The secretary of the Shrewsbury Historical Society, well, actually it's Shrewsbury and The Norman Marches, isn't it?"

"Oh absolutely," I nodded blindly, and waited for more.

"I've never actually met him," he went on, "but he picks them all up and drives them to all those places –"

"Places?" I prompted.

"Their meetings and lectures, or sometimes excavations, all those Norman ruins."

"It sounds great fun," I agreed, "so instructive, too. When does it all happen?"

"They go out a couple of days a week. I'm never here of course, working in the depot every day you know, but there are evening excursions as well, every now and then. I'm very happy for her to have that interest, these friends, so soon after we settled here."

"Of course."

"And then," he added a little apologetically, "I've got this fishing bug, you know, and I'm quite often out right through the night when the weather's right – "

"And the moon?" I suggested knowingly.

"Oh yes, especially on still water – well, you saw me at the canal."

"Tell me this, Harold, and it's important though I can't yet say why: were you fishing last Monday night?"

To my astonishment, he got up and went over to a raincoat hanging on a peg by the door; and pulled out a substantial notebook with an expensive leather cover, emblazoned in gold 'Freshwater Diary 1947'. Admittedly it was a year out of date, but still impressive: Harold had evidently been given it for Christmas by Marina two years ago and was was doubling-up his pescatorial successes economically. As one would have expected.

He thumbed lovingly through the closely-written pages and reached the right month; then, he lingered over some of his entries, in recall of those holy hours on the canal-bank… It struck me that an alternative gold-embossed title might have been 'Death-roll of Shropshire Fish'…

"Yes," he said at last. "Little feeding in shallows – paste g-b." He looked up helpfully. "That means ground-bait. We throw it in, then fish it after about twenty minutes, it works well in a canal." He turned back to the book. "Moon good, no wind. Nothing rising. Try bottom."

I think he must have sensed my raised eyebrows.

"If they aren't feeding up near the surface we adjust the float and try to get the ones that feed further down."

To my surprise, this dredged up from my mind the memory of something I'd read years ago.

"Tench!" I cried. At last I could join in this conversation.

Harold was thrilled.

"Yes!" he enthused. "How did you know? Have you been a fisherman?"

I had to disappoint him, reminding him that it was only as a boy, long years ago, with my Grandad in the sluggish Mole at Hampton Court. But it was that very lack of flow that had cemented in my brain a quotation, from some poet or other who was a committed town-dweller but had an urge to seem to love the countryside and all it held dear, especially when it had paid off so well for people like Wordsworth and that crowd. He had written a poem in which he unwisely praised quite the wrong sort of freshwater fish.

"The tench leaps up to take the fly," he wrote. The flow was irreproachable, but the content was hopeless. Of all fish, I'm told, the tench must be the least energetic, an aquatic cousin of the giant sloth: so far as I know it feeds, idly, on the bottom as it lumbers along the riverbed; if it should ever, perchance, swivel its eye upwards to see a fly splashing about on the surface, I imagine it just shrugging its scaly shoulder and scrabbling along for the next misguided worm, and having trouble even catching that.

As you may now imagine, I was getting on well with Harold. I ended by assuring him that his Marina would be back with him soon; and if she should ring him, or if anyone else, at all, should call in on that phone, I must be told at once: *must*. Did he have any contact number or other helpful information on the Norman Marches Historical Society? No, nothing at all, just the driver's name was Curly and he was the historian who organised all these activities, apparently day and night.

I left him, taking the four folders, and went to find Helen in her tilly.

As we drove back to Donnington, and I was flipping through the folders despondently because they didn't seem to promise anything much, I remembered to ask her what was the thing she had recalled about last Monday night.

"You know, as we got near to Wem, we went through a village, and a big Army car came past us going the other way?" Of course, I said.

"The street lamps were shining. I could see the driver. A white face. He had a green hat."

I thanked her and said I would file it away for future reference. Doesn't anybody talk sense any more, I asked myself as I cycled from the motor pool back to House Four and flopped on the bed.

XVI

There was, as I might have guessed, no such organisation as the Shrewsbury and Norman Marches Historical Society, though the rather cute County Assistant Deputy Sub-Librarian, who coyly hid her attractions behind tortoiseshell glasses in the approved Hollywood manner, said that there certainly ought to be. Such fun, she said, and I found it easy to agree with her.

If the Society didn't exist, who was Curly?

Did the non-existent Society in fact have any other members? Was Marina being hoaxed into joining an outfit that was bogus? Or was she the only member? And if so, did she know she was? And if that was so, wasn't she simply giving herself a clever alibi, a cover for her work as a 'sleeper'?

I had to look through those four folders, but I must bear in mind that she had left them behind, therefore they were probably innocuous.

When I began to examine them more closely, some unexpected facts began to emerge, the chief of them being that the main story was laid bare in those title labels...

The file which Harold had described as B-one was in fact written: Bi. And again, the one called D-one was really Di. I only cottoned on to this when looking at the third file – D-zero – which was actually written Do. That surely meant Donnington...

I looked back at the travel details I had received from my Agency friend. When Harold had been fishing around Oxfordshire, evidently Marina had also been busy on her rented bicycle. The Di file had Wallingford written on it, as I would have expected, and inside it was a plan of the castle ruins and earthworks spreading for hundreds of yards alongside the river; but just a few miles away was the major Ordnance Depot of Didcot, as big as us and perhaps even more militarily important – but no papers about it inside: Marina must have taken them with her. Next, the Bi file.

I was gratified to see that she had indeed chosen that little motte-and-bailey as her excuse, next to the church at Middleton Stoney; but of course, as I had already spotted the other day – could it really have been only yesterday? – she would have been almost within sight of the gigantic Ordnance Depot of Bicester. My nascent suspicions had been side-lined, just hours ago, by my personal sudden and more important alarm about Bobbie's disappearance, but now, for the moment, I had come to terms with that. I didn't think our Marina was a killer. Excusably paranoid, perhaps.

However, I knew that COD Bicester was our most vital base of all, designed in such a way that it stood ready for immediate transportation lock, stock and barrel anywhere in the world as an Advance Supply Depot whenever the need might arise. This Bi file had nothing inside, except for a one-page sketchmap and some measurements of Otmoor, the flat marshland south of the Depot, showing the old Roman road that crosses it.

The third file, Do, was also empty now although it showed signs of having been stuffed pretty full. No castle nonsense on the cover, either: unnecessary, of course. But scribbled on the back in pencil there was a telephone number… I wrote it down hopefully.

File number four, LM, had three names on the cover, two of which – Warwick and Kenilworth – had later been crossed out. The third just said 'L.M. Fosse?'. But then I looked inside, at the lone postcard which I had assumed to be from Marina's family and misfiled...

It was made from a coloured photograph, and showed a ruined castle towering against a blue sky; in the foreground, perched on a shrub, was a swallowtail butterfly. An inviting picture. I turned it over.

The stamp was French and the date a couple of months ago. Posted somewhere in Var, but the town name was too smudged... Marina's address (no mention of Harold) was in a neat educated hand. The message simply read "LM.X". The signature just 'H'.

From my job back in Building Five, I knew that the next largest Depot we dealt with was Long Marston, a mainly vehicle store not far from Warwick and, for that matter, Kenilworth; but also it lay just off the old Fosse Way, close to which there would undoubtedly be a whole range of small ruins – as I told myself cleverly, just up Marina's street. Was the message "Don't cover Long Marston"?

★ ★ ★

I took all my ideas and evidence across to the DC, and found him skimming through the latest Codonian. The Major was alongside, and had shed one or two bandages. I was incautious enough to ask him how the Sergeant was. Mending, he said, mending nicely. At that point we both glanced across at the DC but he was deeply involved in sorting a tray of paper-clips and trying valiantly not to listen to anything regimentally inappropriate.

At which, to my astonishment, Major Parrott winked at me. A new bond formed?

I showed them the empty folders with the notes written on the covers. But – just for now, I promised myself with my fingers crossed – I had removed that French postcard. All in good time…

"Well," said the DC, "what you must do now, Topps, is stick close full-time to Harold, so that you can pick up as much new evidence as possible, and the moment you get a real lead, don't bother to check back with me, just go in however you can to rescue your girl –"

"And while you're doing that," the Major assured me, "Get a message through to me and we'll rush our people in to support you." He took a quick look at my uniform and the side pockets. "You're armed?"

I still had the rather neat and almost feminine pistol I'd been sent so reluctantly by Captain Dick Barton, he of the twisted lip.

"Know how to use it?" The Major was recovering well, I thought, from being blown up, and getting his swagger back. Yes thank you, I told him. I'd never fired the thing, and hoped I'd never have to. I had been well trained in the rifle, ever since school – indeed, I'd been taught to fire a two-two when I was seven, out in Kenya. I'd won a second prize with the Army's routine three-o-three last year on Salisbury Plain. I'd wholly enjoyed using the deliciously-smooth Bren as part of my primary training; and I'd nearly taken three toes off with the crazy Sten which seemed to have been thrown together by a drunken blacksmith somewhere at the wrong end of the Balkans, and which pulled down to the right if you fired repeats instead of singles. And by the way, they weren't my toes, either, they were Sergeant Murphy's. So, "Yes," I lied, I knew how to use it.

"We're getting close now," the DC commented. "It's pretty clear that this girl Marina has panicked. She'll know full well that she ought to have held her nerve – to kidnap Bobbie because she was probing too much, was very silly indeed; and," he added comfortingly, "Now that she knows how stupid she's been, she certainly won't want to make things worse by kill-"

218

" – By mistreating Bobbie in any way," Major Parrott kindly translated. And the DC quickly agreed.

"When this is over," he said, "we must reward Bobbie, to compensate. Perhaps..." he looked vaguely at the Major, being at a loss when it came to presents for women.

"Perfume," said the Major. "What does she like –?"

I racked my memory, never having got into the heavy end of cosmetics, and beyond the simple Yardley's Lavender preferred by my grandmother with whom I had spent the war years. Then I remembered something my three-thousand-miles-remote mother had told me in one of her air-mail-form photo-letters we had been limited to during the war.

"Chanel Number Twenty-two!" I told him. "Yes, that's it."

He wrote it down, but looked at me drily.

"From what I hear," he said, "after the relief of Paris, you'd be more up to date asking for Chanel Number Seven-one-two-four." It was forty years before I got the joke, when the details emerged about Nazi Agent code numbers...

The DC put down his Codonian.

"I'm glad you've explained away the Wem explosion," he said approvingly, perhaps forgetting that the wording had been largely his. "But, you know, Topps, now that we've set our trap and it's been sprung, we really have little further use for the paper. The War House won't continue to support your twelve pages or whatever it is."

"Yes, of course I accept that, sir. Shall I gradually unwind?"

"Well..." He looked uncomfortable, and shifted in his chair so much that the embroidered antimacassar, or whatever the hell it was supposed to be, slid off and dropped to the floor. The Major retrieved it.

"The fact is," the DC began, "Whitehall is a bit unhappy about the mistakes in the reporting..."

"Mistakes?" I said.

"Mistakes," the Major put in, quite loudly. "About the radar. Whitehall thinks –"

"But I was instructed –" I began.

"Whitehall," said the DC as kindly as he could, "is saying that a Depot newspaper covering such a large readership, about six thousand isn't it? –"

"About that, sir, now that I've built it up so well –"

"Yes, well, Tim, they feel it needs to be run under a more senior Officer. After all, you know, at the end of the day –"

"And the end of the day will be very soon, I suppose, now we've sprung your radar trap?"

"Tim, you're due for demob in a few months. You're not a Regular. They think we ought to have a Regular…" He ran out of steam, so I saved him. He had been a good friend to this unmilitary little subaltern, and I must make it easy for him.

"Would it be permissible, sir, for me to offer you my resignation as the Editor of the Codonian, with immediate effect, in exchange for your permission for me to give up my Building Five duties and devote my remaining time to pursuing our suspected sleepers, still entirely covertly?"

"Yes," he smiled, much relieved. "That sounds an ideal solution, and you've worded it so well, it must have been rehearsing in your head for quite a while. Put it in writing and I'll write back agreeing, so it'll be official. But then, this will be a Security matter." He turned to the Major.

"Oh yes, I entirely agree. Take full control of this sleeper business, Topps, especially as I'm not very mobile yet. But always come to me for support."

I thanked them both.

"But before I go, sir, and I'm just off to check with Harold Colman, as I will every day, do either of you know anybody whose name or nickname is Curly?"

Neither of them could help with that, though they were

keen to help. Major Parrott thought we should search for a driver with a full mop of hair. The DC was better at tangental thinking or whatever they call it: he suggested it was most likely a completely bald man we were looking for…

I left them debating it.

★ ★ ★

Harold was sitting at his desk as usual. I suppose a dedicated angler is used to doing tricky things like attaching hooks to gut, and then extracting them from the lips of fish so that the pain doesn't show too obviously? At any rate, I saw that he had meticulously mended that snapped Government pencil with several rounds of black insulation tape which must have cost the War Office far more than the pencil. A microcosm, I thought, of our bureaucracy. An echo of the mindset that demanded a senior officer, with far too many things to think about, to replace an energetic and under-employed junior as editor of a flimsy local rag which, as in the past, would soon revert to being a mere guide-leaflet to the local cinemas…

But enough of that. Harold said he had still not heard from Marina; but he had a feeling that she may telephone this evening: first, it was payday, so there might be things to discuss about her job with the Travel Agency (whom she had apparently asked for "a few days leave", no more, and she hadn't said anything about giving up the job). Second, the Codonian had come out and she may want to know whether it said anything of import. (I quietly interpreted this as Harold's newly developed fear that she might have been involved at Wem, but he was much too scared to say so). And thirdly, the end of the week was the time when, in most families, bills had to be paid. Most simple hire-purchase agreements were drawn up with husband and wife as joint guarantors, therefore, if

221

Harold should refuse to pay, Marina would be in trouble with The Law – the last thing her mysterious Controller would tolerate.

I was more than ever convinced that her disappearance with Bobbie had been a knee-jerk reaction to the suspicion that we were, one way or another, on to her. I guessed that she was now wishing she could undo that rash development; and it would be sensible – especially now that I apparently had 'carte blanche' from the powers-that-were, to press ahead – to stay close to Harold.

"When you knock off tonight," I said, "never mind the bus, I'll run you home, but then I need to stay at your place all evening, in case you get a call."

He agreed. I went across to Printing & Pubs, at Building 18. I saw they had repaired the broken window, until now boarded up with a square of plywood which, when wet from the Wrekin's constant weather, had taken on in its curious graining a ghoulish shape of a skull with a twisted mouth. I was never quite sure whether to call it Dick or Bart. Or whether to write an editorial about it. No chance now.

I went over to the Codonian desk and found Private Brown. This being Friday, he saw it as his day-off, and was relaxing with a cheese and watercress sandwich and a copy of the latest 'Reveille', as we all did when we had the chance.

But he got up at once.

"They've told me, sir. I'm dreadfully sorry. It wasn't your fault. You were set up. The fall guy."

"Well…"

"No, really. I don't want some stuffy colonel telling me what to do," he said. "I'm going to request a transfer, a posting."

He, too, was due to be demobbed quite soon, so I didn't argue. I was glad that he had been involved in our expansion, no matter how artificially spy-related it had been; and I was sure he would make the most of the story when he eventually hit Fleet Street.

★ ★ ★

Shortly before five, I went over to the Motor Pool and found Bob Blackmore. This time, he was upright rather than flat underneath a car; and almost free of oil. I told him I had an important patriotic job for him, and he preened at once.

"I need you to drive me to Wellington again," I said, "and hang on right through the evening because we may have to drive further afield and make an arrest."

"Are you going to arm me?"

"Bring a big spanner and a starting-handle."

In due course we picked up Harold, and in the square I left Bob sitting in the car; he had sensibly brought along one of those new portable Roberts radios, so he was happy to wait. It was just as well.

I sat with Harold on his fraying settee which had long distressed threads trailing off it, and quietly wondered how long it would be before the landlords of such squalidly furnished apartments would be enabled to update their outworn furnishings, given the strict controls on rents. And anyway, nearly everything was still subject to rationing, or to coupons, or to some other sort of restriction. Across the Channel, they were all pulling themselves together so quickly, so efficiently... And we were giving them financial transplants whilst bleeding to death ourselves, all in the traditional cause of "*victor oblige*" or whatever the smug phrase was that had been seized upon and twisted by all those left-wing university dons, set upon undermining us at our most vulnerable time. Admittedly, the neurotic Communist witchhunt was surging way over-the-top across the Atlantic (I had seen evidence of

223

this even back in 1946 when I went there); but here, in our gently plodding UK, I wondered, would our traditional laidback old-fashioned gentlemanliness be hijacked by these hotbreath firebrands? Very likely.

Harold realised that he was reluctantly doomed to be my host for a long evening. He made us both some very commendable baked-beans-on-toast, and followed it up with a big mug each of coffee. No sooner had this been done, that the telephone rang with that irregular urgency which indicated a long-distance call being handled manually by a girl at the local exchange...

We both reacted with the sort of nervous spasm one used to get at the shrill sound. Harold grabbed the handset. I rushed across, embarrassingly close to his right cheek, so that I could at least partially muscle in on the conversation.

The voice was unmistakeable, and despite myself, my left knee twitched.

"Harry darling..."

"Oh Marina," he cried, and I choose the verb advisedly, "Where are you?"

"You mustn't worry, carissimo, I am doing a thing I have to do."

"But surely, you must tell me why this is happening?"

"People have been asking many questions about you," she said, "And I cannot keep having them bothering us. I had to go away to hide from them, and I took with me this Bobbie woman..."

"Yes, my dear, but why? It is not sensible to take anybody away, it is called kidnap – our laws don't permit –"

I detected a plaintive note entering into Marina's voice. She was probably regretting her spontaneous reaction to our hassling of her?

"She is in no harm. She has food, and I have given her

some of my – how you say – change of clothes… We talk…
Harry, I like her, she is nice. But I was told I must take her as
– what word is it? – as '*ostaggio*' – to stop all those '*intrusione*',
those '*interrogazione*', you know, darling, as in those last days in
Nice."

"Yes, of course," he was nodding as though she could see
him along the line. "You told me, I remember. But are you all
right?"

"Si, yes. It is difficult, but I can come here to call you. To
this box."

"Where are you?"

"I mustn't say –"

That suddenly put a different light on the affair, and I
whispered to Harold: "Why not? Is she under somebody's
control? Ask her who."

"My God!" he whispered. "Marina, darling, why can't you
say? Are you a prisoner too?"

"Well – ," I could hear her breathing, as she paused
wondering how to answer. "Harry, don't worry, I will be OK,
and I can call you some evenings."

"Who is in charge of you? Is this anything to do with
Curly?"

Another long pause, more breathing, but no response.

I said to Harold: "Let me speak to her – after all, it's
Bobbie's problem too."

He said to her: "*Momento*," and passed me the phone. At
this unrehearsed moment's notice, I had to come up with
something innocuous to say, so that she wouldn't immediately
hang up.

"Butterflies," I said. There are few things less nocuous than
that.

"*Che?*"

"Are there butterflies?" I repeated in a chatty tone. "You

know, Marina – *farfalle*? *Marsina*? *Coda di rondine*?" (I had spent half-an-hour in the inadequate garrison library looking up 'swallowtail', and had the words on a piece of scrap library paper).

She was so taken aback by this that despite everything that was going on, she burst into laughter.

"*Mamma mia*, even in this country, moths do not usually go around wearing – how you say? – dinner-jackets. Next, you will put them into Sam belts."

"Marina, you lovely girl," and I took a quick look at Harold but he was finishing his baked beans. "Tell me, please, is Bobbie all right?"

"I am with her, and she is OK. Mr. Topps, Tom, I am sorry this has happened, it was not my intention –"

"Marina, if you are both being kept prisoner, I don't need to know the background right now, just where you are?" Something else occurred to me. "And how are you able to telephone?"

"I come to get food." I supposed that was reasonable.

"But where –?"

Again she laughed: if she was a prisoner, it didn't seem to be scaring her much. "In a castle, of course."

"But –"

"You must come and find me, Tom –"

"Tim."

"But you have to bring your own butterflies, there are none in these ruins." There was another quiet giggle. "As you know, all the best castles are ruins. So, be quick to pass your test, then come on a big white horse or a big brown Hummer to rescue me and get a big kiss." Then, but only as an after-thought: "Oh, your Bobbie surely sends her love, too."

"You must give me another clue, Marina." This was becoming ridiculous, I knew, but if she was in such an outrageously flippant state of mind, I had to make the most of it. Reality seemed to have gone out of the window. "Is Curly with you?"

A pause: she was searching for a trick reply.

"I am at Curly Castle, Tom."

"Tim."

"Yes, I am at Curly Castle. That is good." Another giggle. "You, with your Codonian, can think about it. But now –"

At this absurd moment, the operator in the manual telephone exchange, wherever it was, interrupted: "Your time has run out, please insert further coins."

She didn't. She just said rapidly: "I will call next wee – " and the line went dead.

I patted Harold on the shoulder, and saw myself out, after checking with the telephone operator: the call was untraceable but it had come from a phone-box more than 25 miles away, because of the tariff-rate. Most likely from Ludlow: Hereford would have been too far, and Shrewsbury not far enough.

★ ★ ★

Getting back into Bob's car, I felt that the night's excitement was over. I had at least established that Bobbie was probably safe, mainly because of my success in provoking a sort of light-heartedness in Marina. It seemed pretty sure that they were both being held in a fairly benevolent detention: the aim, I had come to suppose, was to hold them incommunicado, away from the Press, while something-or-other illegal, or antisocial or anti-governmental was about to happen.

These, as I have said, were the days when half the Western world was neurotically twitchy about Communism, and sure that 'The Reds' were infiltrating everywhere, set upon destruction of our relaxed laid-back tolerant lives; while the other half didn't really, quite honestly, give a 'Tinker's Cuss' what happened in the wider world, so long as we could buy our daily bread, keep body-and-soul together without the awful embarrassment of insolvency, and get through to a pensioned old age after, one hoped, doing a lifetime job that was interesting rather than an utter murderous bore…

So, I sat back and asked Bob Blackmore to drive me home. He let me stay quiet for a few miles, but then asked where I wanted to be dropped.

"My billet," I said. "Just past the HQ Mess, on the left. House Four: it's got a blue door, you can't miss it. God, I'm tired."

He missed it. We were moving on up the road.

"For Christ's sake," I shouted, over-weary I must have been. "What's the matter? I said the blue door. Number Four."

Bob reversed. We drew up alongside. He pointed.

"It's green," he said. "Look."

He was expecting me to get out and bugger off to bed, but I just sat there. I was thinking…

★ ★ ★

It's strange, though I'm sure you've experienced it: even if you are worn out, and more than ready for bed, something can happen which gives an unexpected twist to your dozy thinking, and at once you become alert, ready for a good few more productive hours before your head sinks on to the eventual welcoming pillow.

One feature of the Officers' Lines, that being the pretentious name given to my road of houses, was the excellent night-time street lighting… Very clear, very chemically reliable yellow light. But, I now noticed for the first time, it had the effect of turning blue into green.

I vaguely remembered our Art master at school, recently arrived from Austria with Nazi blood as well as painters' oils under his fingernails, telling us, we insular receptive idiotic fourth-formers, about the interaction of colours. Fritz Gross, I remember you so well and your bulging-eyed enthusiasm, which we so arrogantly disregarded, and went on to dismiss as the outpourings of an exile non-starter. His work is now treasured by the Ashmolean, but from those days all I remember is that blue – when yellow is applied – gives green.

I didn't get out of the car.

Instead, I asked Bob to take me to the motor pool, where he spent all his daytimes. Admittedly, it was now nearly midnight, but Bob's patriotism and his kiplingery could be relied upon, I was pretty sure – it was worth banking on.

I was remembering, as you may recall, one or two disparate and seemingly ineffectual facts, and now, when put together, they threatened to add up to a most alarming picture.

Our four suspects had been distilled from an original reservoir of civilian workers. The DC had understandably commented that the military should be omitted because (a) they could be presumed to be loyal to the Crown; and (b) they tended to come and go, posted here and there, and thus were not a good bet as a longterm sleeper…

But blue looks green under a yellow light. My ATS driver Helen had said that the staff car emerging from Wem just before the explosion had a green-hatted driver under the street lights. The man at the gate had told me that, on the night of the break-in, there had been "only the usual comings-and-goings" including the Garrison Adjutant. And that was my unpleasant superannuated Captain who wore a blue beret. I'd never liked the man, my "Bart Dixon" and now it seemed to be incumbent on me to do some checks.

I would have to take Bob Blackmore into my confidence.

As we headed for his Motor Pool office I asked what records they kept of the various staff cars' coming and going. He assured me it was all on paper in the office.

"Am I allowed to know anything about this?"

"Not much," I told him. "But I need to find out some facts and figures about mileage, and servicing, stuff like that."

Once we were sitting amid all the utterly boring pages of invoices and reports, indents for petrol, accident statistics and the rest, and I was completely bemused, Bob suddenly swept them all aside and looked at me.

"Nothing," he said. "Not a thing."

"Explain?"

"We don't have any record at all of Captain Barton's staff car. It doesn't come here for servicing, he never claims for petrol use, or anything else. For all we know from our routine records, he and his car don't exist."

I slowly realised that I may have found Curly. The DC had been right – I remembered that the Adjutant, on top of all his other age-expired deficiencies, was as bald on top as a billiard-ball. The ginger was only a sort of all-round fringe.

From the Pool, where I had left it at teatime, I pedalled slowly on my bike, bidding goodnight to my reliable Bob and went into the Mess.

It was now two in the morning, and nobody was around except Tillie and the Padre, each of them taking a little while to recover from some crisis or other. Nobody seems to mention, when writing about the Forces, those unexciting but so vital services performed by officers high and lowly – and non-commissioned too – in relation to the soldiers who are "under their command". That phrase is so often taken to mean one's actual tactical movements in the field, under gunfire; but if you spare a moment to think about it, the meaning is far deeper. When you have a group of disparate men serving under you, each of them an individual who may well be hopelessly mixed-up inside (why else did he join?), and you are responsible, front-line, for the welfare of all of them (and in the Army the minimum is a platoon of more than thirty of them) you have a fulltime job. They will bring you all their troubles: you are their social worker who will later take them into battle, see them killed, and then answer to their parents, wives and sweethearts. And still you are committed to all this, now, in what is called 'peacetime', whilst being belittled and jeered at both by well-heeled Left-wing journalists and by slobs on State benefits, all of them living at their homes in relative (or extreme!) comfort, always with the sly support of greedy, sleazy lawyers playing both sides against the middle. (God, Shakespeare's Dick the Butcher was so right: kill them all, first thing): except for mine, of course: excellent chap.

I sat and pondered this as I watched little Padre Jones, at this unearthly hour, scanning through some papers as no doubt he worked upon the problems of one of his – our – my – flock; his parish was confined to the walls of the depot and the Army camps that surrounded it. He was one of four or five padres, and I believe they shared out their work geographically in the first instance, no matter whether the soldier was C-of-E, RC, Jewish, Methodist, or of some splinter group; then they would shuffle their cards and deal them to one another as seemed most appropriate. Padre Jones once, on a late evening similar to this, opened up to me over the second glass of port. Living here at the Officers Mess, in this luxury only two years after he had seen men torn apart by shellfire, and had first to pray over them and then visit their loved ones, he confessed that he was deeply embarrassed, and longed for the sackcloth and ashes of a more simple and straightforward life of service. I felt that if given the choice, he would escape the artificial pomp of the weekly official Mess Dinner, and live and eat humbly at the

NAAFI over the road. (And I learnt years later that he did escape, and join a Community of monks. They were based only a mile from where I subsequently lived, but I never knew that until I read of his death. I would have liked to visit him – but I wonder whether he would have wanted it, a reminder of those sumptuous days?)

I then looked across at Captain Kitson. Even the essentially kind-hearted DC made fun of Kittie ("two poached eggs…"), but no matter what he looked like, and no matter what was causing it, here was a man expert in his speciality: to organise the feeding of a multitude… He took personal responsibility, no doubt, for our day-by-day culinary enjoyments in the Officers Mess; but aside from that job which resembled catering for a select London hotel, he had to keep a controlling eye on the daily hunger of a thousand-or-more young men up at the camps, bursting with testosterone (oh, and several hundred ATS girls equally afire with whatever the opposite is)… He had the ultimate control of the brews their five-or-six cookhouse chefs came up with, for two miles in every direction. On top of that, he was also the ultimate target for everybody's wrath if bromide really was being put into the tea. I sometimes wondered if the amorous pairs who populated the slagheaps were all coffee-drinkers: worth research?

All these drifting thoughts were, I realised, my brain's effort to avoid facing up to my immediate problem. I pulled myself together: there was this other Depot character – caricature, almost – I had to focus upon…

First of all, I had to admit that I had never liked Captain Barton. I must guard against being biased, not only because it would cloud my judgment but because when – if – I reported back to the DC and the Major, they would seize upon it.

Further, this was a much older and more experienced officer, a tested veteran of the war, and however unpleasant he

232

had become (and who knew why?) he was infinitely superior to me in every conceivable way. As he had uncouthly pointed out on my first arrival, I was a mere part-time ex-schoolboy filling in a couple of risk-free years before the equally State-supported hedonistic delights of Oxford.

And yet, there were these unavoidable pointers to Captain Barton. The blue beret might be quite harmless, a trick of the light – again; but why was his staff car and his use of petrol not recorded? How, away from our Motor Pool, was he able to get that fuel? Come to think of it, if anybody else was 'Curly', how would that person be getting access to all the fuel needed for visits to castles, given the strict limitations of the time?

It now seemed to be my duty, despite my lowly position as a National Service short-timer, to demolish in real life the senior long-serving officer whom I had already flippantly demolished in fiction a few months before. I assure you that I wasn't happy about it.

I decided to sleep on it, then do some more research before I went to the DC or anybody else. My only consolation, at this early-morning point as I sat entirely alone, down at the wrong end of the Mess, was that on the telephone, despite the bizarre circumstances of the call from Marina, she had seemed quite relaxed and easy – mischievious even – to talk to. If, in reality, she and my Bobbie were both in some way prisoners of 'Curly', and if, again in reality, this 'Curly' was indeed our superannuated Depot Adjutant who had disembraced from 'The System' and gone over to Communism, where the Hell do I go from here?

And who would listen to me, I wasn't even the editor any more?

233

XVII

I slept, fitfully as was usual now, on all this excess of alarming information; and at six in the morning I went down in my pyjamas to see my trusted quarter-batman.

"Edwards," I said as officially-sounding as I could at that hour, "I have a job for you."

"Sir?"

"I know it's early, and it's Saturday, but you'll be doing us – the entire Army – a favour."

"You want a higher polish on the belt?"

"Nothing so important as that," I told him. "I want you to go to Captain Barton's house and bring me his left Wellington boot."

"Of course, sir."

I realised this was pure soap-opera. (The expression had just been invented across the pond, but it perfectly summed up the position I was in with him).

"Would you like his underpants as well?"

"Edwards," I said. "Despite how I look, I am not pissed. For reasons of deep security, I need to see the Captain's boot, Wellington, left. And quickly."

I suppose he must have detected a note of genuine urgency in my eye, bloodshot though it was. He suggested that I might like a cup of his special-brew tea first of all; and while I sipped this, and it was excellent, he disappeared up the road…

My brown paper parcel was upstairs. I fetched it. The boot, when it arrived, fitted perfectly. We had found the man with big feet, bald, and with a blue beret. I had got Curly, it seemed. Bart Dixon of all people!

But who could I tell? As Edwards sneaked the infamous boot back to its treacherous owner, yet to be accosted, I was completely confused over what to do next.

If I took my suspicions to the DC or to Major Parrott, it couldn't be till Monday, but then even if I was believed, the whole thing would be blown up into a public disaster and – for all I knew – Bobbie could be caught up in some sort of gun-battle, or even seen as a collaborator?

For the moment I must pursue these leads myself, quietly.

★ ★ ★

I went across to Building 18 – being respectable white-collar people they were again at work on a Saturday morning, while the sweaty sons of toil in the warehouses had their rest and the weekend cleaners came in to mop up the widespread detritus. To be fair, though, most of those sweaty military storemen would be limbering up on the parade-ground and being shouted at by the once-a-week sadism of bellowing sergeants, who were no doubt doing their non-commissioned best to conceal their hearts of gold, as required by Hollywood.

I found Private Brown sitting morosely at his desk, he was beginning to clear it of all his accumulated notes and papers. I told him to stop it: maybe I was no longer his editor, but exciting things were about to happen and he ought not to miss out on them.

He reluctantly put stuff back, stubbing out his cigarette in the dregs of his coffee, as I'm sure he had seen done, only with a fried egg, at the cinema.

"Tell me about the exciting things," he asked; but I felt that I should bring The Chunk into the frame as well, now that I was myself heading out of it. I went across to her part of the Building.

"Peggy," I said, "two young and attractive women may be captives of a rough and renegade Army Officer, somewhere remote along the Welsh border."

"Disgusting male behaviour," she said, or something like that, following me back to the Codonian corner.

"Scandalous," echoed the nubile Goodbody who had followed us, and who was at once dismissed to make us all some more coffee. Milk and sugar…?

"Two lumps," said Brown thoughtfully as he watched her go.

Anyway, I told them both, I have to rescue the girls somehow, and for this, though I am no longer connected to the Codonian, I must have a base from which to work; and my main problem is that my chief suspect – here I paused and looked from one to the other meaningfully – is a senior long-standing official of the Depot.

That is the point at which, in all the best fiction, one hears a sharp intake of breath. I didn't actually detect any such thing, more a fidgeting of the fingers which passed me the message: "Get on with it".

"One of the prisoners is a suspected spy."

That worked, they were attentive now.

"The other," I announced with suitable emphasis, "is my intended wife." And yes, I now had them on my side. What could they do to help?

"Two things, one for each of you," I said. "First, Peggy, can you privately ask HQ to install here in the building, a telephone line with a direct connection, so that it will come in straight through our depot exchange but the incoming call is registered and can be traced back? It doesn't work on our normal lines."

The Chunk was pretty sure it could be done.

"Right away? And in secret?"

"On Monday. Don't worry. I'll say it's for immediate access by all the national media."

"And Brown," I turned to him, "You were at School in Shrewsbury –"

"At," he corrected me.

"Eh?"

"At Shrewsbury." He sort of tutted me. "The School."

"Ah yes. I remember. When I was researching Wem the other day, I saw –"

He interrupted me rather quickly.

"How can I help with your local history, sir?"

"Castles," I said. "All those Norman castles that seem to litter the whole of this part of the country. I have to research them over the weekend."

"Do you have any particular district in mind, sir?"

This use of 'sir', I was well aware, was aggressive. I pressed on, grimly, as one does. I told him that I simply had to spend the weekend searching to find a less well-known, but presumably still habitable, old Norman castle where these two lovelies were being, so to speak, 'held' by the un-named Army officer. From a telephone report it would seem we should centre our thoughts on the Ludlow area; but the main county library for Shropshire was of course over in Shrewsbury. Ought I to go there for my researches? I told myself it was somewhat urgent, now that I had the blue-bereted suspect in my sights.

Brown thought for a while, then made a very sensible suggestion, which even I have to acknowledge. He had done some history at that school of his, not bad in its way…

"So far as abandoned or lesser-known Norman castles go," he said as he lit a second nonchalant cigarette without offering the packet to me, "I think you ought to be looking further south."

I both wanted, and resolutely refused, to ask him why.

"Because," he was answering me anyway, "in the days immediately following the Norman Conquest, William's barons were granted vast areas of land to be their personal domain." He looked up at me. "Everybody knows that," he told me, and there was a pause… "But," as I was expecting, "in Herefordshire itself things were different. Because of the need to defend the Border against the rebellious Welsh, the land-owning barons were given permission to build castles, both to defend their lands and as a base from which to counter the Welsh. They were specifically allowed, by the King, to castellate. That means –"

"So you think we ought to be looking further south?"

"That's what I'm suggesting, sir." Private Brown looked at me and raised a languid eyebrow. I realised at once that what he was suggesting was his educational superiority. I couldn't allow that. On the river, maybe, sometimes; on the pitch, very rarely, (and then no thanks to me, I didn't tell him). But when one dug into deeper and long-term traditional things, the record spoke for itself.

"At Wem," I said, quietly but slowly and mercilessly, "I learnt that it was the birthplace, home, and constituency of the dreaded Judge Jeffreys –"

Brown had blanched.

"An alumnus of yours, I believe?"

"Well," he said, "You get these reports…"

"Terrible vicious man," I reminisced from my history books. "Shocking Salopian background…" I smiled at him. "We had John Bunyan probably, you know? What a splendid chap."

"Wasn't he in prison for years, in the middle of a river?"

I think that was the point at which we called it a draw, and went on to give more sensible thought to my need to study the Border castles over this weekend…

"We were told by the telephone exchange that the call must have come from –"

"Yes, sir, around Ludlow, I know; but you see, Ludlow sits right on the Herefordshire border. And in those early days it really was a border, because of the – er –"

"Special dispensations?" I knew some long words too.

"Absolutely. Or very close. Do you know, in Herefordshire there are more than a hundred and thirty castles?"

"Good God!" This really did floor me.

"Nearly all now just ruins, or the grassy remains of a motte-and-bailey, of course."

"Of course," I echoed. What could be more obvious?

I went and got on a bus to Shrewsbury. The reference library was open till late on a Saturday and I delved very deeply into castles. But, as I might have expected, their books and references were almost exclusively concerned with their own county. In case it helped, I made copious notes of castles from there down to Herefordshire and across to Wales; but nothing emerged that would be very useful to me.

Even more frustrating, although they had a copy of the Victoria History of their neighbour Herefordshire, I had forgotten that it was just a single Volume One: it had been published, doubtless to the sound of trumpets, around 1904, and Volume Two was still awaited... I could well become an expert on geological shifts, or even a range of extinct beetles; but of defensive sites built by humans, Norman or otherwise, nothing. (Volume Two? Wait another fifty years!).

So, having got that far, it being a pleasant weekend, I caught a train down to Hereford, and booked myself in at the Green Dragon. Clearly, I wouldn't be in time for the County Library.

And old and much-liked schoolmaster of mine, Mr Thomas, had moved on, years ago, and was now running the Cathedral School. I rang from the hotel and was immediately asked to supper. We chatted about the castles, and he lead me across to the School library, where local history occupied three groaning shelves…

It's "who you know", isn't it?

★ ★ ★

I went back on the Sunday morning early, armed with the library key, and had those shelves all to myself while the kids were audibly and pleasingly at choir practice; I also had the OS map which extended satisfactorily down into the North Hereford castle-rich areas.

The Thomases very kindly brought me a glass of their post-matinal sherry, then another which was intended to be pre-prandial; but having done all the available research, I made my apologies and headed for the station.

I got off at Ludlow, which was alive, for me, with all the vivid memories of that lovely holiday with Bobbie: still my favourite town of the whole country, as it will always be. I still covet that lovely house at Ludford, down past the bridge, but I didn't have the time to relax and soak in the happiness – I wanted to follow a hunch, and I went to look for a bicycle shop.

Being a tourist centre, I suspected that the place I sought would be open on a sunny autumn Sunday; and so it was. Yes, they had recently hired out a lady's bike, to a young woman with a foreign accent. Spanish, was she? French? It had been a week or so ago, paid in advance for a month. No, no local address, just a travel agent up in Wellington. Was there anything else?

There wasn't really: I'd had no lunch, so I wandered down to that splendid but almost over-timbered Tudor watering-hole The Feathers, and opened up my OS map. They had brought me a coffee but the saucer wasn't big enough for my researches, so I said to the girl that I'd like a cucumber sandwich.

"Just the one?" she queried – I must have been looking gaunt and troubled.

She was a nice girl, and I wondered whether anyone was taking her for walks along the Teme. Such a waste if not.

"You're right," I said. "Let's live dangerously, I'll have two. But on a big plate, one that'll stretch from –" I measured on the map – "from Craven Arms to Tenbury."

She leaned over to look.

"What you want is a dustbin lid."

"You're probably right, Lucy," I said. "It is Lucy, isn't it?"

It wasn't Lucy, but she went off with a big smile and I settled down to look for ruined castles within cycling range of Ludlow: most of them were over to the left, which was only to be expected since that way lay Wales...

But then she came back, bringing me a pencil tied to a foot long piece of string.

"There you are. What you do, you hold the end of the string at us here, and then you draw –"

"A circle, brilliant."

"I learnt that at school," she told me, "And it's Jennie."

At that moment, a very large and burly young man came into the room, kissed her, and they went off with their arms around each other. But at the door, she did look back. So that was something.

And wasn't it an appropriate name, remembering Leigh Hunt's lovely verse?

★ ★ ★

I had with me all the notes I'd made down in Hereford. I started by putting a mark against every castle I could find within about ten miles of Ludlow: the place was crawling with them.

However, stage two was to cross out any which I was pretty sure would not be relevant. I had to bank on Marina's word, and it might have been malicious but I preferred to see her as frivolous, so much so as to be playing with me on a level field: she may be teasing me – indeed I was quite sure of it and my best bet was to play along with her – but I didn't think she would spoil the game by outright lying. I felt somehow that deceit would spoil her fun…

At the same time, I was on a knife-edge. No matter how dizzily scatter-brained Marina might be, she and Bobbie were essentially under the – Under what, exactly?

This basically unpleasant and generally unliked Captain Barton, hiding behind the position of Garrison Adjutant, was clearly in a state of terminal disillusionment at the damp-squib ending of his Army career. I had gained that sort of impression the very first day at Donnington, when he was so rude to me, and I remembered his sidelong glances at his whisky-bottle across the office, well before ten a.m.

But then, the DC did much the same…

Ah, the DC though had achieved the rank of full Colonel and would no doubt go on to Brigadier soon. Both of them much the same age. My point made.

So, Captain Dick Barton was rotting away, failure gnawing at him as he sat amid his over-the-top maze of assistants and jobsworths in that grim little Nissen hut at the centre of his web. Was he just a member of our Big Shit's network, in a similar position as our flippant Marina? Or was he, himself, covertly the Shit? It would be so nice to think so.

It was still the weekend, of course, but I didn't think I could handle this much longer on my own… On the other hand, if Barton was our man, or even a 'sleeper', while a regular Army officer, whoever could I trust? Major Parrott and his 'Security'? Even the DC for heaven's sake? And why did nobody ever see the Brigadier himself – was he really spending all his time at the pictures with my cinema vouchers?

Too much research is a bad thing at the weekend, I decided. I paid my cucumber bill to an immensely ugly old waitress who couldn't have been walked along the Teme for fifty years, and went to the station.

I'd missed my train.

There was a cross-country bus which limped along a diagonal minor road to Wellington, and I sat on the long back seat so that I could carry on with my studies. Local people looked at me mirthlessly: *they* knew where they were.

From what Marina had told me, I had to assume that I could eliminate any castle which was well-known, active and flourishing. So I crossed out Ludlow itself (far too popular); Stokesay (delicious, but unspoilt, unruined and anyway open to the public); Downton Castle (I knew it, Bobbie and I had visited as we walked towards our Mill, and been shown around by the caretaker occupants: it wasn't ruined in the least – and anyway it only dated from the 1700s); and one or two which were apparently completely phoney, but don't tell the owners I said so.

After that, nearly all the sites I had circled seemed to be lacking in one way or another. In the area I had drawn with kindly Jennie (had they gone up the river?) there were dozens of 'castle mounds', 'castle earthworks', 'mottes and baileys', and suchlike, all in the OS Gothic script but unpromising as a place in where two young women could be kept in shelter and in food. I crossed them all out, but at this stage only in pencil (yes, I'd stolen it, string and all, what's the point you're making?).

How many of Marina's Norman castles were left to me? I tried to add them up as we bumped along beneath Wenlock Edge and then swung left. If she was at all knowledgeable about all these ruins – and it seemed she was – I needed to draw up a short-list, and one day very soon indeed, I must get Bob Blackmore to take me on a tour of them...

I picked as our first call the apparently very impressive castle at a village south of Shrewsbury called Acton something, or Aston – I couldn't read my scribble and had to search for it on the swaying back seat. I was in trouble at once: everywhere in Shropshire and Herefordshire seemed to be called Acton or Aston. (I looked it up later, and found over twenty of them: they mean, respectively, the settlement-by-the-oaktree or the settlement-to-the-east, which didn't help me much. What I really needed was "the-settlement-in-the-ruined-but-still-habitable-somewhat-remote-old-castle-accessible-by-bicycle-from-Ludlow").

There didn't seem to be any of those, though it might have been more likely over in Wales, from what I had read about places like LlanfairP.G. What did strike me was the number of these little castles that were named after their originators; making short work of many hundred years of history, the castle at Cheney Longville was a 14th-century fortified manor established by the Cheney family; Moreton Corbet castle had been inherited in 1235, already 150 years old, by Richard de Corbet, become another fortified manor house, and had fallen into disrepair generations ago, but it was still owned by the Corbets! Brampton Bryan castle had been owned by a whole string of Brian Bramptons but in their case, it seemed, they had taken their name from the place, which was pretty common in the middle ages, when if you lived in a bothy on a hill you might well be Harry Upcott, or Roger Atwood if your house was among the trees. Also on my list was Richard's Castle, whoever Richard was; and Bishop's Castle, more interesting: a chap rather cruelly called Edwin Shakehead, who suffered from a palsy, prayed to some saint or other at Hereford Cathedral and was cured; so he gratefully gave some of his land in the far reaches of the Marches to the Church; a later Bishop then built a castle to keep those nasty Welsh away, some time around the end of the 11th century quite soon after William had moved in. It seems that a little town grew around it, as one might expect; and over the centuries, as the castle fell into disuse and crumbled, the town sort of expanded inwards, swamping the initial castle itself, so that in the 1550s the site included fifteen rooms mostly roofed in lead, a stable, a prison tower and a dovecot. By the eighteenth century much of the foundations had been overbuilt as a hotel, which was owned by Clive of India, and the castle was lost apart from the name…

It goes on, and I hope I'm not boring you, but isn't this what England is all about? If Marina, despite her background which must have stretched right back to the first Romans, had become so enthralled by our Norman history and all these exotic side-spread roots I was now uncovering for myself, she couldn't really be involved in such antisocial activities as spying on us for the benefit of The Kremlin, who planned to wipe us out? Could she? It was pretty clear to me that she had in some way been swayed – corrupted even? – by my chief suspect in his pale blue beret and lack of grace, indeed highly antisocial himself.

But should I expose him? The question continued to nag at me, right up to changing buses and eventually arriving with all my notes and the flapping map, back at the depot.

Walking along that well-trodden path to the Mess, I looked as usual across to the ATS CRS. What was happening to Bobbie? Tomorrow was Monday: I was fairly sure she was not in actual physical harm, otherwise Marina would not have been so chatty, or would probably not have spoken to me at all; but I must get ready to do something – whatever it was.

XVIII

The ground was cut from under me. The officers up at our Army camp, where all our soldiery lived, ate, and had their off-depot being, were purely military-minded, which in my book meant not very minded at all.

We were technically a Company, so the man in charge at the camp was a Major. (There were three Companies at the Depot in total, and that makes a Battalion, which has a Colonel in charge. Three of them make a Brigade, but I won't bother you with any more of that). Our own Major had had a pretty good war, running storemen at various Depots well behind the front lines, so that he could rattle his sabre where the enemy couldn't hear it. To compensate for this inactivity and lack of campaign medals, he now insisted on furious warlike activity for the rest of us every weekend: the men had to go out into the nearby swamps and marshes, charging through canals and deep ditches in pursuit of imaginary Reds (I supposed, or were they still the Germans or the Boers or the Fuzzy-Wuzzies?).

That had been all very well so far as I personally was concerned, because luckily I was not just a store supervisor and an occasional (though co-operative) platoon commander when it concerned my men's welfare and home problems: I was the immensely busy editor of the Codonian…

But now, and cruelly quickly, the Major had discovered my release from that job. Awaiting me was a note to advise me of a special two-day "Field Exercise" starting this Monday, where the whole Company was destined to venture out at eight-thirty to attack and destroy an imaginary invasion by vicious but unspecified baddies who had landed by parachute on top of The Wrekin. (I remember hoping they'd brought their umbrellas). We would dig into trenches overnight. My platoon, thirty men with rifles plus a machine-gunner and a mortar-man, all under my old-timer sergeant with his medal-ribbons that always put me to shame, would be awaiting me up at the camp at eight-fifteen.

Shit!

At six a.m. on Monday morning, Edwards looked at me sympathetically, but he had all my kit ready. No spit-and-polish this time, just the rough khaki appendages to buckle around me, designed by some nameless Whitehall wizard to contain ones ammunition, map, goggles, morphine, compass, first-aid kit, revolver, and all the trappings of war; or, in this case, a bottle of Tizer and some sandwiches to get me through until we bivouacked.

The first day would be spent in a fairly authentic replica of most World War Two films without the actual bullets and only some harmless explosions. But in the brief hiatus before it began, when I had a couple of minutes up at the Company Office, I used the phone.

I rang the number I had found on Marina's file, scribbled in pencil.

It was a few minutes past eight o'clock and I just thought it might be a good idea.

The number rang about five times. Then a gruff male voice answered.

"Yes, Marina?"

I didn't say anything.

"Hello?" I was pretty sure I knew the voice. I thought I'd risk it.

"Dick Barton?" I said, speaking a bit clipped.

A pause. Then:

"You will never, ever, use this line again." Much more clipped than me. And he hung up.

I went forth with my thirty men to attack the enemy up on The Wrekin, and we killed them by the thousand. We visited a pub that evening, killed thousands more on Tuesday, it was a good campaign. I came back feeing almost like a soldier.

★ ★ ★

Wednesday, I woke up aching in every muscle: crawling through mud was acceptable, I conceded, in the interests of national security; so was hurling oneself across ditches and through thick hedges; but not both at once, and all day, two days. I wondered if I could find some other excuse to avoid all this – as an ex-editor, would Reveille or Titbits take me on?

But apart from all that, the exercise hadn't been completely wasted. It gave me time to think; and you can do that, in a new-dug moist-earth-smelling trench at midnight under a few feeble stars, I found.

So long as anybody else, huddled beside you, will shut up.

That rather sly phone-call I'd made, had finally established Captain Dick Barton, my erstwhile pea-brained victim of the Codonian serial, as being Curly. To say the very least, I had under-estimated the man. This was either our actual 'sleeper', or much more likely, a junior controller of Marina, himself a lieutenant or subsidiary to the Big Shit we had to look for.

His "Yes, Marina – " on that private phone number had sealed his fate but how was I going to prove it? I really must, now or very soon, go and tell the DC or our official Security Officer, Major Parrott. And yet …

I found myself asking again: if the Garrison Adjutant was a Communist traitor, who else?

Writing now at this long distance of time, my predicament and my suspicions may seem idiotic. But you must set the story in the context of its day.

Churchill's 'Iron Curtain' had just swished down upon Europe, where Soviet troops had swept ahead of the West to seize Berlin. Atomic bombs had pulverised Japan's cities and if the secret was leaked to the Russians – who had no compunction, under Stalin, in wiping out millions of their own people – what chaos could they inflict on us, we who were utterly exhausted by our success, and pretty much broke?

You must remember that Red spies were already leaking secrets from us (in Canada, I had cause to remember) to the Soviets. The US had rescued certain Nazi scientists in order to work further on rocket science. The poisonous seeds of Macarthyism were already sprouting among Hollywood's elite...

Here in England, admittedly, we took Communism with a big pinch of salt, and tended to laugh (though perhaps a shade nervously) at people like Harry Pollitt; up in Scotland and over in Wales, he was taken more seriously, but then, the Celts have always been a bit extreme – perhaps as a means of asserting their importance?

All the same, given all that background uncertainty, I felt I shouldn't yet unburden myself to anybody about Dick Barton. Except, surely, the DC?

I snatched a quick breakfast, that Wednesday morning, and headed for his office. But I stopped. I had to get my personal priorities right. And, even more so now that I had been kicked off the Codonian, and with my demob approaching, that top priority was to rescue Bobbie. I decided not to trust the DC just yet, nor for that matter Major Parrott, bleeding from a thousand wounds though he might have been... Or even Mac for Heaven's sake: Reds had no sense of the ridiculous, we all knew that, so with her wit hadn't she giggled herself out of suspicion?

I realised that I was nonplussed and playing for time…

I stopped off at HQ to see whether Shiela was back at her desk; but no, not yet. She was mending, and they'd sent her flowers. In her hospital bed at the ATS, she'd had lots of them, they told me; understandable – a popular girl. And visits, too. The Security Major had called in several times, wasn't that nice of him? Not half, I thought.

Oh, and the Adjutant, too. He'd taken her a big bunch of grapes, goodness knew where he'd got them from, these days, but how kind. Conscience, I wondered?

As I walked out of the building, somebody tugged at my sleeve.

It was Harold.

"Mr Topps, sir."

"Yes, Harold, what is it? Have you got some more news from Marina? Is Bobbie OK?"

Well, he told me, it was now Wednesday and he thought Marina was likely to ring him this evening. If so, what did I want to do about it?

If she was going to ring, I had to make sure I got the call diverted; so I lied to Harold that I was sure his wife would be back with him soon, and made a beeline for the Chunk at Building 18.

Peggy had not been slow to set up the special phone-line, and to arrange for all calls to Marina's Wellington number to be automatically diverted to Brown's desk.

I went over there. According to the note stuck on his typewriter he was "out on a story", which I took to mean, as usual, that he was sleeping off the excesses, whatever they might be, of the previous evening. I sat and wished that I was still a journalist and not suffering from the healthier but agonising excesses of my two Field Days.

While I waited, I dug out from Peggy Chunk's archives a whole stack of old Codonians, dating right back to the paper's start three years ago, when it had been founded by an obscure and usually absent Colonel with an obsession for sport but with only scant journalistic pretensions. It had always been the practice to run a short piece on popular officers when they were posted away, but I was wondering whether senior people had been mentioned upon being posted in. Apparently not, other than the Brigadiers themselves, who came and went pretty frequently, either unhappy or too happy in our backwater. So, no hope of any clue here, as to Dick Barton's origins.

How else, I wondered, could I check on the man, while avoiding any exposure to other senior officers? I had a sudden inspiration and went across to the HQ building where our old Polish suspect Paul Klenov would be sitting at his desk in Records Section. He was still using that name, since he had no other. He was innocently pleased to see me…

I had remembered that he was in the filing department: did they have all the files on the depot military?

"No, I'm afraid not."

Sadness…

"Only the officers."

Happiness after all. Yes, they were over there, and all their pay records, too.

While I sat amid the dozens of busy typists, the air throbbing with unimportant messages being sent from one bureaucrat to the next and back again, our memory-lapsed musician was across the room delving into cabinets. As one always finds with string-players, he was meticulous: they have to be, don't they, until they get famous? Wind, the wood and brass can puff and blow and an occasional wrong note is called 'creative', especially on the horn (I've even heard a blatant mistake in a Borodin overture hailed as 'unbearably plaintive'); percussionists just hit, too-loud or too-soft being just a personal statement; even a concert pianist can get away with ham-fistedness, known as temperament, or 'idiosyncratic' if he's Canadian; but if you're a fiddler and one of the crowd, it's got to be right all the time, until you've developed into a 'well-loved eccentric' soloist, grown your hair very long or very short, and if possible turned it ginger. Then, you've got it made.

Paul Klenov came back into my wandering consciousness, disconsolate, shaking his head.

All the depot's Army officers were fully recorded, one file each. Moreover, a separate set of files listed them all and their pay details alphabetically. But there was nothing for Captain Barton. Not a mention, anywhere.

Not even payslips? No record: the Captain must be paid elsewhere.

Too bloody true, I thought. I swore Paul to secrecy, and went for a drink very thoughtfully indeed.

★ ★ ★

So very badly, I needed somebody to talk to. I read once about a young subaltern who had escaped from people he thought he could trust, and was stumbling in the dark through a minefield, blindfold… Not the ideal way to locate the Big Shit.

And yet I was certain that Barton wasn't that top man. He must simply be the second-in-command, or just a level associate… Where the hell was I?

I went to see little Padre Jones.

He had an office, as one might expect, alongside the corrugated Garrison Church which had been positioned by some hopeful moralistic planners in the 1930s between the

lascivious Garrison Theatre and the licentious NAAFI –
presumably in the days before they began putting bromide in
the tea. I found the Padre at his desk guiltily reading the
scurrilous 'Reveille', and enjoyed shaking my head at him as I
sat down.

"I need to keep myself abreast – ," he began, then tried to
rephrase it.

"Your research and your secret," I said, "are safe with me."

I told him my problem: I had been appointed to search for
our covert enemy 'sleeper' and it seemed I'd found him, plus
a young woman who was probably under his control. But
what, now, was my ethical duty? As this man was a senior
Depot officer, should I expose him to other senior Depot
officers who might also, for all I knew, be covert agents? I then
told him that they had Bobbie as a captive…

He didn't hesitate.

"Tim," he said, "you kept that fact until last, and it shows
that you have a keen sense of duty to your country, as your
training has instilled in you." I was duly though perhaps
mistakenly flattered by this. "But, ultimately," and he flapped
his hands as he tried to find the appropriate quotation, "at the
end of the day as they say, and it must say so somewhere in the
Bible but," with a despairing shrug, "I'm buggered if I can
think of it, lots of other people can take care of the country and
its ethics, but only you can look after Bobbie."

I can't tell you the relief Padre Jones had given me. And he
went on.

"Politicians come and go," he said. "Political ideals and
enforcements come and go; not just governments but whole
nations come and go, and we – the poor bloody infantry of
every country – have to come and go with them, we have to
drift with those ideals to and fro, we can't swim against the tide,
and if we try to, they wipe us out. The gas ovens of the Nazis

were only the extremity of the verbal gas ovens of democracy…
If you don't comply, you'll be snuffed out, one way or another."

"So, you think –?"

"Look after your Bobbie. Keep all your findings to yourself until she is safe. Once you've got her back, do whatever your officer's duty requires of you, but look after her first," said Padre Jones. "And then, when you're ready and she's out of an ATS uniform and 'acceptable' to these pompous Blimps, I'll marry you."

I got up to go; but then I looked past him, to a collection of old postcards on the wall.

"Padre," I said, astonished, "where did you get that?"

He turned and looked. I was pointing to a card showing a ruined castle, with a swallowtail butterfly in the foreground.

"I've no idea. It's been up there ever since I arrived, it must have been sent to my predecessor. You know how these cards get pinned up, and stay for ages. Why do you ask?"

I beckoned to it. "Please?"

He passed it across to me. It had been posted in Toulon, nearly two years ago. It read: "Many thanks for the send-off. Settled here. Best regards: H."

Yes, of course I could have it, if it was any help. Maybe, he said, as I left, one day I could tell him what this was all about? At the wedding?

★ ★ ★

It was now Wednesday afternoon, and for a week Bobbie had been a prisoner, somewhere. From Marina's flippant comments, she was – they were? – being held at some ruined Norman castle. Within cycle distance of Ludlow…

I went despondently back towards Printing & Pubs. at Building 18, for no real reason except that I still felt more at-home at my old Codonian desk than in the soulless Receipts-and-Maintenance-and-Issues of Building Five. I nevertheless felt a slight spark of remorse for having so thoroughly abandoned poor Mr.Whatever-his-Name-was… Ah, yes, Stanway, God, I was forgetting everything: all I could remember was his gummy smile after losing all his teeth… It was high time I got out of this crazy life. Thank God it was teatime.

Private Brown met me with a sense of unusual urgency, as well as a steaming mug.

"Your little man Harold has been trying to contact you," he told me. "He went home at lunchtime, and came back with this."

He handed me a postcard. It was addressed to Marina, from France. It was a picture of a small, rather distressed-looking fishing port, with a few tattered boats and a long quay, and an unimposing tower over at the right-hand side.

I turned it over. In the same neat hand I had seen before in Marina's file, the message simply read: "p/q court-ct? v.exp vite". Signed as before: 'H'.

I sat and looked at this for a while, as memories of schoolday French slowly seeped back, because this wasn't about minding one's ps and qs: this was 'pourquoi', especially given the question mark… At the end, it was 'please explain quickly,' wasn't it? But the middle bit?

"It's 'short circuit'," Brown told me, about half a second before I was going to say it to him.

The writer, who was so evidently our Big Shit now, was referring to our Wem article in last Friday's Codonian. The message could mean nothing else. But this was impossible, given the time-scale.

I looked at the postmark; again, it was Toulon, but that was just the postal centre for foreign post: our Big Shit could be based anywhere along that still under-developed coast west of the Top People's Riviera, where little houses clung to the red Maures hillside and the fisherfolk mended their nets amid the olives and the cork-oaks.

But the date was the impossible thing in all this: the card had been posted on Saturday.

In itself, that was quite normal: four days in transit was unremarkable for letters from France, now that services were beginning to return to normal.

What was alarming me, was how that message could have been written on a Saturday, quoting the Codonian which was only published on the previous day.

It was alarmingly obvious to me, that the wording of my article must have been conveyed to the Big Shit *before* its publication date.

XIX

I hunched alongside the Codonian desk for the rest of the afternoon, feeling more alone than ever: the only people who could have sent the Wem article wording to the Big Shit in advance of Friday's publication-date were all the ones I was supposed to trust. Why had the DC so quickly clipped my wings by removing me from the editorship? Had Major Parrott faked his Wem injuries? Was Peggy Chunk a Red feminist, as so strongly approved of, we were always being told, up in Moscow? Or if not her, how about her nubile assistant-cum-receptionist: perhaps Communist women weren't all so concrete-and-spanner-built as we had been led to believe? And then there was my Private Brown himself: perhaps it was fashionable at places like Shrewsbury to lean to the Left, it certainly had been for a good number of my own schoolmates, I remembered from our Debating Society and indeed from a few of the younger masters, as they all limped back from the war…

Yes, I was on my own. I did, now, seem to have in my hand a clue to the Big Shit, as I sat and looked at the picturesque postcard. But who could I show it to without running the risk of sounding an alarm? Nobody. It was now my personal problem.

Brown was leaving me well alone, but I thought I should test him by setting him a research task: if he showed any signs of alarm, I would know he was a suspect.

"From all these notes I've made about castles in north Herefordshire," I asked, "can you please draw up a list of them in their date order, right from the start of being built when the Normans first came?".

He had been busying himself with next week's layout. There was quite a good editorial lamenting the two-day Wrekin exercise, the sarcasm of which would probably have got him kicked off the paper if he hadn't resigned already. He had also – very neatly I was the first to admit – snookered the "GC" (as he termed our incoming editor, the "Gruesome Colonel") by slipping into the centre pages, this very last week before the take-over, a piece praising all the local cinemas and launching a very simple competition which promised masses of free seats and would run on for a guaranteed six months. I particularly liked that idea, as it would secure the backing of all the cinemas, promise them continued advertising, and the free passes which would see Brown through – in the back row prior to the slagheaps – until his demob. It would also go a long way to undermine the GC's plans to cut out our essential cinemas and concentrate on his boring and superficial inter-battalion sport...

Brown went off to another desk to work on my castle request.

I had decided that enough was enough. Tomorrow, I would undertake a lightning tour of all the most likely Norman castles around Ludlow, find Bobbie and rescue her from this mysterious kidnap.

I rang Bob Blackmore at the Motor Pool and asked him to pick me up at nine a.m. at my House –"

"The one with the green door?"

"It'll be blue by then," I said, "the lamps will be out. And bring that starting-handle, we're in for a heavy day."

★ ★ ★

If our Big Shit was sending postcards from the South of France, as he clearly was, what did that card on Padre Jones's wall indicate? He must have been here, in the depot, at some time. Did he then recruit Captain Barton? But perhaps he had already recruited Marina in France, then followed her here, before returning to the Maures Riviera or whatever that undeveloped coastline should be called?

Whoever else had he recruited to "The Cause" while he was here? And if he was using Marina to spy on our depots at Bicester and Didcot, where else? How did Dick Barton really fit into all this: just as a parallel agent, or as a superior, a valued second-in-command? I had to attack all this head-on, if only to rescue Bobbie. I just had Marina's word for my girl's safety and wellbeing... No matter what corns I trod on, I now had to stop pussyfooting about to please my seniors (who might well be under suspicion themselves in any case) and blunder in for my personal reasons. I looked forward to a full day's reconnaissance tomorrow...

No matter that I might well be wading about in a whole seething nest of spies, sending secret messages from my Codonian to their Red controllers, I –

This ridiculous reverie was interrupted by Peggy Chunk, who had her coat on and was heading for the exit. Her arms were full of small packets.

"Anything for the SMP?"

I had never even heard of the SMP, so I shook my head vaguely and wanted to go on thinking about spies and Norman castles.

But then at the last moment, as so often in my erratic military career, something struck me.

"Just a moment, Peggy." She was halfway out, but put a foot against the door and turned.

"Tell me about the SMP."

"Special Military Post – don't they teach you anything at Tidworth?" She came back in. "It's been going for donkey's years, our own postal service, in case ordinary postmen go on strike or something. In Victorian times they used to print special stamps for it –"

"Yes." I remembered from my collecting days, 'army official' overprints. "And I think they still did it right up to the war, in Egypt, a sort of label?"

"I wouldn't be surprised," said Peggy. "Nowadays it goes by air, any stuff that's fairly lightweight on the scales but heavyweight in importance, that's how they teach it to us." She put all the packets down on the desk so that she could wave her arms about. "All over the place, post-haste literally. Whether it's Hong Kong or Nairobi, it'll be there tomorrow; it's alongside the good old Diplomatic Bags, you see…"

I knew I was grasping at a straw, but it was just possibly worth asking.

"Could you, just maybe, send Codonians out with it?"

"What, with the SMP? *Special* Military Post? Don't be –"

But then she stopped.

"Wait a moment, Tim… We've a very short mailing list for Codonian subscribers outside Donnington. They go to other depot magazine editors, like Bicester and the obvious ones; and to big BODs abroad; but you know," and she gave it some thought, "there is a tiny list of individuals, people who have left here and asked us –"

"Peggy. Let me have that list, eh?"

She went across to her files; and within two minutes I knew that I could breathe again, and regain faith not just in Peggy, her lovely acolyte, and my old pal Brown, but also the DC and the perforated Major. They were all pure as snow.

I knew who our Big Shit was.

★ ★ ★

I was still sitting by the Codonian desk as night fell and everybody went home. Brown had done a good job with his list of suspicious castles from 1066 through to the 1300s, that is, everything one could describe as Norman. I had my map spread out, and was sketching out a tour for tomorrow.

But most of all, I was waiting for the telephone to ring: the special line we had persuaded Security to lay on, diverted from Harold's flat.

Six o'clock passed... Seven... Eight... I had to read Reveille twice. (But that was usually worthwhile. Some years later it was incredibly rewarding, with a splendid sideways-on double spread in the middle pages, of young Brigitte at her sublime best, pinned up in nearly every student room I visited in the course of my insurance business).

Then at about eight-twenty, the phone suddenly screeched and I jumped a foot. It must be a semi-local call again to judge by that hand-manipulated ring: coming in from an operator outside our own automatic area, but less than thirty-or-so miles away. Yes, it was around Ludlow again.

"*Ciao, cheri,*" it said. The mixture of French and Italian I've always found irresistible, not just sexily but historically – it derives from the close relationship of the northern Italians with the southern French; after all, Nice was Nizza until quite recently.

I didn't say anything, just yet.

"*Carissimo mio?*" Just slightly hesitant.

"Probably not," I said.

"Oh my God," said Marina. There was a pause, with some breathing. "I want Harold," she went on. "Why are you at my house – "

"Marina, I'm not at your house, you are at mine." I had to play this as carefully as I could, chiefly because her actions had been so eccentric and she might well have become deranged by the pressures that Curly must have been putting upon her.

"I am only ringing," she went on, "to talk to my Harold –"

I wasn't trained in this sort of thing, but I felt I needed to somehow disrail her, just to see what would happen.

"Your Harold," I told her, "doesn't want to speak to you." Let's see what that turns up, I thought.

"*Ai*". I believe that is the way you are supposed to spell the Italian cry of distress. I only know a double-dot as being a German umlaut (why don't we ever use it when writing about Goering or Goebbels?); but my classical friends tell me it simply isolates the letter over which it hovers; so – "*Ai*" is what she said.

"No, Marina," I pursued. "Harold is so upset, he has asked me to answer your telephone calls, until you come back home to him."

"But, Tom –"

"Tim."

"*Mamma mia*. Tim, Tom, I am only acting to save my dear Harold."

What sort of bluff was this? She really did sound genuinely upset.

"Quickly, Marina, before the telephone money runs out, you must tell me."

"I cannot, I mustn't talk –"

"Don't be silly. Where are you? Where is Bobbie? Who –"

"Oh Tim, you are so – *come se dice*? – so English. You know we are at Curly Castle, I have told you."

"I have a list of all those castles. I am going to visit every Norman castle near to Ludlow, so you might as well tell me."

She was laughing: that lovely little French-Italian sexy giggle which had always melted me, no matter what. I could see her eyes, the tilt of her neck, the uplift of the shoulders. Oh, what a woman – Oh, stop it!

"What makes you think Curly's is a Norman castle?" she said. And hung up.

★ ★ ★

At the start of our phone conversation, I was intending to tell Marina that I was in possession of the latest postcard; but in a few moments her continuing attitude made me sure that it would be much better to withhold that knowledge in case I could use it later, as some sort of bargaining-point. I put the card into my pocket, together with the list of Norman castles from Brown and the short list of Codonian external subscribers from Peggy. And gathering up my OS map of the Ludlow area, I went over to the HQ Mess.

The DC was in his usual antimacassared chair, and smiled at me, but it was quite obviously a guilty smile: he knew that he had been forced to dismiss me from the Codonian, he knew I resented it, and I'm sure he also knew that the new incoming Colonel, though dripping with Establishment laurels and commendations, was going to be the kiss of death to The Codonian.

★ ★ ★

My alarm clock went off in good time and I was fully ready for Bob when he drew up outside my blue door at nine next morning. I took my map and my notes. Oh, and my gun. As one does… But I decided not to wear uniform.

"We're going to explore some ruined Norman castles," I told him as we sped towards the main A5 road.

"Oh, good," said Bob without much enthusiasm.

"Because," I continued, "one of them is the base for a secret nest of spies threatening our national security."

263

"Oh Christ!" He didn't say anything for a while after absorbing this. I let him think about it.

"Turn left," I said after The Wrekin, "we want to cut straight down towards Ludlow."

The road came out at Church Stretton, which had no noticeable castles, just the bleak hilltop remains of pre-Roman forts remembered only by their grassy mounds and ditches, where the tough wooden defences had rotted away through two thousand years.

I waved a hand up towards those immense green ditches, the perspiring work of a multitude of slaves. Couldn't he imagine the ghastliness of it, I asked. The tiny huts full of vulnerable innocents huddled together in terror; the constant, everyday anguish of murderous invaders; the perpetual –

He interrupted me as he swung left on to the main Ludlow road. Was I describing my old school or his prison?

As far as I remember, I didn't reply to that, but buried my head in the depths of the OS map. I had made, from Brown's chronological work, a short list of the Norman castles I ought to take a close look at – all of them within ten miles of Ludlow, which meant that a call from any local phone-box would be routed through that exchange.

I had also just decided, since we were making such good time, and it was still only mid-morning, to go first of all to the furthest point South; then work our way around Ludlow to the West, because presumably the castles sponsored by the Norman kings would chiefly be over by the threatening Welsh… (Except those in Ilford).

So, quite soon, we had sped through Ludlow and were approaching Brown's entry of Ashton (one of the many, you'll remember?), where a 'Castle Tump' was marked right alongside the main road, and also a wide expanse labelled 'Castle Ground'.

This seemed very promising until we got there and I walked about. I knew that 'tump' is a rather rare, west-midlands word for a mound, but I had hoped that the important-sounding 'ground' would reveal a spread of old ruins and the sort of hiding place I was looking for. It didn't. We turned west, aiming for the fully-spelt-out 'Croft Castle', and enjoying along the way some of the delightful place-names: a little village called Eye, another close by named Luston – we wondered whether the latter had been given its name by voyeurs in the former. Perhaps that was (up on the hill) 'The Riddle'?

Croft Castle, even at first glance, took us violently in the wrong direction altogether. We found a greasy-spoon café on the main road and had sausages and chips while I read about Croft, aloud, to Bob. Then we drove up just to look. True, it had been established very soon after 1066, so that Brown was arguably right to include it; and astonishingly the De Crofts were still there the notes said; but the whole place had been pulled down hundreds of years ago and the gigantic present structure dated only from the eighteenth century. We zigzagged cross-country to a much more promising site: Wigmore.

This excited me the moment I laid eyes on it; it even aroused Bob – it was all in ruins, but draped across the entire end of a hill, and how evocative! Brown's notes dated it to "pre-1075, when taken over by the Mortimers; probably very soon after 1066, probably one of FitzOsbern's." I loved that 'one of'. ("Yes," said FitzOsbern casually, "that's one my castles, actually…") Being a Top Norman couldn't have been too bad.

We explored thoroughly, and it took two hours, the remains of towers, the leaning curtain wall, hints of a gatehouse, all of it smothered by weeds and drapes of ivy… There were none of the signs of life that I had been hoping for. We ended up looking at the mound which still held aloft the broken shell of the keep. I found myself searching the mound fruitlessly, in the hope of a hidden entrance to some underground dungeon that had been newly made habitable; but of course there was nothing whatever.

We went back to the car and I looked despondently at the map. Our next stop was just a few miles due north, but it was merely described as a 'Castle Mound', and I felt it meant no more than that; in any case, we were nudging my ten-mile limit from Ludlow. Better start to head east?

There was another 'Castle Mound' at Downton, but I knew that one from my Bobbie holiday, and that's all it was. Then, Downton Castle itself, I also knew – like Croft all over again, it had been thoroughly and pompously thrown up in the seventeen hundreds, so of course it wasn't on Brown's list anyway…

But something was bothering me.

I remembered Marina's teasing words on the phone yesterday: *What makes me think that Curly's Castle is Norman?*

"Hold on," I said to Bob. "I need time to do some thinking, let's go and find a decent pub."

Was it called The Wigmore Arms, or something? I don't remember, but it was open late afternoon because it called itself a hotel, whereas pubs would be closed till six. Moreover, it was very cosy, they had splendid pickled onions to go with the pork pies, and we indulged ourselves with a pint of the local tangle-foot.

Herefordshire cider can be dangerous stuff, especially to beer-drinkers. A favourite village pub of Bobbie's and mine, had a mixed clientele; and there was an occasion once, over a Bank holiday weekend, when the beer ran out. All the beer crowd were forced, muttering disdainfully, to go on to the local apple-juice. Over the evening we noticed that they were going

266

out, one by one, to the lavatories in the yard; but they weren't coming back. The landlord went to investigate. He found them lying in heaps…

… So I made sure that Bob drank his pint carefully, and instead of a second round I bought him a bag of crisps. It was good thinking.

Good thinking, also, was what I managed as I thumbed through my notes.

Suppose Marina, with her admitted knowledge of early castles, but probably none at all of so-called late ones, which were in any case not defensive structures but just pretentious country houses… Suppose she wasn't so much teasing me but outwitting me?

I dug back, not into Brown's list, but into my own sketchy scribbling after my Hereford trip. Not post-Norman, but what about pre – ? Yes – a brainwave!

I read that *before* the Norman Conquest, some visitors from across the Channel had been invited over here by Edward the Confessor, and they had brought the castle concept with them. It was believed that just four pre-Conquest castles had been built, with Edward's blessing. Of these, three had been in Herefordshire, with the evident idea of defence against those Wretched Welsh. One: in about 1050, a little place called Ewyas Harold, down in the far south at the bottom end of the lovely Golden Valley, destroyed after a few years of being put up but leaving a big mound thirty feet high and two hundred feet across. Two: at Hereford itself, completely wiped off the face of the earth by a Welsh invasion a few years after its building in 1052…

And three: Richard's Castle, ho-ho, only four miles outside Ludlow, is a remote large village which may well call itself a small town, and whose castle is even more remote, now that I could study it on the OS map. Not only that, but where we sat with our pies, it was on our direct route.

I realised that Marina was being even more subtle than I gave her credit for: "Curly's Castle" was Richard's Castle because Curly was Dick Barton and Dick means Richard… Clever girl.

★ ★ ★

Can there be any other civilised country, other than in the mountains, where nearby places are so difficult to reach? When I had dragged Bob away from his empty tankard and the crackling fire, and pointed him in the right direction, I took a closer look at the roads we needed. I also took a look at my watch: it would be getting dark within half-an-hour, which wasn't a bad thing because I reckoned night-time would be best for me. But the obvious minor road from Wigmore to Richard's Castle, which must in its time have been a well-worn thoroughfare between two flourishing Norman neighbours, now simply petered out. The first four or five miles were fine, but then we would be going through or at a tangent to interesting-sounding settlements like 'The Goggin', 'High Cullis', 'Brightall', and if we weren't very careful, 'Woodcock Hill' and 'Yeld's Hill' where the yellow contours were huddled together as if terrified of their own vertigo. I didn't show any of this to Bob, as he was already leaning forward or swaying quietly sideways in his seat, and had turned on his headlights far too soon.

But we got into the village or small town or whatever it was; and then out of it again for nearly a mile, before drawing up at an excessively minor crossroads, one limb of which carried a worn sign to an old church and, ultimately it seemed, to the castle.

It was now close to twilight. I suggested that Bob should park the car a few yards up a track directly opposite the one I needed: that way, he could see what went on – if anything did, I hastily added – I didn't want to alarm him, this was none of his business. To reassure him how calm and peaceful everything was going to be, I took my pistol out of my pocket – what a relief to the hipjoint – and left it in the car's glove compartment.

"Stay put," I said. "I should be back within the hour."

And I headed off, up the hill, past a few cottages, then between ragged hedges on either side and, at last, an aged tower and then the old church.

Not a soul in sight.

I came to the beginning of the castle ruins: as at Wigmore, they were evocative and impressive, with very high remains here and there of the outer walls; I detected what must have been several towers built into those walls; as I felt my way onwards, there was a muddy patch in the middle of the overgrown path, and I was thrilled – no other word will do – to see a wide range of identical bicycle tracks.

But still, no signs of life.

I was starting to lose heart: had Marina been nastily teasing and misleading me after all? Was I never going to rescue my love – and if so, whatever was going to happen to her – to me – to us?

Then, through the encompassing gloom and against a darkening sky, I was just able to see that those cycle tracks continued, past the ruins. Over to the right, was the considerable mound upon which the main keep must have stood. I moved clumsily towards it through a forest of nettles; but the tracks veered across to the left, so there was no point in looking at the mound for signs of life.

Over to the left, beyond the end of the residual curtain wall, was a building.

It seemed to be partially in ruins, though surely of a later date than a Norman builder would have recognised, let alone one who had come across to live among the Saxons. It was not big, but it was quite square; also, I realised in my entirely amateur way, it had no castellations or whatever they were called; and where a castle would have slits, this had some – modest to be sure – windows. I went up close.

There was a set of stone steps which wound down to a lower floor. At the bottom, after a small courtyard, there was a big wooden door. Cycle tracks led inside. There was a light.

I took a deep breath and flung the door open.

It was a large room, quite well-furnished with second-hand wooden stuff. In an inglenook (probably later than Tudor?) a log fire simmered happily, and a big old black kettle steamed on the edge of the grate.

Bobbie was sitting reading a book, close to the fire, with one ankle attached by a handcuff to the leg of a heavy oak table.

"My love," I cried. "I've come at last to get you!"

"Go away," hissed my beloved.

"What!!"

"Piss off," she said, "You'll ruin everything."

XX

Quick and quiet as possible, but in utter bewilderment, I slid back outside, stumbled up the steps and sat down thoughtfully, and painfully, in the dark on a mass of brambles that were upholstering a big chunk of fallen masonry. pre-Norman, High Dutch, Deco, who the hell cared?. I found that I was fast losing my appreciation of old ruins.

Somewhere, there had to be an answer to this development. As the bats circled overhead, I looked at the various options:

Bobbie was working in secret with the lovely Marina, innocent as she must therefore be, against this evil Captain whom nobody liked, whom I had made a personal enemy by ridiculing him in my newspaper, but who was evidently an agent of the Big Shit whom I was about to expose.

Or Bobbie was, inexplicably, doing the exact opposite.

Or, she had some secret scheme of her own, to escape from both of her captors.

Or she had been driven completely insane by the horrors and rigours of her imprisonment; more likely drugged, suffering delusions…

Or… There must be a number five, somewhere.

I had to get back in again. Apart from anything else, I was getting thorns in my bottom and it was starting to rain. But I thought I'd better stay put for a bit longer in case anything else happened.

It did.

The door opened, casting a shaft of light on the steps. Marina came out, with her bike; looked at the weather, went back for a raincoat; and called out "Won't be long" as she shut the door. She hauled the bike up dextrously, and rode off into the murk.

I ran across and down to the door. I opened it and walked straight into Captain Dick Barton. He didn't have the blue beret on. His head was shining. No wonder they called him Curly; I suppose he preferred it to my Bart Dixon?

"Come in and shut up," he told me.

★ ★ ★

Bobbie was shaking her head, giving me a despairing look.

"Why couldn't you keep out of this? I said in my note –"

"The only letter I got, told me you'd been posted away to Catterick –"

"What! Catterick? I wrote and said I had a special job to do, but mustn't talk about it."

Captain Barton coughed.

"If you'll both be quiet –" We did. "I stopped your note, I didn't want this silly man putting his nose in –"

"So why did you send me that stupid Catterick thing?" I asked him.

He didn't know what I was talking about.

"I am hunting for an enemy agent," he began self-importantly, "and I needed –"

"You? The DC put me in charge of that. We've used The Codonian to –"

"I told him," said Bobbie.

"Pointless waste of time, silly little bogsheet."

"I don't believe you," I said to the Captain. "You did the break-in at Building Eighteen, I've measured your boots. You did the Wem explosion, your hat was seen in the car. You get your petrol and your servicing away from the depot."

"My word," he sneered. "What a smart-arsed little Sherlock."

"And what's more," I ended triumphantly, "you aren't even on the Depot strength, are you, you miserable –"

Dick Barton reached into his pocket and, truth to tell, I was expecting a bullet; but all he pulled out was a small wallet. He flicked it open and showed an identity card with his ugly face on it.

"Any fool can fake an ID these days," I told him. "They'll do one while you wait in Brixton market." I'd never been anywhere near Brixton, let alone its market if there is one, but it sounded good.

To my surprise, he smiled. It wasn't a very pretty sight but it did seem to ease the tension.

"I'm sure you're right," he said, putting it on the table for me to read. "But it's the best I can do. The War Office can't afford to pay for forgeries."

It said something about a Government Department, it mentioned three letters starting with 'S', and gave a London phone-number to ring if any proof was needed. I didn't recognise the 'S..' thing.

"We call it MI6 nowadays," he said, putting the card away. "We have to operate outside all the normal routine establishments, that's why Depot HQ doesn't have any file on me. The Brig and the DC think I'm just the Garrison Adjutant, and a pretty bloody useless one according to you and your idiot newspaper."

"Well – " I began uncomfortably, but again he smiled.

"It wasn't bad really, your serial thriller," he said. "The wife loved it. I suppose, come to think of it, it's improved my cover. But listen, we must talk fast. I'll fill you in."

He sat closer.

"I've been on to Marina for weeks. We know she's been put in as a sleeper, the CIA tipped us off but they got the sex wrong." He grinned. "Can't think how, I'm damn sure I wouldn't…"

"Yes, but her controller –"

"No, shut up and listen. It's absolutely essential that I trace the top man who's running her, as we call it. The Controller."

"But I know who –"

"Do shut up, Topps. I've got her to believe I'm also a sleeper but superior to her. I'm sticking with her, and encouraging a whole string of minor events so that she'll divulge the name. She won't given me a clue yet, and –"

"But I know –"

" – I'm pretty sure she fully trusts me now and she'll drop the controller's details soon. Especially after I got her to kidnap Roberts here. I'm sorry about that, but Roberts agreed, so no harm's been done. I convinced Marina we had to silence your girl because she was getting too close for comfort, and I had a big event planned. That Wem thing was just a dummy-run, you see: it wasn't meant to hurt anybody, I'm so sorry about Bill Parrott and the staff sergeant, in fact –"

"Yes, you've taken them flowers and stuff, that was suspicious too."

"Why?" He was genuinely alarmed by that.

"Out of character." That was a point to me. He had started to be rather irritating, and was so dismissive of my Codonian successes that I decided, for the moment, to give up on my attempts to tell him about the Big Shit. It could wait. Besides, the man was still talking.

"It was supposed to be a minor incident with nobody around. I had no idea Wem's little security corporal had reported an intruder. But I just had to kid Marina along, so she'll trust me. Then, soon, she must come up with the name of her controller."

I opened my mouth and shut it again.

"But I've always tried to leave a hint here and there, so that the DC or somebody at the depot will realise MI6 have put a man on the job –"

"For instance?" I still didn't really want to trust him. I was nearly ready to spring my surprise on him, but I had to wait for Marina to come back from the pub or wherever she'd gone.

"Well, look at that Codonian break-in. I got us inside by using my master-key, then –"

Bobbie interrupted to say yes, we had worked out that the glass was on top of the footprints, so it must have been an inside job. She had told him already that the small boot-print had led us to Marina –

Barton looked at the door furtively.

"That brings us back to her," he said. "I must insist that you keep up the deception, at least until I've got that name out of her." That name: *I had it.* I sighed but nodded. "She should be back any minute."

"One last thing," I said. "Well, two, really. Why isn't there a file at HQ Building on you, just as Adjutant, I mean?"

He shrugged as if it didn't matter in the least.

"I nicked it. Nobody was likely to look for it under normal circumstances, those files can lie there for years until somebody's dead or posted away. I'm not paid through Donnington in any case, and as you've spotted, my car expenses are taken care of direct from Baker Street." I supposed I had to believe this. "What was the other question?"

"Have you got a picture of a swallowtail butterfly?"

It was his turn to open and shut his mouth. Before either of us could say any more, we heard the curious sounds you make when dragging a bicycle down the stone steps of a Saxon castle cellar. Or the house next-door to one.

★ ★ ★

Dixon hadn't reacted to my last question, he evidently had no idea what I was talking about. A slight puzzled expression, and he briefly shook his head at me as Marina came in, dripping from the rain, with a big bundle of waterlogged newspaper.

She took a startled step back when she saw me, but recovered quickly.

"Tom," she said with a big smile, waving her parcel. "You like cheeps?"

"It's Tim," said Bobbie from her table-leg enchainment, and there was an edge in her voice. "And yes, he likes chips."

"*Bene, bene.*"

"If your Harold was here," Bobbie added, "we could have feesh."

"Ah, dear Harold," Marina sighed. "You have a message for me, Tim, no?"

Dick Barton looked across at me with surprise all over his shiny upper face.

"Not immediately." I thought I ought to play for time.

"What's all this?" Barton said. "How have you been in contact with each other – "

"It's far too simple for you to understand, down there in Baker Street," I told him. "We just use an invention they call a telephone."

"I ordered you," Barton said to Marina angrily, "only to telephone Harold, at your flat. Or else me on that special numb-." He broke off and swung round to me. "And how the hell did you ring me the other morning? Where did you get that number?"

This was fun.

"When you took all Marina's papers from her files in the Wellington flat, you should have taken the outside folders as well."

This was a shot in the dark, but it worked. Marina was the angry one now.

"You took all my papers?" This was to Barton.

"Yes, yes, dear. I have to report all your work back to our controller, surely you understand that?" The Captain was well-trained, evidently, in fast reactions.

"But does Harold –"

"Harold knows nothing, you've told me that. He was at work, I made sure."

"You broke in!"

Barton sighed. I felt he needed some help to maintain his credibility, just for the moment.

"What a shocking, un-British thing to do!" I cried. "What foreign power are you working for, swine?"

The Captain looked at me gratefully.

"Marina," he said, "if you disapprove of my actions, I suggest you simply talk to the controller. Or shall I?"

She was on her guard again at once. She gave a very continental pout: I don't know what that did to Bart Dixon, but it certainly gave me a little twinge. I glanced across to Bobbie, but she was deep into her chips.

"I only talk…" Marina admirably corrected her grammar. "I talk only to my controller. This is his instruction. You know so."

So the Captain still wasn't getting anywhere. I felt inside my jacket for the comforting crinkle of the pages given me by Peggy. It was time to fire my missile, as soon as we had polished off the rest of the meal… I took a deep vinegary breath.

"That was really good," I said, wiping my mouth on my damp sleeve; and they all nodded in the usual polite English, or maybe Franco-Italian way.

"Real chips. Something you can't get," I told them, "in any little seaport in Var."

They all looked at me with various expressions: Marina's was the most alert.

"Not even," I went on, "at that little artistic enclave, what's it called? Saint Something or other?"

Still general bewilderment, though Marina was twisting her hands.

"*Sainte Nitouche*, would it be?" That was a subtle message for Marina, being the mythical saints-name used in Southern France to describe somebody who is utterly, extravagantly innocent, just too good to be true as we say.

But now I was getting too clever for my own good.

"I know," I said brightly, at last firing my missile, "Let's ask Hugo."

"*Aï!*" shrieked Marina.

I was expecting that reaction, because Hugo Hallam was the Big Shit.

But to my horror, Bobbie had shrieked too.

Well, I'll come back to that.

★ ★ ★

My first observation was that my performance had meant nothing whatever to Dick Barton, and he was completely out of his depth. This demonstrated that he was not only innocent of any involvement-with this spy network, unless he was very clever indeed, but that I seemed to be – despite myself – in charge of the situation, ahead of MI5 or MI6 or S-something, and all the Captains and Majors and denizens of Baker Street and Long Service and Good Conduct and all that hoo-hah. Here, I thought sadly, was the ultimate Codonian scoop that would never see the light of day because of the dreary local-league-football-obsessed editor due to succeed me next week.

Nevertheless, for the moment I was in control.

I indicated with a flick of the head to Captain Barton, that it would be useful if Marina wasn't around for a while.

"Also," I told him, "can you release Bobbie from her vicious chains?"

Barton unlocked the footcuff, handed it to Marina, and said: "Go and wait in the car, sweetie, and we will talk later about our next move, after I've checked with the Controller."

"I will myself talk to the Controller," she replied defiantly; but she was still shaken after my mention of Hugo.

"Leave this Hugo person to me," said Barton firmly, not knowing what on earth he was talking about, and I really did have to admire the man for that neat display of *sangfroid*. Whatever they taught them down there in Marylebone, must have provided a pretty sound foundation, however stupid they might seem on the surface.

When the door had shut behind Marina, he turned at once to me. I was carefully picking the last wizened chips out of the News Of The World and simultaneously pointing out to Bobbie some of the exciting scandal on its oily pages, while she rubbed her ankle.

"Who in Hell," asked Dick Barton, "is Hugo?"

It would take a while to explain to him, I said, and was there anything around to lubricate my recollection of the facts. He took the hint and disappeared into some age-old room at the back of this proto-Norman enclave, or whatever it was.

I said to Bobbie: "We'll be home soon, then we can talk more."

The Captain came back with a most welcome bottle of the usual golden liquid, and two glasses.

I rebuked him. His prisoner, I pointed out, was probably

even more in need than we were. The prisoner confirmed this. He fetched a third glass and a jug of water. We sluiced it down and though it wasn't Laphroaig, it wasn't at all bad.

"So," said Barton. "Enlightenment time?"

"You yourself," I began, a touch sycophantically because it would please him, "you are ultimately the cause of my success in unearthing Hugo."

"I am?" And then: "What success.:?" And next: "Who; for the love of – ?"

I pulled out of my damp pocket the fishing-port postcard, and – much more important – the list Peggy had given me.

"When you made that cock-up at Wem, I had to print some sort of excuse in the Codonian, and last Friday we mentioned an electrical short-circuit. Today, this card came for Marina, and it quoted the article…" And I went on to explain how the short-list of Codonian subscribers and the Special Military Post –

"Yes, I know about it. So?"

I handed him the postcard with its *'pourquoi'* message; and the list.

"As you'll see, there are just a few individual overseas Codonian subscribers," I pointed to them, "and only one in France. Down in the Midi, and in the postal catchment, or what you call it, of Toulon. Hugo got the paper and replied at once."

He looked. "Ah," he said.

I let him read the entry for himself, because I didn't want to hear any reaction from Bobbie, for some hidden reason which I so far couldn't understand.

The entry on the Codonian's external subscriber list said: "Major Hugo Hallam, RAMC (retired), c/o Post Restante, Cavalaire-sur-mer, Var – via Toulon, France."

This had been the much-loved Senior Medical Officer, so devoted to his tasks around the Depot a couple of years ago; so happy to visit the vulnerable – even the non-military – in their hospital beds, and chat and commiserate…

Or so Bobbie had told me, in those early days together when I was drafting articles about Depot personalities. She knew what a good man he was – she had known him.

She had quickly taken the hint from my whisper earlier, and said nothing. But it was high time we got out of this cellar and back into the relatively fresh air of Donnington.

Captain Dick Barton had been sitting rather quietly, looking at my exhibits and, I suppose, wondering how a pathetic National Service upstart could have out-manoeuvred him. But I had to interfere yet again, and did so apologetically.

"If you remember Marina's startled reaction when I used the word 'Hugo'," I pointed out, "isn't it likely she will panic?"

He had pulled himself together.

"The fact that you didn't try to stop me saying it," I continued, "She will have thought that very suspicious of you. Quite obviously you didn't know him. Not knowing Hugo, you will have lost any trust she had in you, don't you see?"

"I covered up –"

"Yes, but it won't have rung true with Marina, I'm sure she suspects you now."

"Perhaps I ought – ?"

"She's gone to your staff car, can she drive? She said not, to me once, but –"

We were both dithering at this point. Would she try to run away? Where to? Maybe there were other members of Hugo's network where she could hide? Bobbie didn't think so: she would simply go back to the home comfort of gentle fishy Harold –

The door burst open and Bob Blackmore fell in, dripping wet but flourishing my pistol.

"Back against the wall," he cried fiercely, "all of you."

We looked around for a wall to be back against.

"Oh," he said in a sort of diminuendo. "Well, Mr Topps Sir, are you OK?"

I thanked him.

"It's just," Bob explained, "I've waited much longer than the hour you said you'd be; and –"

I thanked him doubly. It struck me that Bob had taken a colossal personal risk in bursting into the complete unknown. This might well have earned him the MC to which he had pretended.

"Anyway," he went on, once we had all sat down again and lowered our arms, "I need your help."

We asked why – he seemed pretty self-sufficient so far as we could see.

"There's this foreign girl," he told us. "She tried to get into my staff car, but she was carrying some handcuffs so I fastened her to my steering-wheel and I haven't got the key."

Dick Barton went back with Bob and transferred Marina to the right car: those Army Humbers all look the same in the dark. He drove off to Donnington and locked her up.

Bobbie and I were taken back to Donnington in Bob's car, and didn't say very much, for the moment. It was all a bit too confusing.

I don't know who turned the lights off, or closed that heavy basement door; nor, for that matter, whether MI6 kept the place going: I know they have "safe houses" but that was ridiculous.

We were all required to meet the DC and Major Parrott, next morning.

XXI

The first thing that happened after we got back to Donnington, was unexpected. Bobbie came over to House Four from her CRS and said: "I'm being demobbed." We had both completely forgotten that she was imminently due to leave the ATS. Her three years were up, and she had to go to Preston in a couple of days' time to get her official return to Civvy Street.

However, we were due in the meantime to present ourselves this morning at ten in the DC's office; and this I did, together with Captain Dick Barton.

"I'm sorry Corporal Roberts isn't able to be here," I told the DC, "She's in the process of getting demobbed."

"Is she all right?" He remembered her involvement in visiting all our suspects, and ultimately my alarm about the 'kidnap'.

Barton quickly explained how he had been told about Bobbie's curiosity by Marina, and then as swiftly as possible he tracked her to the CRS and persuaded her to play along with his scheme.

"All this," asked the DC in some puzzlement, "was in the hope of coaxing the controller's name out of the Marina girl?"

"Yes sir."

"And did it?"

"Er – " said Bart Dixon.

I put in a helpful word. "It made an enormous contribution, sir."

The DC and Major Parrott nodded thoughtfully.

"Anyway," said the DC, "it's an extraordinary story. This Senior Medic, of all people. I never met the man myself, he left just before I came here." He turned to the Major. "Did you –?"

"Knew him vaguely. Mind you, I never liked the chap. Worst –"

"He was generally very much liked, I understand…?"

"I gather he kept himself to himself most of the time," said Barton. "Never seen in the mess."

"That's a bit strange."

"They loved him at all the sick bays and the hospital," I pointed out. "I think he mixed more with the other ranks – And among the civilians, I'm told."

"My God," the DC suddenly said, "He was recruiting sleepers!"

Barton shook his head: "I've no evidence of that, but –" He stopped shaking it, and looked at me. "Roberts!" he said. "Bobbie Roberts must have known him. What do you know about that, Topps?"

Now they were all looking at me; and as for myself, I was remembering the quick cry of surprise when I first said: "Hugo" at the Castle yesterday.

"Nothing." My turn to shake my head, but I tried to do it nonchalantly.

★ ★ ★

The next few minutes of that meeting are still somewhere in my head but only as a kind of mist. I know they went on to discuss what should be done with Marina; and it was decided that she should be allowed to return home to her Harold, and stay in her Travel Agent job; but that the telephone should be monitored, and she be required to report every day to Barton's office. Apparently she had told him that she knew of no other

284

appointees by Hugo, and – most interestingly – that he had recruited her in the south of France as soon as she had hitched up with Harold.

Barton understood that Hugo had performed some very generous medical service to both her and others of her family, and it was that indebtedness, plus a Leftwing family background, that had led her into the sleeper network. Barton said he was continuing to 'work on her', now that she knew his true identity; and a certain amount of gentle brainwashing (I didn't enquire at all closely into these Baker Street habits) was expected to 'turn' Marina. In any case, she was no longer a threat.

Was Harold to be brought into the picture? Not a good idea. Barton, I remember, gave one of his little coughs. It appeared that Marina's relationship with Major Hugo, RAMC, out there amid the gunsmoke and chaos of the Allied landings, had not been entirely medical, if we knew what he meant. We knew, we knew... So Harold could fish on blissfully, which was nice, I thought. Ignorance would do what it was supposed to do.

Next, as I gradually came back into the proceedings, they moved on to the main problem: how to deal with our Big Shit.

At first sight one would have thought this to be a job for Dick Barton and his Heavy Mob; surely they had all the know-how, the necessary connections, and – quite literally, I thought with a slight shudder – "the tools to finish the job" as Winston had once said.

But "No," said Bart Dixon sadly, the CIA said this had to be dealt with by us ourselves, "extreme rendition in-house"; and now we *all* shuddered, not so much at the implications as at the ghastly phraseology.

When the DC asked why, we were told that MI6 had larger fish to fry; they would wait for us to eliminate Major Hugo, then observe the ramifications among the higher echelons of treachery – it became apparent that the Baker Street Boys had their sights set on Shits whose Bigness we couldn't even imagine. No splash whatever.

At this point, Captain Barton had to go and speak with his bosses; so I stayed in my seat opposite the almost unplastered Major and the DC, who was already halfway across the room.

"Shouldn't encourage Captain Barton," he told us as he opened the bottle. "He needs all his residual in-house brain cells."

It was quite like old times. I gave them a short lecture on pre-Norman castles; I digressed briefly to say how Bobbie and I were going to get married as soon as she was demobbed, because my own National Service was expiring within the month, and we planned the wedding during my four weeks' official demob leave. They both, as old hardened bachelors themselves, seemed very interested.

Then I found out why.

★ ★ ★

Suddenly they were smiling at me and refilling my glass though not theirs, and this is always alarming.

"Unfortunately," said Major Parrott the Security Officer, "I am still a bit lame after the Wem affair…"

"Regrettably," the DC agreed, gazing out of the window, "my duties here – and of course I never knew the man…"

The awful pause lasted only a few seconds, then: "Look upon it," the DC said benevolently, "as a paid honeymoon."

"You do still have your pistol?" asked the Major.

"Bobbie will clearly recognise him?" said one of them. "Of course, you'll catch him when he calls at the Poste Restante to collect his mail?"

I began to remonstrate; and full of sympathy and concern, Major Parrott assured me that he didn't in the least want our married life to begin with the military court-martial of a probably entirely innocent young ATS NCO, just because of her connection with –"

"She just knew him," I protested. "Like people know their doctor."

Both of them nodded. "Of course, of course, that would all emerge eventually…"

At which point they did both refill their glasses, though not mine.

★ ★ ★

Little Padre Jones did marry us, but up at Ulverston in the Lake District rather than in Donnington. We both already felt a bit remote from those earlier days, exciting because illicit, when we had to go for walks in civvies and in the dark to dodge the stuffy military authorities; and we realised that attendance at the Garrison Church would have been not just embarrassing but wickedly hilarious, with Bobbie's ATS other-ranks on one side and my lot in their service-dress (and one blue beret?) on the other. Nevertheless, up north, to be worthy of Bobbie's sensational New Look outfit in maroon and silky grey, I did for my last time appear in that splendid barathea; and Edwards had been invited, and brought a gleaming Sam Browne with him. My erudite literary colleague came as well, and I hoped he'd brought his notebook; and Marina, reporting dutifully to the local village policeman whose day was made by the encounter – probably more than his whole war; Harold had come with her, and advice from the policeman led him to hire a rod and they stayed for three days up in Coniston with Harold knee-deep in the streams; I don't think Marina found any castles, it's not too far from Hadrian's Wall though, so maybe she went a bit further back into history and found a link with her ancient Roman cousins? Bob Blackmore drove them all up and back again, and mercifully he wasn't wearing his MC.

Peggy Chunk sent me a bound volume of all the Codonians from No. 1. The DC and Major Parrott sent a nice bouquet, a bottle of the usual, and with it a small packet containing half-a-dozen cartridges suitable for my pistol.

How thoughtful.

★ ★ ★

My Best Man was a huge muscular gorilla from Baker Street whom I'd never seen before: he had been more-or-less parachuted in by Dick Barton's bosses, to make sure that "all went well". I had no idea what this meant, at first, simply going along with the weird over-the-top security obsessions that emanated from those tight-arsed people in Marylebone. It was only later that I realised I really was under threat. Or was it Bobbie?

A police car took us away from the church. I'm told there was a reception, a rather delayed 'Wedding Breakfast', but we weren't at it. By mid-afternoon we were in a small but very fast RAF plane, about to be dumped at the airport in a small place east of Toulon, called I think Hyeres.

Somebody in a grey suit met us, and took us to the local hotel. We were told we had to stay in our room, having no passports, but they sent up a glorious meal by British post-war standards: they must have been told we were newly weds. It started with potage-aux-everything and went on to all sorts of garlicky fish that would have enthralled Harold – and probably had done a few years back.

Early next morning we were given return tickets, and a bit of paper with instructions on recalling the aircraft when we had "completed the operation".

The rail journey was something to remember, a quiet leisurely chug along the coast. Our two-carriage train hauled itself precariously on the cliff-edges, with a whole series of rocky creeks on our right, where the deep blue Mediterranean spread out into the background; and on our left, a changing pattern of the local life. First there were busy fields of lavender; then plantations of aged cork oaks, small private vineyards, regimented rows of date palms in the background...

Every few miles, a stop. One or two locals got on or off, sometimes with a batch of gabbling squabbling children, more often with a cage of chickens or a goat... All seemed at peace, the timeless peasantry of the Midi, and it was very difficult to imagine those beaches and inlets full of scrambling men in khaki and the waters behind them a great mass of pitching landing-craft just four years before...What an incredible recovery.

We would have to get Hugo's memories of this later on, if ever we found him: or rather, I would. We agreed that – all being well – Bobbie would covertly point him out, but then I would be the one to accost him. Although in innocent civilian clothes, I was still technically an Army officer, whereas Bobbie (though now an official 'Army Wife'), was a civilian, and could claim no rights legally to take any action on behalf of the Allied military... This had all been carefully and boringly spelt out to us before we were put on the plane, and as it took off we had turned to each other and said: "Can you remember any of that?".

But I remember those little 'stops' – hardly deserving the pomposity of 'stations' – so clearly: and it has to be just memory because a few years later the line was closed: there was

Lavandou... Bormes... Canadel... Rayol... And there was another, which I am not going to include because we went back and lived there, years later, and in the high season we used to let out our little house on its tiny rocky creek by advertising it "for quiet people who can keep a secret"...

After which, we pulled up at the far more businesslike station labelled Cavalaire-sur-Mer, and this was our destination. A long, shallow-sloping sandy beach, a sleepy hotel at one side, and no indication whatever that a few years ago this had been the main centre of the 1944 invasion: "Operation Dragoon", as it had been re-named by Churchill because he wasn't in favour of it and had very reluctantly been persuaded, 'dragooned' into it. But, as he had to admit eventually, the landings had proved enormously successful; and a visit to Cavalaire by M. le President De Gaulle, to the waving of flags and the sound of trumpets, soon became an annual event. One does privately wonder to what extent the acid De Gaulle regarded those celebrations as a juicy dig against Winston, who perhaps wished he had called the affair Operation Frogmarch?

We strolled around the centre of town, which was not difficult because the railway station sat plumb in the middle of everything, surrounded by a lively open-air market and adjacent to the main – and almost the only – street. There was a cafe opposite the post office, and we settled there with a coffee.

I had taken the precaution of sending Hugo two or three short messages a few days before, from the Codonian, each of them innocuously asking our overseas subscribers to tell us whether they were happy with this-and-that. Of course, it meant nothing at all but it ought to bring the late Major to the surface when he collected the letters from the Post Restante.

In France, in those days as – I believe – even now, you could sit for ages over a single cup of coffee, chatting to your friends and coming out with your timeless *bons mots* which some lurking diarist would scribble down for next week's literary magazine. Pay the bill at the end of the day? Mon Dieu, here, let me give you a little impressionistic painting I've just dashed off, it'll sit nicely on your walls, *mon ami*.

To be truthful, as I must, after two of those coffees and no result, I gave in and we both had a couple of pastis. This made us feel continentally good – you couldn't get it in England and it pretended to be decadent like the absinthe from which it was bastardly descended... Bobbie felt it seeping into her consciousness somewhat, but with my long-built-up accommodation to Scotch, it didn't do much harm to me. We continued to sit and watch the Post Office. And then:

"That's him."

★ ★ ★

I looked across at a medium-height man, just a little portly, dressed in clothes which I suppose were rather traditionally British: the jacket was a heather-mixture Harris tweed and the trousers were that grey flannel that always goes with a blazer. I supposed that the blazer itself would only come out on special days.

"Are you sure?"

"Of course," said Bobbie. "I knew him well enough."

This was no time to probe into my hidden worries, but I did anyway.

"How well?" I demanded, like a fool.

She turned to look at me.

"How well did you know that Mac woman?"

Oh really, I thought. We're supposed to be here on business – and pretty blood-letting business, too. We're supposed to kill that man.

"I knew Mac pretty damn well," I said airily but lying.

"Oh, yes? And what does that mean?"

I took another deep breath.

"Look," I said, "sticking to facts, Mac isn't here, but Hugo is, and we're here to kill him. There he is, over the road. He is apparently a big security risk to us. Do pull yourself together."

"I loved Hugo," said Bobbie.

★ ★ ★

According to my watch we hadn't even been married twenty four hours yet. I huffed across to Hugo's side of the road and stood behind him at a bus stop. The corner of my left eye told me that Bobbie was still sitting at the table, and appeared to be asking the waiter for another pastis: this could be bad news, but just then the dusty bus drew up, and I got on to it after Hugo.

I was acting mechanically and had no idea what I should do next; but he was handing the driver some change and getting a ticket; so I gave it a couple of seconds, then said: "*Même chose*" or something like that, and worked my way down the gangway. As it happened the seats were mostly taken so it was quite natural for me to sit right next to my quarry.

How to start things? I had the pistol in my pocket but I could hardly shoot the chap on a bus in full daylight and get away with it. Besides…

I thought he looked interesting. He had smiled pleasantly when I sat down. And it was becoming more and more uncomfortably apparent that we had some things in common. I decided to make contact.

I shifted in my seat so that I slightly bumped him – with the pistol in that pocket, which struck me as ridiculous.

"Oh, sorry," I said in English.

"Not at all." Nice voice. Then: "Oh, you're English?

"Yes, I am," I smiled. "You on holiday too?"

"Not me, I live here."

I told him how lucky he was. Yes, he said, a most beautiful part of the world for gracious retirement, but it was soon going to be spoilt, everybody was planning to build here. He himself had discovered it towards the end of the war...

I thought the invasion had been a French affair, with some Americans thrown in to supply the necessary dollars and chewing-gum?

"Mainly, yes, but we dropped a brigade or two, a little way inland. I came in with them, I was a Medic."

"And you've just stayed on?"

"For several months, there was a lot to do – among the civilians too. Many of them had had a bad time." He shook his head sadly. "No point going on about it now. Of course, as soon as the war was over, everybody along the coast emerged as heroes of the resistance; you'd fall over them wherever you looked, the *maquis* must have been as thick as the cork-oaks hereabouts, from what they tell you..."

"But then you went back home?"

"Yes, for a while, to serve out my time. But I knew I'd come back."

We watched the scenery unfold; I noted that the bus had turned inland and was moving up into the foothills. He observed my interest, and asked where I was heading for.

"Nowhere. Well, anywhere really," I answered casually. "When I'm on holiday, I like to get on the first bus I see and go wherever it's going. In the Army I used to do the same thing but by hitchhiking – I'd flag down the first lorry that came along and go wherever it was headed. On a good weekend leave I'd get from Tidworth down to Cornwall and back, maybe ten lifts... Great fun," I remembered.

"Who were you with?"

"Ordnance."

Slight pause.

"Don't know much about that lot."

Change of subject: I asked him if his family were out here with him.

"No," he said sadly. "I've never had a family, really. Married once, but she was killed by a bomb in London. Worked for a bank. One of their functions: she'd been ordered to attend, they were trying to impress some puffed-up clients. She was the only one killed. Bank didn't offer any help – and I was abroad as an Army doctor. Couldn't afford any assistance, times hard – bloody banks, bloody capitalists…" His voice trailed off.

"Some nasty things must have happened, so often," I muttered.

"Still," he said, "We showed them, didn't we?"

"I beg your – ?"

"Attlee. When we all came back from the war, looking for that 'Land Fit For Heroes' Churchill and his crowd had promised. It was us, returning from the war, the Forces, that kicked them out. But," he shrugged, "you're too young to know."

"You think Labour – ?"

"They don't go nearly far enough," said Hugo. "The country has to be taken in hand. Well, no, not in hand, but really led –"

"By the nose?" I couldn't resist that.

He was getting up.

"This is where I live," he said. "It's called Grimaud. Come and see, we can have a drink."

★ ★ ★

294

We walked along the road, it was hilly and there were one or two little shops aimed at the burgeoning tourist industry, though those would almost exclusively at that time have been people from the north: Parisians driving in the middle of the road, Belgians still apologetic for their early failure in 1940; plus a few Italians equally apologetic for their wartime role, for failing first to hang Mussolini, and then to hang him the right way up...

Suddenly, we came in sight of the ruined castle of the postcard.

"I live right opposite this," Hugo told me proudly. "Isn't it splendid?"

I asked if we might go and walk around. Of course; and he led me through a leaning rusty gate, to the foot of the keep which I already knew so well.

The setting was superb. The little village was sleeping in the midday heat; a few crickets were rasping gently in the unkempt undergrowth. Only a lone chugging taxi went past...

"Did Marina like this?" I asked him.

I had my pistol out.

Major Hugo Hallam RAMC (ret.) sat down calmly on a bit of stone wall, much as I'd done a few days ago at Richards Castle, only the weather here was an improvement.

He looked at the gun, and laughed a bit.

"Well, well... I suppose I had it coming," he told me evenly. "I know it sounds like a Hollywood film, but may I smoke?"

He lit a Gauloise (I imagine it was, they always are in the films). I waited, and noticed my pistol was wavering somwhat in my hand, so I put it down on the masonry.

"Yes," Hugo said as he blew out a smoke-ring. "Marina loved the castle. She loves all Norman castles, you know?"

I told him I knew.

"Is the girl well?" Yes, she was, and now free from Cold War influences.

"Lovely creature."

"Indeed." Didn't I know it.

"And stuck with that dreadful little fisherman."

I told Hugo that Harold and Marina really were in love, and enjoying a simple straightforward married life, uncomplicated by neurotically twisted communistic threats and menaces; and that this deserved to be allowed to continue, as surely he as a doctor ought to concede, remembering his Hippocratic Oath. I went on like that for quite a long time.

"They really should have come out here, you know. Marina belongs in a warm climate. And Harold could have had the time of his life in one of our little fishing ports. There's a place just down there," he waved towards the distant sea, "it was founded by some saint like those Irish ones who came floating in on an oyster-shell or something, you know? His name was Torpez, but they've got it wrong, I keep telling the Mayor, it's Torpez but they're saying Tropez. Lovely little unspoilt village, though the artists are creeping in and settling and it'll be ruined soon." He sighed, and blew some more smoke rings.

"So they've sent you out to shoot me?"

I told him that was about the size of it.

"Would there be any point in me telling you that I'm acting as a double agent and really passing useful stuff back to the CIA – oh, and MI's 5 and 6 and 7 and 8?"

I told him I didn't think so, I was acting on clear orders I'd had from all of them.

"When that Irish novelist, you remember," he said, "back in the 1920s was it? During what they smoothly call 'The Troubles', begorrah? When he –"

"You're talking about the 'Riddle Of The Sands' author? Erskine something?"

"Childers, yes. Well, when he was up before that firing-squad, he just said –"

"I know this," I told him. I read books too. "He just said to them, 'Come closer, lads, it'll be easier for you'."

"Yes,' I said to Hugo, 'very romantic. But nevertheless, we in the UK have to snuff out people like you who are infiltrating us with snoopers and sleepers and spies. What will happen if Russia gets the bomb? They have no hesitation in wiping out millions of their own people – what can stop them from casually wiping out millions of those of us who aren't their friends?"

"Hugo, for God's sake," I ended, "Can't you see that?"

I'll never know whether he could, for God's or anyone else's sake; because at that moment, from behind me, Bobbie swept in and gathered up my pistol.

★ ★ ★

"Give me that," she said grimly as she went past; but she had it already, and I heard her click off the safety-catch. She waved the gun at Hugo.

Whom she loved.

"Good God, Roberts! What are you doing here?"

"Get up," she ordered him. He did.

"Get up that path." She waved the pistol towards the castle keep. Then she turned and, to my greatest alarm yet, pointed the gun straight at me.

"Stay put."

I did, believe me.

They disappeared round the keep. Silence for a few seconds; then two shots rang out, echoing around the ruins. Several swallowtails fluttered up into the scented air and sank swivelling down again as it all went quiet.

"Let's go," said Bobbie, coming down the path and handing me the pistol. "I've a taxi."

★ ★ ★

We didn't say much in the taxi as it descended to Cavalaire station. There was a strong smell of wormwood, mixed with a slight hint of gunsmoke, and the driver's face in the mirror was a picture. I spent most of the journey wondering what the waiter had put into that last pastis: was the good old original absinthe still on the shelves down here?

We didn't say a lot on the train either, beyond small talk about the new developments and the possibility of coming back one day. I did take a look at the gun: yes, two bullets gone – but gone where? I never asked Bobbie about it, what was the point, it had to be her secret. I just hoped she hadn't shot any swallowtails…

We went back to the depot so that I could hand the pistol and the four rounds back to Captain Barton, but we didn't hang around, except that I did at last have the satisfaction of taking Bobbie into the Officers' Mess (and I've restored its correct apostrophe in celebration of the event). To be fair, the DC did welcome us, at the door, having spotted us coming from his antimacassared corner-seat.

"Are you really and truly out?" he asked her. "Then come in, welcome."

I had a Laphroaig, of course. When he asked her for her choice of drink, to instruct Charles, she said: "Do you have pastis?" without looking at me.

Charles looked, though, with that eyebrow…

★ ★ ★

The Codonian ceased publication a few months later: its new editor never really caught on to the basic facts. The soldiers could just read it in the Company office, and didn't need to buy it; and the civilians made up the bulk of the readership, wanted to know what was on at the pictures, and didn't give a damn about military sports. In its final issue, which somebody sent me – Brown? – much was made of him, but in the full list of past editors they were all Majors and Captains, there was no mention of me, I was just a National Serviceman and, one must suppose, a mere passing aberration: they didn't mention the Paper Caper either. Secret, don't you know, as they say in Baker Street.

I went back not long ago to Richard's Castle. Much the same, but the odd building past the far end, with its steps down to that basement, had been demolished, and no trace remains.

And many years after all these events, Bobbie and I returned to the Hay Mill. That, too, had been demolished: not a trace. I sat on the river bank for quite a long time; her remains were beside me, in a friendly little jar. As she had requested, I poured them into the Teme, just at the spot where that basin had floated away into its future…

One of these days, I'll go into a river too. It may not be the same one, but then, they all flow down to the sea, don't they?

For Bobbie

May Morning 1948 – Gladestry, the pub.

I stood with you on Ludlow Keep
And gazed through history, back and down
To where some proud old Marcher Lord
Surveyed, possessive, hand on sword,
His town - his little huddled town.

I stood with you on Ludlow Keep
And dreamt of times that used to be:
The fortitude, the thrill of power,
That hotspur gift to seize the hour,
The witchery of Chivalry...

All gone. Regrets? There might have been
Had not your voice recalled from sleep
My thoughts; and then I knew at last
I went one better than the past:
I stood, with you, on Ludlow Keep.